THE GOODE GIRLS OF MAPLE LANE

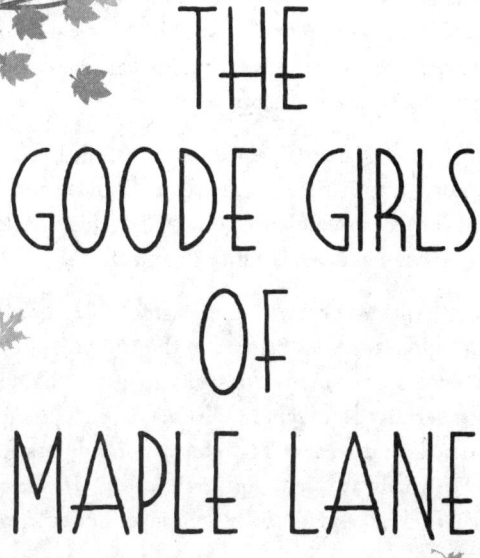

THE GOODE GIRLS OF MAPLE LANE

A Novel

Jacqueline Firkins

An Imprint of HarperCollinsPublishers

Without limiting the exclusive rights of any author, contributor or the publisher of this publication, any unauthorized use of this publication to train generative artificial intelligence (AI) technologies is expressly prohibited. HarperCollins also exercise their rights under Article 4(3) of the Digital Single Market Directive 2019/790 and expressly reserve this publication from the text and data mining exception.

This is a work of fiction. Names, characters, places, and incidents are products of the author's imagination or are used fictitiously and are not to be construed as real. Any resemblance to actual events, locales, organizations, or persons, living or dead, is entirely coincidental.

THE GOODE GIRLS OF MAPLE LANE. Copyright © 2025 by HarperCollins Publishers. All rights reserved. Printed in the United States of America. No part of this book may be used or reproduced in any manner whatsoever without written permission except in the case of brief quotations embodied in critical articles and reviews. For information, address HarperCollins Publishers, 195 Broadway, New York, NY 10007. In Europe, HarperCollins Publishers, Macken House, 39/40 Mayor Street Upper, Dublin 1, D01 C9W8, Ireland.

HarperCollins books may be purchased for educational, business, or sales promotional use. For information, please email the Special Markets Department at SPsales@harpercollins.com.

Avon, Avon & logo, and Avon Books & logo are registered trademarks of HarperCollins Publishers in the United States of America and other countries.

hc.com

FIRST EDITION

Designed by Diahann Sturge-Campbell

Autumn maple branch © Farosofa/Stock.Adobe.com

Library of Congress Cataloging-in-Publication Data has been applied for.

ISBN 978-0-06-344175-0

25 26 27 28 29 LBC 5 4 3 2 1

To Buster, Mocha, Fannie May, Heidi, Ffiona, and Stella.
My heart is carved from the love you let me give you.
And which you gave back a hundredfold.
Every time.

THE GOODE GIRLS OF MAPLE LANE

CHAPTER ONE

It's just past midnight on a Friday, I smell like questionably sourced pepperoni, I'm pretty sure the blister that keeps forming on my left heel burst again, my phone is burning a hole in my pocket with five unanswered texts from my well-meaning but boundary-averse mother, and the man in the elevator with me is carrying a houseplant so large, he's not only edging me into a corner, he's completely hidden behind the plant from the waist up. He's also grunting a little from the weight. I'd worry he's sneaking into the building using a tactic he picked up from a cartoon, but I recognize his blue corduroy pants and faded red Converse low-tops. Also, this is the third time in as many weeks I've seen him haul a hefty houseplant up to his apartment at an unusual hour. Assuming his apartment is a similar size to mine, I've begun to wonder where he fits a bed. I also wonder where he makes his late-night foliage runs. And why.

Naturally, I've dubbed him Plant Guy.

Unimaginative? Sure. But Bespectacled Midnight Philodendron Smuggler is a mouthful.

Also on my floor: a couple really into PDA (The Lovers); a girl who never looks up from her phone, somehow intuiting when she's reached her floor (Phone Girl); a guy who's always awkwardly but apologetically cramming his bicycle into the elevator (Cycle Guy); and a middle-aged woman who carries her tiny black-and-gray Yorkie-poo around in her purse (Dog Lady).

Six apartments. Six twentysomethings and one fiftysomething who all live here because the rent's cheap and the location's convenient. It's certainly not for the character or the views of the narrow alleys that flank the building, though we have a few modern amenities, like the elevator, a parking garage, and an intercom system that lets us buzz friends in from our phones, the last of which I've had depressingly little reason to use. Everyone on my floor but Plant Guy has been here at least as long as I have—a little over a year—and I have yet to learn anyone's actual name. I haven't made the effort, though in my defense, no one has attempted to learn mine.

The dog's name, however, is Pilot.

Something tickles my ear and I swat it away.

Leaves, apparently.

"Sorry." Plant Guy edges farther into his corner.

"It's fine." I edge farther into mine.

This comprises the entirety of our conversation on our slow ascent to the sixth floor. If I wasn't so tired from a long day of classes and a five-hour shift at the pizzeria, I would've taken the stairs. I hate this steel box. Not only do I have to stand near strangers and pretend I don't feel a weird pressure to make small talk, but no one ever scrapes away the blackened gum wads, the overhead fluorescents flicker like they're prepping us for a jump scare, and I swear, I could've solved an entire *New York Times* Friday crossword by the time the doors ding open.

Plant Guy lets out a quiet grunt as he adjusts the weight of his new roommate in his arms. I'm not sure if he's waiting for me to exit first or if he can't see what floor we're on.

"Need a hand?" I ask, realizing way too late that I should've asked sooner.

"Nope. Good. Just. Doors," he says in a strained staccato.

I step out and reach a hand back to prevent the elevator doors from closing.

He shuffles past me, eking out a "Thanks. Night" as he heads to his apartment at the opposite end of the hall from mine. Nothing strange here. Just a man and his plant.

"Night," I call after him, following his lead on the dropped *good* before doing a quick tally. Thirteen words from start to finish. As elevator conversations go, it's practically a record.

My sneakers are off as soon as I enter my apartment, tossing my keys onto the sideboard and dropping my bag on the futon I drown in blankets and throw pillows, lest it become a daily reminder that I could barely afford to furnish this apartment, and everything in it is the absolute cheapest version I could find. While slipping out of my jacket, I flip through the mail I grabbed on the way in. Two charities seeking donations, a new food delivery company trying to drum up business, and a more formal envelope from Cornell's bursar's office. I toss the first three in my recycle bin and put the fourth on a growing stack of Things to Look at Later. Once my student loans hit six figures, the number became oddly abstract. It's already an amount I can't imagine paying back in my lifetime. Why not add another $60K? At this point, they might as well send one of those cards that open up to a laugh track. Or maybe the sound of a falling anvil.

I grab the sole remaining cider from my fridge, which is a wasteland other than a few bruised apples, a partial loaf of bread, a carton of oat milk—I'm never sure which "milk" I'm supposed to be drinking these days—and a dozen half-empty condiment jars and bottles in the door. I like to cook. I just don't have the time and energy. Not when cereal's ready in seconds.

As I close the door, I tap the photo of our family's golden retriever, Lady Marmalade, where I've pinned it to the door with a pewter paw magnet. It's a habitual gesture, and one that still chokes me up, even though she died three years ago now. I've never been good with people, so Marmie was my best friend while I was growing up, and her loss hit me hard. I've done my share of ugly-crying, scrolling old photo albums, and watching heart-tugging videos of dogs leaping into water after tennis balls, one of Marmie's favorite activities. As with all forms of grief, some days are easier than others, and sometimes the sadness surprises me, like when I find a blond hair on an old sweater or when a dent in a throw pillow is about her size, and the sadness drags me under before I can take precautions against it.

On the anniversary of her death last year, I was so bereft, I got wasted and spent the night filling in applications with shelters and fostering agencies, noting that I had a particular interest in golden retrievers. Thankfully, no one called and I didn't have to backpedal. Of course they didn't call. At the time of application, my only assets of note were my enthusiasm and my recent entry into vet school, which were unlikely to offset my shortcomings. A single grad student living in a five-hundred-square-foot apartment with no yard, no caretaking help, no free time, and a laughable monthly income that only partially covers her current living expenses is hardly an ideal pet parent. They know that. I know that. Even the dogs I'll never meet would know that.

One day, when I finish school—*if* I finish school—and I knock at least one zero off my loan statements, and I live in a space that doesn't make my aggressively utilitarian undergrad dorm look elegant by comparison, I'll get a dog. Until then, it's me, the cheap futon, the empty fridge, an impossible mountain of studying, and an even more impossible mountain of debt.

I raise my bottle to Marmie's photo. "Living the dream, huh, girl?"

She smiles back in that way only dogs do, with their entire bodies, nose to tail.

Slumping onto the futon, I reach out to the one friend who's stuck by me since childhood, even though she moved to the UK when we were in eighth grade, and seems to have no intention of returning since she's still over there, currently pursuing a law degree. At least I can text her late at night and know she's up and probably on her tenth or twelfth mile of a morning run. She does Ironman races. She never would've taken the elevator tonight. But since I did . . .

CAMERON: Good morning. Thought you should know. Plant Guy strikes again!

HANNAH: Another one? Was it pot this time? Please tell me it was pot

CAMERON: I think it was a philodendron

HANNAH: You sure that's a plant?

CAMERON: According to the straight A's I got in bio classes . . .

HANNAH: Whatever. It still sounds dirty

CAMERON: There's a bush joke in here somewhere but I'm too tired to find it

HANNAH: Long day?

CAMERON: Long week. Long month. Long year

I take a hefty swig of cider and feel my body start to relax.

HANNAH: Still having second thoughts about vet school?

CAMERON: Try third or fourth or a thousand and fiftieth

HANNAH: But you'll be SUCH an amazing vet

CAMERON: I don't know. The grind is getting to me. And being a vet is so much more about dealing with people than I thought it would be back when I was bandaging teddy bear legs and diagnosing the family cats with catatonia and cataracts

> **HANNAH:** You just made me spit-take my Gatorade

> **CAMERON:** How many miles this morning?

> **HANNAH:** Only ten. I'll do a long run this weekend

Only ten, I think as I prod the raw spot where my blister popped. I can't even imagine.

> **HANNAH:** Maybe you should shake things up? Ask Plant Guy on a date

> **CAMERON:** Pretty sure I'm not his type

> **HANNAH:** Green?

> **CAMERON:** Fun

Hannah sends me an angry face emoji. I reply with a shrug emoji. This is a long-standing argument and I appreciate her perennially generous view of my personality, but I know myself. I'm not exactly the life of the party. I rarely even attend "the party."

> **CAMERON:** Also, pretty sure PG's habit of sneaking large houseplants into his apartment in the middle of the night is a major red flag. Don't you think it's a little weird?

> **HANNAH:** It's the greenest of green flags. And I thought you liked weird

> **CAMERON:** I like

I stop there and delete the text, unable to complete it. It's probably not a good sign that I can't identify what I like, let alone rally the energy to pursue it, but I know this much. I don't have room in my life for dating. I barely have room for a daily shower.

> **CAMERON:** I'm not sure my tween crush on the goth, blue-haired skater boy who worked at Tasteez soft serve should be considered indicative of my adult dating taste

> **HANNAH:** Hey, if you have a type . . .

> **CAMERON:** I promise if Plant Guy ever dyes his hair a primary color, gets a ton of piercings, rolls in on a skateboard, and muddles my ice cream order, I'll at least ask his name

> **HANNAH:** Aww. It's practically wedding bells

> **CAMERON:** You're funny. Enjoy your run

> **HANNAH:** Enjoy your sleep

With a grossly indulgent sigh at the vast disparity between the life I used to imagine I'd be living by now and the one I'm actually living, I set aside my phone and kick my tired feet up on my ugly, thrifted coffee table, settling back into my less ugly, thrifted pillows and finishing my cider at an alarming rate, one I try not to read too much into.

My phone draws my eye as I set down my empty bottle.

I should text my mom back. She's in Oregon, so it's only nine-something her time. But what do I even say? *Thanks for the links to my high school ex's wedding pics. You're right! His wife IS beautiful! And their wedding looks amazing! Definitely something I wanted to see! Also, thank you for offering to buy my plane ticket home for Christmas again this year, but I'm not sure I can handle an entire week of Look on the Bright Side pep talks and not-so-subtle setups with sons of your friends' friends.*

She means well, but I don't have the energy tonight. Or ever, really.

I turn off the volume in case she decides to torture me with good intentions again. Then I flop sideways and curl up to unwind with a bland but entertaining rom-com playing on my TV, drowning out thoughts that would otherwise spiral on repeat for hours. *Dog. Plant. Christmas. Joy. Loans. Blister. Friend. Wedding. Pizza. Tired. Grind. Rut. Sigh.* And back to *dog*.

I don't even realize I've fallen asleep until a noise in the hallway wakes me Saturday morning. It sounds like Cycle Guy, banging his bike around as he wedges it into the elevator while apologizing profusely to Dog Lady, who says it's no trouble but in a way that implies maybe it *is* trouble, as Pilot lets out a single, adorable, passive-aggression-free yip. Such is life on the sixth floor of the Maple Lane Apartments, aptly named for the street they're on, even though only a few of the trees that used to flank the winding street have survived through decades of urban development. Still, we have one right out front, and in the fall, with its bright scarlet leaves, it's gorgeous, and I can't pass it without marveling at its beauty and resilience.

Sitting up and stretching out my neck, I see a voicemail notification. I assume it's my mother, wondering why I haven't texted back, and decide she can wait until I've showered and brushed my teeth, but then I notice the number isn't hers. It's one I don't recognize at all.

Too curious to leave it until I'm fully awake, I go ahead and play the message.

Hi. I'm calling for Cameron Goode. My name's Andy Faulkner, and I'm the shelter manager at Hounds and Hearts in Syracuse. We have your fostering application on file, and while I know it was submitted some time ago, I'm hoping you're still interested. It's a time-sensitive situation, and a complicated one, but if you're still looking to foster, or even adopt, please return my call at your earliest convenience at . . .

He finishes with his number and Hounds and Hearts' hours of operation. I replay the message three times, perched on the edge of my futon, certain I've misheard. He must be trying to reach a different Cameron Goode, one with a lucrative, work-from-home job; lots of free time for long, meandering walks; a dog-loving partner; a big house; and an even bigger fenced yard. But no. Apparently, he means me. And since the message suggests the matter is urgent, I call right back.

A cheerful woman's voice answers, "Hounds and Hearts. How can I direct your call?"

I explain who I am and the voicemail I received.

"Oh, thank god," she says through a dramatic exhale. "This poor dog. I mean, I've just never seen . . . and she's such a sweetheart, and none of us could bear it if . . ."

A throat clears in the background.

"Sorry," the woman who answered says. "I'll let Andy explain."

She passes me off to Andy, who reiterates that he runs the shelter in Syracuse, a little over an hour away from Ithaca by car. I confirm that yes, I am the Cornell vet school student who filled out a fostering application over a year ago, noting an interest in golden retrievers and detailing my relationship with my family pet.

"So, here's the situation," he says, adopting a more formal tone. "We have a seven-year-old female golden retriever in need of a home, and she's had a rough go of it."

I inch forward on the futon, prickling with anxiety. "How rough?"

"She's been chained outside her whole life, on a concrete pad, underexercised and overfed. She currently weighs in at a hundred and twenty-five pounds." He pauses there, as if he knows I need a moment to absorb this, and I do. Not only am I horrified that someone left their dog outside for seven years without space to run and play, and without proper warmth, love, and shelter, but Marmie weighed about sixty pounds for most of her adult life. That's half of this dog's current weight. "Her obesity has left her immobile and fighting hyperthyroidism," Andy continues. "She's not doing great and we're not even sure how long she has. Obviously, this isn't a dog who can easily enter the average family home. She needs medical care, and, if she pulls through, someone who can work with her to regain mobility and social engagement."

I swallow down the sob that wants to emerge. I've always known becoming a vet means dealing with the hard times and not just the happy times. That animals experience pain, illness, injuries, infirmity, neglect, and abuse, and that a vet's job is to make their lives as long, healthy, and happy as possible, and to not fall apart while they do it. But the thought of this poor dog breaks my heart. It's absolutely crushing. How can anyone treat a living being this way?

"Still there?" Andy asks.

"Yeah. Yes. Sorry," I say through a rush of breath. "This is . . . a lot."

"I know," he says, and then repeats, as though his heart is breaking, too, "I know."

We take another moment, not a long one, but a necessary one.

"Your message said this was time-sensitive?" I prompt, already suspecting what that means but silently praying I'm wrong.

"I'll be blunt, Miss Goode. You're not our first call. We've worked through our list of regular foster homes. Reached out to applicants who seemed more . . . secure." The pause that follows is loaded, and I appreciate Andy's attempt to soften the truth—namely, that I'm his last resort—but it's not like I don't understand. If I was in his shoes, I'd be my last resort, too. "This dog needs a lot of one-on-one care. We don't have the funding or staff to provide that here, not with so many other dogs also needing our attention. We've called some other shelters, but they share our limitations. If we can't find a foster home within twenty-four hours—"

"I'll be there," I say. And I know, *I know* this is madness. I'm never home. I don't have a car. Or help. Or time. Or space. Or savings. Or upper-body strength. I shouldn't even pet-parent a healthy little handbag passenger like Pilot. How am I supposed to care for a hundred-and-twenty-five-pound retriever who needs intense rehabilitative care?

But how can I let her die?

"You sure?" Andy says. "She might not—"

"Doesn't matter," I interject before he can finish that sentence in a way that will yank the awaiting sobs from my chest, the ones I'm barely keeping down. "I just need to sort out a ride, but I can come by this afternoon if that works for you?"

He doesn't answer right away, probably rethinking this whole thing since I just admitted I don't have a car. Obviously, this is an added challenge, but not an impossible one.

"We're open until five today," he says. "I'd love for you to meet her."

"Same," I say, and my eyes drift toward the photo of Marmie on my fridge, smiling like she's looking on in spirit and letting me know I'm doing the right thing.

I grab a few more details from Andy so I can arrive prepared. As soon as we hang up, I look up the cost of an Uber. It's almost $100 each way. Not ideal, especially since I'll have to call in sick to Loden and Linden, the upscale furnishings store where I spend twelve tedious but well-paid hours every weekend, selling overpriced candles and textiles to bored housewives and affluent influencers who need tastefully curated props for their highly filtered lifestyle accounts.

A cab is even more expensive. I could take the bus but I'd have no way of getting a dog home with me. This shouldn't be that hard, but my only close friend is on the other side of the Atlantic and my nearest living family member is on the West Coast.

A thought occurs to me. A long shot, for sure, but not an impossible one.

With a quick detour through my bathroom to pee, re-twist my tangled topknot into a slightly less deranged version, and swish some toothpaste, I scurry out my door and to the other end of the communal hallway, pausing before apartment 606. I know very few things about the current tenant. He likes plants. He likes corduroy and Converse. He has a kind smile. He often boards the elevator not from the main entry, but from the lower-level parking garage.

It's not a lot to go on but I don't have many options right now.

I take a deep breath and knock. A few seconds later, Plant Guy opens the door, blinking at me through old-fashioned, wire-rimmed glasses. His loose brown curls are in gentle disarray, the lower half of his face is faintly stubbled, and his pumpkin-colored sweater is rumpled, tugged sideways over a white crewneck tee and moss-colored cords.

A familiar jolt of anxiety sets in, a sharp discomfort with strangers I can't shake off, even during an urgent animal rescue. My fingers flex and curl with a need to fidget, but I decide no one who wears a pumpkin-colored sweater can be all bad. Even if he steals houseplants.

I thrust out my hand.

"Hi," I say. "I'm Cameron. Cameron Goode. I live in 602. Grad student. Veterinary medicine. Sorry if I've been . . . whatever. Doesn't matter. I think you might have a car. And I just got a call about a dog who will be euthanized if I don't go get her right away, and she's in Syracuse, and she can't walk, and I can't lift her on my own, and I *really* love dogs, and I think this one needs me. So . . . any chance you're free and interested in saving a life with me?"

He continues blinking at me, completely nonplussed, and my stomach sinks.

He's going to say no. Why shouldn't he say no? Wouldn't I say no if he came to my door and blurted out a plea to drop everything and go on what might be a completely invented rescue mission? I could be a dealer or a serial killer. Even if he threw aside all logic and decided to trust me, surely he has a job, or classes to study for, or a weekend hobby, or a social life, or a botany documentary series to binge. What possible reason could he have for helping me?

But then his kind smile appears, slowly building as he takes my hand and shakes it.

"Hi, Cameron," he says. "I'm Everett Redmond. Give me a moment to grab my keys."

CHAPTER TWO

Everett's car is a powder-blue, rust-tinged vintage Volvo station wagon he informs me was his grandmother's before she died and left it to him. Then he apologizes for using the word *died*. A silence follows that neither of us knows how to fill, until I say I'm sorry about his grandmother, but think it's nice that he kept her CDs—an assortment of seventies-era light rock heavy on the Neil Diamond and John Denver—and that he listens to them in her memory. He tells me the CDs weren't his grandmother's. Another silence follows, one in which I have a new appreciation for childhood warnings not to get in cars with strangers. Not because I think Everett is dangerous, but because the two of us are trapped in here for the next hour and it only took us five minutes to demonstrate our combined lack of social skills.

I study a tomato sauce stain on the jeans I slept in and should've changed.

He finds a staticky college radio station to replace the music on his CDs.

We leave the outskirts of Ithaca behind and follow a winding surface road through the surrounding farmland and the wooded patches that are just beginning to change color, hinting at the vibrant October hues that are still about a month away but always seem to arrive overnight, and then vanish just as quickly with the first hard autumn wind. When Everett reaches for the volume at the same time I reach for the tuner, our eyes meet, we exchange an apologetic smile that has the fortunate effect of resetting the mood, and I can feel us both rallying to try again.

I'm about to ask if he has always lived in Ithaca but he speaks first.

"So, you're studying to be a vet?" he asks.

"Yeah," I say, thankful for the easy topic. "It's been my dream since I was a kid. I know it sounds cliché to say I've always loved animals, but I've always loved animals. They feel things in a way we'll never fully understand or be able to emulate. Dogs especially. When they're happy, they don't question the meaning of that happiness, dissect its causes, or make ten-step plans for achieving it again. They don't try to moderate their happiness in case the other dogs think their happiness is uncool. They don't perform their happiness on social media, as if they're only happy when their followers notice that they're happy. They don't manufacture their happiness. They don't curate their happiness. They're just *happy*, in the moment, embodying the feeling without restraint, analysis, or pretense. Can you imagine?"

Everett nods as though he's giving my impromptu speech serious consideration.

Or maybe he's tallying how many times I said the words *happy* or *happiness*.

"Sounds like you've given this a lot of thought," he says.

I inch up a stiff shrug. "I have a lot of feelings about dogs."

He slides me a sideways glance. "And about social media?"

"Guess I wasn't so subtle about that." I tug at a loose thread on the cross-strap of my seat belt, an obvious but necessary attempt to anchor my focus and buy myself some time.

Given the brevity of my acquaintance with Everett, I should probably refrain from telling him about my mother, and how social media became a platform for her unrelenting positivity, turning an annoying trait into an unbearable one. She gets sick. She posts about how lucky she is to have a perfect, doting husband who takes such amazing care of her. A friend receives a breast cancer diagnosis. She posts triumphant photos of a charity 5K she ran with a caption about how strong she feels, and how inspired she is by her friend's "journey." Our beloved family dog dies. She posts joyful videos from her long-awaited Italian vacation, the one she can finally take without worrying about leaving an old dog behind. There's always a bright side, with a pretty picture and jaunty caption to ensure everyone else sees the bright side. I find it all exhausting.

"Let's just say I'm not a fan," I tell Everett. "Anyway. What do you do?"

"I'm in marketing," he says. "Mostly social media content and management."

"Oh my god." I throw my face into my hands, utterly mortified. "I didn't mean—"

"No. It's fine." He holds up a hand to halt my protest, a hint of amusement dimpling his cheeks and creasing the skin beside his eyes. "It's a complicated landscape. I get that. But there's a positive side to it. And I don't just mean for selling stuff."

I peek out between my fingers, curious where he's going with this. I spent plenty of time on social media in high school and college, but I have no regrets about leaving.

"You mean all the memes?" I ask, only half kidding.

He sneaks me another glance as he nudges his glasses up the bridge of his nose.

"I mean accounts with real impact like the digital activists informing people about climate change, disability rights, decolonization practices, and health care inaccessibility," he says. "Or fun accounts like the Italian greyhound who's a fashion influencer."

I finally lower my hands, recalling some of the dog accounts I used to follow, though they were all just for fun, made by people who loved their pets, nothing approaching influencer status.

"A fashion influencer, huh?" I ask. "Whose fashion is she influencing?"

Everett's cheeks dimple again. "You'd be surprised."

I'm sure I would be, I think. Also, he really does have a nice smile. It's warm, friendly, and a little reticent to fully bloom, a characteristic I respect in a smile.

Everett soon pulls onto the highway heading north. As we settle into a slightly less uncomfortable silence and as I watch the landscape pass through my window, a low rumble of anxiety begins to roil in my belly, not the kind of anxiety I felt when I knocked on Everett's door or tried to figure out what to say about his assertively musty but gloriously convenient car. It's the kind of anxiety I feel when I know I'm about to face something genuinely, profoundly hard.

The dog we're about to meet will remind me of Lady Marmalade. She'll call up waves of grief I'm still learning to manage. She has also been abused and neglected, which is always hard to see.

She'll need a lot of help and I'll need to be realistic about whether or not I can provide that help. I'll know, while looking into her eyes, that after all she's been through, I'm her last chance, not just for a good life, but for any life at all.

What if I can't do it? What if I have to let her die?

A warm hand wraps mine where I've balled it into a tight fist on my thigh.

"I really want to tell you that won't happen," Everett says, making me realize I spoke those last thoughts aloud. "But I don't know much about animal health and welfare. I've never had a pet. And I don't really know you, either, but I'm going to go out on a limb here and say I'm pretty sure you'll only let her die if you're confident it's the right thing to do."

I bite down hard on my lip, holding back a swell of emotion. Not from the warm hand around mine, or the gentle way Everett expressed his faith in me, or even just feeling a little less alone on this unexpected journey. It's his use of the phrase *the right thing to do*, rather than *the only thing to do*. Because they're not the same, and I'm really glad I won't have to explain that.

"Thanks," I say. "I hope so. I really, *really* hope so."

FORTY-FIVE MINUTES LATER, we're walking through the glass door of Hounds and Hearts. I've deep-breathed myself into a state of relative calm, helped by Everett's rather charming efforts at maintaining a steady stream of distracting small talk in the car, guiding us through random conversational turns about recent TV favorites, growing up as either an only child (me) or the middle of three (him), a Korean restaurant we discover we both like, the origin of his first name from his birthplace near Seattle, and childhood team sports in which both of us did a lot of bench-warming. After we parked, I thanked him for the ride and asked if he wanted to wait somewhere else while I met the dog and decided whether or not she was coming home with us—a nearby bookstore, maybe, or the cozy-looking diner across the street. He said he preferred to come with me, as long as I'd be okay with that. Surprisingly, I am.

A rosy-cheeked thirtysomething woman in a hoodie that says *My dog is smarter than your honor roll student* greets us from a reception desk cluttered with novelty mugs, well-used office supplies, stacks of files with papers jutting from their open edges, jars of dog treats, and a few small houseplants that look like they'll be lucky if they make it to October.

The woman introduces herself as Nora, the shelter administrator, janitor, cheerleader, and backup dog walker. Then she asks if I'm Cameron, her eyes brimming with hope.

"I am," I say. "And this is Everett. He'd like to meet the dog, too."

Everett nods politely while Nora's face lights up.

"I'm so glad you brought your partner," she says. "This is one of the toughest cases we've had come through here. I'm not sure anyone should take this on alone."

"He's not my partner," I say reflexively.

"Sorry." Nora winces. "Hasty assumption. Your friend, then."

I'm about to clarify that he's not my friend, either, when I realize Nora doesn't need a debrief on my hour-long relationship with a guy I thought might give me a ride. Also, calling Everett *my ride* or even *a guy who lives in my building* feels reductive now that I at least know he has two sisters named Dakota and Charlotte, and he likes his bibimbap with extra chilis.

"If there's anything I can do," Everett says, "I'm happy to help."

I smile at him in gratitude. I may not be comfortable calling him a friend, but given how fast he grabbed his keys when I showed up, frantic, at his door, and how patient and kind he's been today, I'm pretty sure he's a genuinely good guy.

After a few minutes of digging through papers while muttering to herself about a desperate need to fully digitize, Nora tells us she'll grab "the boss." Then she disappears through a swinging door labeled *Employees only*. While we wait, I flip through a year-old *Modern Dog* magazine while Everett fusses with the wilted plants, plucking off dead leaves, patting the soil with the pad of his index finger, and sneaking water from a nearby cooler using an empty mug he grabs off the desk. I remind myself to ask about his midnight houseplant routine later, when I'm not about to make what could be a literal life-or-death decision.

Nora soon returns with a tall, lean, serious-faced man who looks to be around forty or forty-five, and who she introduces as Andy, the shelter manager I spoke with on the phone. We all shake hands and make the kind of preliminary small chat I usually try to bypass, but Andy's clearly attempting to make us comfortable and deflect the gravity of the situation, so I ride it out. *How was the drive, so glad you could make the time, did you find the place okay*, etc., etc.

Soon enough, he's guiding us down a hall and into a brightly lit room lined with partitioned cages on each side, stacked two high. Almost all are occupied, most with smaller, mixed-breed dogs who wag their tails or bark at us as we pass, looking eager for treats or attention. A basset hound with particularly large ears rests his head on a dish while following us with his eyes. A scrappy Chihuahua mix with a funny tuft of hair between his ears spins in giddy circles.

There's a dog with a bright pink cast on one of its back legs, and another missing an eye.

At the end of the aisle, in the bottom cage on the right, on a padded mat covered with an old, striped towel, a russet face rests between two paws, looking straight ahead with lifeless eyes, and my chest constricts so tightly, I forget to breathe.

A gentle hand finds me for the second time today, this time resting low on my back.

"You okay?" Everett asks, his voice quiet and tender.

Absolutely not, I think. But I can do this. I can do it for every dog I hope to treat in my professional life, assuming I actually do finish my degree. I can do it for Lady Marmalade. I can do it for this beautiful, unhappy dog, who so desperately needs someone to love her.

I take a deep breath and crouch by the cage. The dog doesn't even look up.

"Does she have a name?" I ask.

Andy shakes his head. "We keep trying. She hasn't responded to anything yet."

"Treat?" I say to her. "Walk? Dinner? Ball? Squirrel?"

Nothing. Just a blink, and after a few seconds, another blink.

Andy opens the cage and I move closer, dropping onto my knees. I suppose there's no worry about the dog running out through the open door, and not only because she's currently unresponsive. She's very overweight, and according to Andy, barely mobile, only able to inch herself onto her haunches with a great deal of effort. Between her girth and her long hair, her back legs disappear against her sides, while her sweet little face looks like it belongs to another dog entirely, like a mix-and-match that wasn't put back in order.

Sections of her fur are missing where they've been chewed away, eroded by her living conditions, or affected by sores and illness. But she has a perfect little black nose, and long, reddish hair that curls up in the cutest way at the base of her floppy ears. Her brows twitch when she blinks, and while that might be as expressive as she gets right now, it's not nothing. Some days, all I can do is twitch a brow, too.

"Hi, girl," I say, and when she still doesn't respond, I reach a hand forward for her to smell before running it over the top of her head and rubbing her ear. She's *so* soft, despite the problems with her fur. And her coloring is beautiful, a deep red tone with a lighter undercoat.

Everett crouches beside me, eliciting another twitch of the dog's brows.

"Goldie?" he tries. "Rusty? Fozzie? Bear? Winnie? Ruby?"

"Bella?" I chime in. "Lucy? Lucky? Daisy? Gracie? Lola? Ginger?"

Again, the dog merely blinks, her head still resting between her paws.

I ask Andy if I can give her a more thorough examination. He fetches a rudimentary medical kit before removing the entire front of the cage so we can pull the tray-like bottom forward and into the center aisle. The dog lets out a low groan of discomfort at the movement, so Everett rubs her back while Andy and I move the tray together, easing it forward more gently. This is quite the process, with three of us, making me all too aware of how unprepared I am to manage a dog like this on my own. I could use a sling to lift her, but getting her in and out of a car, or even in and out of my building's elevator, would be a serious challenge.

I check her heart rate, ears, eyes, mouth, joints, and glands. Her heart rate is weak. Her breathing is shallow and labored. Her nose is crusted with discolored mucus and her temperature suggests a high fever. Aside from the more extensive sores I find on her legs and haunches, one of the most obvious signs of her poor living conditions and treatment is her bald and scabby tail, which looks almost ratlike with only a thin layer of golden fuzz running down its length. It's not surprising if her thyroid isn't functioning properly, and if she's been sitting on her tail, pinned between concrete and her substantial weight, but it's still discomforting to see. Another mix-and-match that doesn't seem quite right, because, of course, it isn't.

I want to tell Andy and Everett all she needs is a little TLC. Or even a lot of TLC. A carefully monitored weight loss plan. Dedicated, long-term physical rehabilitation to rebuild her mobility. A soft bed to sleep on. Toys and activities to help her reengage. I want that *so* badly.

Instead, I brace myself and tell them, "We need to get her to an emergency vet. Now."

CHAPTER THREE

Six hours later, Everett pulls into our underground parking garage. We don't have a dog with us, though our situation does have an actual bright side. The dog is in intensive care back in Syracuse, receiving the attention she needs. The vet confirmed she has pneumonia, and there was no way I could care for her at home. Everything happened so fast. After my announcement, and a brief, heartbreaking conversation about potential expenses neither Andy nor I could afford, he made some calls and got ahold of someone at Ruff 'n' Rescue, a local rescue organization in Ithaca. They didn't hesitate, telling us to get the dog to emergency and we'd sort out the cost later. I didn't hesitate, either. Andy, Everett, and I got the dog into the back of Everett's station wagon and across town immediately. The emergency animal care staff took over from there.

I check my phone for the millionth time.

"She's in good hands," Everett assures me, also for the millionth time. "They were optimistic. And they *will* call if there's anything to report. Dr. Kong was very clear about that."

I pocket my phone and blow a frustrated breath toward the vinyl-covered ceiling.

"I'm trying really hard to not hate the people who did this to her," I say. "But I hate the people who did this to her. If I knew who they were, I might hire a hit man. Or if hit men only exist in movies, I'd at least slash some tires."

Everett pulls into a parking spot, shuts off the car, and turns to face me.

"Not that you need it," he says, "but you have my full permission for murderous rage."

This makes me laugh a little, though probably more for the tension release than because it's funny. Today has been long and hard, and the days ahead aren't likely to be much easier. I have a stupidly full schedule for the week so I can hardly run back and forth to Syracuse every day, but I've already grown attached to this dog, started to picture her in my apartment, and in my life. If she doesn't make it, it's going to crush me. And I really will look into hit men.

I unfasten my seat belt and pivot to face Everett, pausing for the first time today to fully appreciate the man beside me. This morning, I couldn't have imagined exchanging more than thirteen words with him, maybe a shy smile. Then he dropped whatever he had on his schedule, drove me to Syracuse, comforted me when I was freaking out, assisted in hauling a hundred-and-twenty-five-pound, immobile dog into the back of his car, brought me a cup of tea at emergency care, waited by my side until I got a diagnosis and talked with the vet, and drove me back to Ithaca, all without a single complaint or even a muffled sigh of annoyance.

Now he's sitting beside me with russet dog hair all over his beautiful pumpkin-colored sweater and rich mossy corduroys. His *Neil Diamond's Greatest Hits* CD just stopped playing "September Morn" after cycling through several other songs I liked more than I thought

I would. His hazel-now-that-I'm-looking-at-them eyes sparkle with the same kindness as his quiet smile, watching me behind his Benjamin Franklin glasses, giving me space to just *be* for a moment.

It strikes me without warning that I might've formed more than one attachment today, though my brain doesn't have sufficient space to give that thought the consideration it deserves. I can only hope the next time someone calls Everett my friend—assuming there is a next time—I won't feel like I should contradict them.

"Thank you," I say. "For everything. I'll give you some gas money. And dry-clean your sweater. And vacuum your car. And if there's anything else—"

"Cameron," he interjects, his brows lifting with bemused surprise and disappearing under his shaggy brown curls. "I'm fully capable of operating a vacuum or laundering a sweater. The gas is on me. Just take care of yourself, okay? And keep me posted about the dog?"

I open my mouth to protest—because surely, I should protest. He doesn't even know me. I didn't just borrow a cup of flour or whatever neighbors usually do. I even made fun of his music and criticized his job, tangentially and accidentally, but still . . . why is he being so nice?

But he gives me a look that brooks no argument, and I don't actually want to argue. I want to shower, change my clothes, and take a long, hard look at my schedule so I can free up time to head back to Syracuse this week. I'll sort out something nice to do for Everett later.

"I'll let you know as soon as I hear anything," I say. "And thank you. Again."

"You're welcome. Thank you for asking for my help. And for letting me come."

We exchange a smile, a simple, tired, long-day-ending one. Then we get out of the car and trudge over to the elevator. He presses the button but the elevator's slow to arrive, because of course it is. It might only be starting its descent from the ground level, but since it appears to run on a single volt of electricity and the power of wishful thinking, we wait.

I'm sorely tempted to tip my head onto Everett's shoulder. I'm pretty sure he wouldn't mind. He might even put his arm around my waist and tuck me against his side.

"You're right. I might," he says, and *dammit!* I've spoken my thoughts aloud again. I have *got* to stem this habit. It's going to get me in serious trouble if I don't watch it.

Thankfully, the elevator doors open, diverting our attention to the couple making out in the corner. It's The Lovers, also known as the residents of 605: a tall, blond, fair-skinned woman currently in jeans and a cropped satin letterman jacket, and a short, dark-skinned woman with natural curls and a sexy red retro dress that makes me think of *Mad Men*. Despite the ding that accompanied the opening doors, the pair doesn't stop kissing. I suspect some residents find this behavior off-putting, but the couple always seems to be enjoying themselves and since they're not hurting anyone, I find it kind of refreshing. I certainly wouldn't complain if I met someone who couldn't keep their hands off me, as long as I wanted to mash faces with them, too.

I'm not sure what Everett's thoughts are on the matter, or if I should be thinking about what his thoughts are on the matter, but he waits as patiently as I do until the doors start to close, at which point he steps forward and blocks their movement with an outstretched hand and a quiet "oops" that alerts The Lovers to our presence. They break their kiss and turn toward us, still half entangled and as unaffected as if we were a pair of traffic cones.

The tall one lifts her chin. "Oh. Hey," she says flatly.

Everett musters a polite smile. "Hi. Um . . . are you getting off here?"

The Lovers exchange a look, breaking into muffled giggles that must make Everett realize what he just asked at the same time I do, because his cheeks go pink and he backs away.

"Sorry," he says. "We can take the stairs."

"No. We're sorry." The short one stifles her giggles and looks around as though she's only just now noticing where she is. "Parking level? Yeah. This is us." She drags the other woman into the garage and they jog past us, leaving the elevator empty for us to enter.

Everett and I step in and I hit the button for the sixth floor, initiating our painfully slow upward journey, accompanied by the usual flickering overheads and the low whirring sound I associate with intense mechanical effort. We both face the doors and go silent, though it seems weird to default to these habits now that we're not strangers.

Everett must have the same thought, because we both speak at once.

"Do you have—"

"Are you—"

"Sorry. You first."

"No. Go ahead."

We both go quiet for a beat as the elevator continues inching up toward the ground floor.

"I was going to ask if you wanted dinner," he says. "I kind of forgot about lunch, and I imagine it wasn't top of your mind, either, but now, I'm guessing you might be as hungry as I am. I thought I could maybe pick up takeout from The Lotus. You know. For both of us."

"Oh." I blink through my surprise. I was going to ask if he had a busy week ahead of him.

"Not, like, as a date," he clarifies, probably because I'm blinking at him like an idiot.

"No. Yeah. I know," I stammer, suddenly flustered by the word *date*, even when prefaced by the word *not*. "I just . . . I need a shower. And want to kick back for the rest of the night."

"Of course. Sure. If you already have something to eat at home . . ." He tucks his hands into the pockets of his corduroys and watches the G light up over the doors as though it's the most interesting thing ever. His face is still flushed and he looks like he's chewing on the inside of his cheek. He's also drumming his thumbs on his thighs from where they hook over the edges of his pockets. I find his nervous tics endearing, maybe because I have so many of my own.

With that thought, my brain finally catches up with my mouth.

"Actually, I don't have anything at home," I say. "But will you at least let me treat?"

His thumbs go still and the corners of his lips twitch with the threat of a smile.

"I've got this," he says. "You can get the next one."

FIFTEEN MINUTES LATER, I've showered and changed into cozy lounge pants, a plain white tee, and a bottle-green cable-knit cardigan that saves me from looking like I'm ready for bed. Everett's picking up takeout while I scramble to tidy my apartment, tucking away the teetering stack of mail I let pile up on the counter, shifting the laundry basket into the closet, and putting the acne gel I leave on the rim of the sink into the medicine cabinet.

Everett knocks as I'm straightening the pillows and blankets on the futon, and I open the door to find him holding a bag that looks far too large and full to contain two orders of bibimbap.

He catches me looking at the bag. "I forgot to ask you about appetizers."

I sputter out a laugh. "So you got them all?"

"I got options. Anything we don't eat tonight will keep." He looks nervous again, which means I find him endearing again, and I step back to invite him in, gesturing toward the coffee table, which I'm glad I cleared, given the size of our impending feast.

Together, Everett and I unpack the mains and half a dozen appetizers, settling in side by side on the futon, which is my only available seating. While we eat, we talk about how the dog might fit in here, where a cozy dog bed might go if the futon nudges closer to the wall, and where I might put food and water dishes, and also pee pads while we sort out a toilet routine, given my schedule and her mobility issues. It's nice, fleshing out the image of her future with me, even if I know nothing's definite.

I also tell Everett about growing up in Roseburg, a small town in southern Oregon, where my parents still live, and about summer vacations we spent at a cabin on the coast. He tells me more about his childhood, how his parents were—and still are—both academics, hunting for tenure-track jobs together but settling for short-term visiting positions as they've opened up in one field or the other. He and his sisters were shuttled from city to city, always for only one or two years at a time. His older sister, Charlotte, was born in Charlotte, North Carolina. Everett was born in Everett, Washington. His younger sister, Dakota, was born in Vermillion, South Dakota, where his parents were kind enough to adjust their naming routine.

"Was it hard?" I ask between ravenous mouthfuls of rice and veggies. "All that moving?"

"Challenging, sure." He pokes at a slippery chunk of avocado he's been trying to pick up with his chopsticks for a full minute now. "My sisters and I got along pretty well, which helped, but we never had much money and moving costs were always a consideration, so we traveled light." He finally manages the avocado slice and takes a moment to eat it. "It's a first-world-problem kind of thing, obviously, but where I'm going with it is that I think it's why I hold on to things now. Things other people might get rid of without a second thought."

"Things like a forty-year-old Volvo?" I ask.

"Exactly. And like this sweater, which was Charlotte's." He gives the front a little tug. "And my glasses, which were my great-grandfather's, re-lensed, of course. And the CD collection my old neighbor was throwing away when she retired and moved to California this summer."

I choke on a mouthful of rice but quickly recover with the help of some water.

"The CDs were your neighbor's?" I ask once my throat's cleared.

Everett laughs a little as his cheeks go pink again.

"I should've told you," he says. "But I would've felt like I was only doing it because I know the music's not cool. And I don't really care if it's cool, if it's something I like."

I gape at him, openly impressed. Not that I make great efforts at being cool, but I definitely try to hide my non-coolness from people I don't know.

"The Volvo isn't set up for Bluetooth," he continues. "It only has that terrible, no-signal radio and the CD player, and I didn't have any CDs of my own. I was happy to have something to listen to. Also, I really liked my neighbor. The music *is* something to remember her by. Now I'm used to it, I like it, and I know all the words to 'Sweet Caroline' and 'Take Me Home, Country Roads.' So the CDs *are* mine." He shrugs sheepishly while working hard on another piece of avocado, with his brow furrowed, his floppy curls, his old-timey glasses, his sister's sweater, and a pound of dog hair on him, all of it together setting off a little red warning light in my mind. *Be careful*, it says. *You might start to really like this guy. And you do not have time for a guy right now.*

I glance at my door, picturing the hallway beyond, and the door to 606 at the far end.

"Is your place crammed full of stuff other people were discarding?" I ask.

He shakes his head. "I'm not a hoarder. I swear. I'll show you sometime."

The red light goes off again but I quickly extinguish it. He's only suggesting a look inside, maybe a visit or friendly hangout. My brain needs to knock it the hell off.

"And the plants?" I ask. "The ones you bring in late at night? What's with those?"

He gives up on the avocado and reaches for a fried seaweed roll instead.

"I feel like I should have a good story here," he says.

"I'm pretty sure anything would be a good story," I toss back.

He nods as he eats the roll and gestures for me to take the last one, which I do.

As I chew, I make a little *mmm* of enjoyment that brings out the smile lines beside Everett's eyes. He watches me savor the roll, and it's a nice feeling—sharing joy—one I haven't felt in a long time, but I make a motion for him to get on with his story. I've been waiting weeks to hear this. He can be all cute and sweet another time.

"I work in a building that houses several other arts and arts-adjacent studios and offices," he says. "There's a team that does styling for print ads and short videos. They go through a lot of props, and their storage space is limited, so they put anything they're unlikely to reuse and don't have room for in the back alley near the trash. Furniture. Rugs. Rolls of fabric. Small appliances. Random statues. This city is full of scavengers, so most of it disappears pretty quickly."

"But not the plants?" I guess.

"Not the plants," he confirms. "And since I often work late . . ."

"You smuggle them in at midnight," I finish for him.

He feigns affront. "I wouldn't say *smuggle*."

"Fine. *Carry*, then. You *carry* them in at midnight. Because you have a thing for plants."

He goes quiet, serious, tapping his chopsticks on the edge of a take-out container until he realizes he's doing it and rests them on the table instead.

"I just think . . ." He pauses and pivots to face me. "I think the world is full of disposable things. We've grown used to them. *I've* grown used to them. It's modern life. But that doesn't mean we should let something die if all it needs is a little care and attention."

This time, when the red warning light goes off, I let it flash away, completely ignored.

CHAPTER FOUR

On Sunday, I work my usual shift at Loden and Linden, peddling scratchy but aesthetically pleasing, naturally dyed, hand-woven flax blankets and organic candles with names like Summer Kisses and First Blush, which have always struck me as suspect because I'm dead certain none of my kisses or blushes have had a distinct scent. When I check in at the end of the day, Dr. Kong says the dog is stable, but still running a temperature and nonresponsive.

Monday through Thursday, I attend the anatomy and physiology, immunology, and pathology classes I'm barely keeping up with, grateful we're not working with cadavers this week because I'm not sure I could hold myself together. I also work my shifts at the pizzeria.

Every evening, I check in.

Every evening, Dr. Kong updates me, though any changes are minor.

Every evening, I force myself to stop picturing the dog bed and the dishes. I have to quit thinking of this dog as mine. Her poor body has a lot to contend with, as do her mind and her spirit. Stressing about her health won't help her. My energy would be better spent preparing for what's feeling more and more inevitable as her health fails to improve.

Friday morning, when I find myself seriously considering if the nutritional contents of four leftover take-out packets of ketchup and six remaining saltines in an otherwise empty box will get me through to lunch, I make a quick run to the grocery store, returning with a discount loaf of almost-stale bread, a few packets of bland but unobjectionable ramen, and a jar of off-brand peanut butter, desperate to save every penny until I know what's happening with the dog.

As I step into the elevator from the lobby, a soft voice calls for me to hold the doors. I reach out to halt their closing, and see Dog Lady speed-walking toward me. She's a short, stout Asian woman with a tidy blunt bob, currently sporting cropped linen pants and sandals that look more suitable for summer, which she seems to be making up for with a heavy knit top, a bulky cardigan, a long, tailored jacket, and two cotton print scarves loosely twisted together and looped around her neck. Her Yorkie-poo, Pilot, is poking her tiny tufted head out from a padded shoulder bag while Dog Lady's hands are filled with mesh totes of vibrant produce that makes me glad my dismal, vitamin-deficient groceries are well hidden within canvas.

"Thank you," Dog Lady says as she joins me, a little breathless.

"You're welcome," I reply.

We exchange a brief smile. Then we do what we usually do: settle into position facing the doors with a polite amount of space between us, going quiet as the doors close. However, I can't help glancing over at Pilot, who's watching me with her tiny black eyes alert and her tiny pink tongue hanging out. She's so cute, and so quiet, and she always seems so happy, tucked in her quilted bag.

Next thing I know, I'm thinking about a golden retriever left outside and alone on concrete, and a lump is rising in my throat, and if I don't say something soon . . .

"How did you pick her name?" I ask, clearing my throat when the words come out raspy.

"Oh!" Dog Lady turns to look at me, her face awash with surprise. "You mean Pilot?"

"Yeah. It's sweet," I say. "Kinda different. Do you fly planes?"

Dog Lady laughs as she gazes affectionately at the tiny, happy face by her shoulder.

"I'm an English professor," she says. "With a focus on nineteenth-century women's literature. Pilot's the name of Mr. Rochester's dog in *Jane Eyre*. It's always been a favorite."

"You're a professor?" I can't help asking, because really? Living *here*?

"Adjunct," she says with another laugh. "Like everyone else these days."

I don't know what to say to that, so I just smile again, though I suspect it comes out forced. It's depressing enough to live here as a student. As a professor? I can't even imagine.

When we reach the sixth floor and head in the same direction off the elevator, grappling with our bags and keys, it suddenly feels silly that I'm still thinking of her as Dog Lady.

"I'm Cameron, by the way," I tell her. "Grad student in Cornell's veterinary program."

Another flash of surprise crosses her face, followed swiftly by a warm smile.

"Minh Ha," she says. "Unless you take one of my classes. Then I'm Professor Huynh."

"I can't really see myself studying literature."

"Well, you never know. But it's nice to meet you, Cameron."

"You too," I say, and hope she knows I mean it, even if my introduction is long overdue.

AFTER BREAKFAST, I manage to pay attention in my morning classes, but later that afternoon, when I'm on my way to my usual shift at the pizzeria, I get the call I'm dreading.

We don't think she has long. If you want to say goodbye...

Doesn't matter that I've been half expecting it. It's still a battering ram to the heart.

I step into the nearest alcove, take a minute to collect myself, and call my boss to let her know I have a personal emergency. She's flexible about schedules in general—the biggest perk of an otherwise uninspiring and far from lucrative job—but she's angry about the last-minute notice, especially on a Friday night, and I'm forced to endure a scolding, one that ends with an order to "make sure this doesn't become a habit." It's literally the first time I've called in like this, but I keep the comment to myself, anxious to get off the phone and get going.

My next call is to Everett, who I exchanged numbers with on Saturday and have been updating daily, often after he sends a sweet, heart-pinching text like How's our girl?

> **CAMERON:** They think this is it. I need to get there stat. Any chance you're free?

Everett doesn't answer and the ellipses don't appear. It's almost 7 p.m. He said he often works late. He could also be out with friends or on a date, a thought that grates more than I'd like, especially since I have way more important things to focus on right now.

I check the bus schedule but it'll be ages before I get to Syracuse, so I go ahead and book an Uber, wincing at the cost, though if there was ever a time to splurge . . .

Within ten minutes, I'm in the back seat of a tidy Prius while Jared, my driver, bobs his head to the base-heavy music he dropped to a low volume for me. I like base-heavy music, but not when it feels like the soundtrack to my anxiety, thumping along to my too-fast heartbeat.

I picture her little face. Her cute black nose. Her sad eyes. Her twitching brows.

Hold on, I think. *Please, hold on. We can do this. Give me a chance to love you.*

When I'm halfway to Syracuse, Everett calls.

"Sorry, sorry," he gusts out as if winded. "I was in a meeting. Am still in a meeting. On a break. West Coast client. Time difference. Where are you? How are you? How is she? Do you need my car? If you can come to my office, I'll give you my keys."

He sounds as stressed as I am, which I have conflicted feelings about.

"I got an Uber," I tell him. "I don't know how long—"

"I'll drive up as soon as my meeting lets out," he interjects.

"You sure?" I ask. "You might not even get to see her. You know. Depending."

He doesn't answer right away but I can hear him breathing as he mentally fills in the spaces we keep leaving in the conversation.

"I'm glad she won't be alone," he says. "But you don't need to be alone, either."

My throat gets thick and I struggle to swallow before speaking.

"Okay. Thank you," I say. "If I leave the vet's, I'll text you where to find me."

We say goodbye and hang up. After a second or two, Jared reaches around to hold out a travel-pack of tissues. I take a few and thank him, and because he doesn't follow up the gesture by asking me to give him a five-star rating, I tap it into my phone as soon as I exit the car.

THE DOG IS being kept comfortable—or as comfortable as possible—on a large mat covered with a fuzzy blanket on the floor of a consultation room. One of her front legs is shaved where she's had an IV, though she's not currently hooked up to anything. She's lying on her side this time, with all four legs stretched out and her eyes closed. Even with her sores, her weight, and her hairless tail, she's absolutely perfect. Because she's a dog, and all dogs are perfect.

A vet tech in lavender scrubs is sitting by her head, stroking her ears. She says they've been taking turns, keeping the dog company and monitoring her vitals while encouraging her to hold on until I arrive. Everyone here is an animal person. I don't need to explain why I'm so attached to this dog after briefly meeting her in a shelter a week ago. They all get it.

"I'll give you some time alone," the tech says. "Be back to check on you in ten?"

I nod, because it's all I can manage. Then I take her place on the floor and she heads out, shutting the door behind her with the softest, gentlest click as the latch catches. It's so quiet, but my nerves are so taut, it might as well be a thunderous gong, ringing out from a mountaintop.

"Hi, girl." I run a hand over the dog's ear and down the back of her sweet, soft, perfect head. "You're not having a very good day, are you?" I lean a little closer, bury my fingers in the thicker hair at the back of her neck. She's not wearing a collar of any kind. I wonder if she ever had one. If someone, early on, before they decided *this* was acceptable pet-parenting, picked out a color, and the shape of a little metal name tag, and got her name engraved. "Millie? Harley? Honey? Bailey?" I give each name a moment to settle before I try the next. "Cocoa? Kiki?"

She doesn't open her eyes. She doesn't whimper or snort. She just breathes, and I can only hope the sound of my voice and the feel of my hand in her fur are a comfort to her.

I don't really know what to say. One of the things I've always loved about animals is that they don't expect you to say anything at all. There are no awkward elevator silences. There are no awkward anything silences, but all I have right now is my voice and my touch, and after a lifetime of being given so little of what she needs, this dog deserves everything I've got.

I pull my phone from my pocket, and while I pet her with one hand, I scroll a baby name site with the other, reading through names from *A* to *Z*. The vet tech checks on me somewhere around *F*. I tell her we're doing okay, which is a pretty big stretch, but code we both understand. She assures me the room is ours as long as we need it, so I let her know I'll pop my head out and call for someone if anything changes. Otherwise, I'll hang out here for a while, which I do.

For the next hour or so, I read names, ask the dog what she thinks, and will her to live.

"Zelda? Zoey? Zora?" I try as I get to the end of the list.

No response, other than shallow but even breathing.

I turn off my screen and rest my phone in my lap, squeezing my eyes shut and letting a quiet whisper of a curse slip through my teeth. I'm thinking about slashing tires again, and this is not the moment to give in to my murderous rage. I can return to it later.

"Maybe I'm going about this all wrong." I open my eyes and look down at the dog, still petting her head, her ear, her neck. "We shouldn't pick your name off a list. We should make it special. Lady Marmalade was named after my favorite song at the time. I used to holler my way through it, missing every note. My poor parents." I smile a little, but only a little. "We could pick a song for you. Or a musician, or a character from a book, like Pilot from *Jane Eyre*, or even an author, though I'm not much of a reader these days unless it's an anatomy textbook. As a kid, though, I used to pore through books. I remember checking Agatha Christie mysteries out of the library five at a time because that was the limit for kids under sixteen. I loved the—"

I stop short, my rambling halted by the gentle nudge of a nose against my thigh.

And then she opens her eyes.

She opens. Her eyes.

At first, she stares straight ahead, like she did at the shelter, unfocused, but after a few seconds, her eyes shift until she's blinking up at me. Her head is still resting on the blanket, her body otherwise unmoving, but she's definitely looking at me, with her tufty brows twitching and more life in her eyes than I saw last weekend. They're a warm, dark brown, almost black, each with a pair of highlights from the overhead fluorescents and a tiny crescent of white at the base.

"Hi," I say, a barely there breath of a word, and again, "Hi."

She blinks, and her nose inches forward to tap my thigh again.

A rush of emotion races through me, though I'm not sure which emotion. Relief, or maybe fear, because it's only a nudge. It could be a goodbye, but also . . . it's a nudge.

I scoot closer so I can lift her head onto my lap. There's hair everywhere at this point from all the petting so I pluck away a few strands that are stuck to her nose. Her wet nose. Her no longer hot and dry nose. Her nose that twitches as I clear it of hair.

A nudge *and* a twitch. And open, curious eyes.

My hope surges.

I stay with her, rambling nonsense for several more minutes with her head on my lap as she adds a twitch of a paw to her repertoire, and then another, and then a faint but happy groan when I rub the inside of her ear with my knuckle. After several more minutes, when I find myself laughing through tears at some random observation I make about how it's too bad neither of us can reach the treat jar sitting on the counter on the opposite side of the room, tucked among examination equipment, I hear the quiet thump of a tail hitting the mat.

This is how Everett finds me as he's ushered into the room with another vet tech: cry-laughing with a dog whose tail thumps for a second time when he kneels and asks how we are.

"I think she might pull through," I say.

His eyes sparkle behind his glasses as he pulls down the sleeve of another beautiful sweater he probably inherited from one of his sisters, and uses it to dab at my eyes.

"Yeah?" he asks.

"Yeah. And she has a name. She doesn't know it yet, but she will. I hope she will." I bend down to kiss the top of her head and then whisper near her ear, "Hold on, Aggie. Hold on and come home and have the life you should've had all along."

CHAPTER FIVE

Three days after the trip to the emergency vet's, I get word that Aggie can come home with me. Dr. Kong puts our call on video so I can see for myself. Aggie's still barely mobile but she's alert, holding her head up and looking around with interest, perking up her ears, gently wagging her funny little tail, and eating her food without hesitation. She also looks like she's smiling.

I reach out to Andy and fill out adoption papers, because once this dog comes home with me, I can't imagine anything that would make me let her go again. We share a laugh about how I might be the fastest foster fail ever, but it's a failure that feels *so* right, I run with it.

Before I pick Aggie up, Andy connects me with Ruff 'n' Rescue, the rescue organization he contacted in Ithaca. There, I meet Sam and Sariah, who look like I imagine Ken and Barbie might look if they gracefully aged into their late forties or early fifties: white, tanned, tall, fit, blond (with a little silver), neatly attired in brightly colored sportswear, and possessing a kind of natural, cheerful charisma that makes them easy to talk to. More important, they both have a lot of experience rehoming dogs and cats with serious health issues. They're also deeply invested in Aggie's case already and want to help her adjust to a new and happier life.

They set me up with a heavy-duty sling and a strappy harness for lifting Aggie from a prone position and supporting her weight until she can support her own. They also provide me with a starter kit of carefully selected food and a large, sturdy storage bin, demonstrating how I can turn it upside down and place Aggie on top of it so she can mimic a standing position, reducing stress on her hips, backside, and tail as we work on her mobility and get her weight down. They talk me through techniques of using both the harness and the sling, as well as what I might expect in the coming weeks, and how to adjust the food plan if I discover any digestive problems or unforeseen allergies.

I pick up a big puffy bed, two dishes, two balls—one squeaky, one not—and a cute stuffed monkey toy I grab on a whim by the register, where a particularly adorable selection of toys has been carefully placed for suckers like me. None of the items I buy are fancy or top-of-the-line, but they'll do until I figure out what Aggie likes. I'm trying not to think about my bank account right now, though I can't completely *not* think about it, especially not with significant expenses ahead of me and the prospect that I'll be cutting back on hours at one or both of my jobs so I'm not leaving Aggie home alone all day, every day. Dr. Kong and Sariah have been talking all week, and the rescue organization is generously covering the cost of Aggie's recent vet bills. They'll even provide some free rehab check-ins at the rescue center, but now that I'm adopting Aggie and she's mine, all further veterinary expenses will be my responsibility.

"They're covering *everything*?" Everett asks as he drives us to Syracuse on Tuesday afternoon. He sorted out a part-day off, which allowed me to attend my morning classes. Once we were both free, we scrambled to put the dog bed in the back of the Volvo along with the monkey and the mobility equipment, and we hit the road like two kids on their way to Disneyland for the first time, though with a *slightly* different soundtrack playing.

"The exams, the overnight care, the meds she needed during her stay," I confirm. "For now, I just need to cover the prescriptions I'll bring home today. Rescue workers are seriously the best humans on the planet. It's not an easy job. Most people only see the success stories, or the happy endings that come after a lot of hard work is done."

Everett nods in understanding while drumming his fingers on the steering wheel to the tune of "Girl, You'll Be a Woman Soon," which is a very strange song to have ever hit a pop chart. Still, the music's growing on me, though I suspect anything I hear in this car with this man will grow on me. There's something about his rebellious un-coolness I find very cool.

"What do your parents think of all this?" he asks. "Are they excited, too?"

"You mean because of Marmie?"

"It sounded like she was important to all of you."

I nod as I consider my reply. I told Everett about Marmie when he saw her photo on my fridge the other night. We've been texting regularly since then, which is all our schedules have allowed. I don't need to dump all of my family issues on him, but I guess we're past the Brand-new Acquaintance stage, so I don't need to hide those issues, either.

"They don't know," I admit.

His brows rise, disappearing under his mop of floppy curls. He's in jeans today, not his usual corduroys, with a plum-and-viridian-striped sweater over a crewneck tee.

"My parents are challenging," I say. "My mom likes to put a consistently positive spin on everything, which might sound great in theory, but in practice doesn't leave room for anything that's not bright and shiny. If I tell her about Aggie, and even hint at the potential difficulties ahead, she'll gloss over it all, saying everything will be great, she's so happy I won't be lonely anymore, and when will I post photos on Facebook so she can share them with her friends?"

"And your dad?" he prompts after a beat of quiet consideration.

"My dad will ask how I'm affording it. That will be his first, last, and only concern. He'll suspect I can't do it on my own, and accepting financial assistance of any kind equates to a demonstration of personal failure and poor decisions." I pause long enough to soften the note of irritation I hear in my voice. My relationship with my dad isn't unloving. The love just gets buried under so many lessons and lectures. "With bringing Aggie into my home, money's a legitimate concern, and I can't honestly say I'm not worried, but I also don't want to start a relationship with this beautiful, glorious being focused on the cost and not the love."

This draws out the creases beside Everett's eyes, letting me know he's smiling even when he's not really smiling. The look remains while he passes an agonizingly slow U-Haul and eases us back into the right lane, checking every mirror and resetting his hands at ten and two.

"Sounds like you have your priorities right," he says, and I could hug him for that, for accepting everything I just told him and rolling with it. "Though if you do decide you want to post anything about Aggie, I know someone who can help with graphics and content."

I catch his eye and tell him with a look that I know which *someone* he's referring to.

"I'm pretty sure I could handle a selfie and a few words about a dog," I say.

His smile eases into view as if he's fighting it, but not fighting very hard.

"I'm pretty sure you could, too," he says. He's teasing me, which I like more than I probably should. He's also leaving a door open between us, which I might like even more.

INSIDE THE RECEPTION area at the vet's, a technician leads us to the closed door of a consultation room.

"Are you ready to see your dog?" she asks.

Your dog. Two simple words that almost knock me over.

Everett sets a hand on my lower back. "I think she's ready."

I don't know what my face looks like right now, but from the glance the two of them exchange, I'd guess it's pretty clear that if the technician doesn't open the door before us in the next two seconds, I'm going to wrench the damned thing off its hinges.

Thankfully, this isn't necessary. She opens the door and there's Aggie, lying sphinxlike on a mat with a blanket, facing our direction. She's upright and her mouth is ajar, with her pink tongue on display. Her eyes are bright. Her naked tail thumps quietly against the mat.

For a moment, I stand completely still, overwhelmed by emotion, with my fists balled together against my chest and Everett's hand on my lower back. This dog and I are about to weave our lives together in a million ways both big and small. She will be changed by me. I will be changed by her. We will be each other's family. We will become an *us*.

I inhale slowly, exhale slowly. Then I crouch by her side, letting her smell my hand before I run it over her head and down one of the supersoft ears I'm already obsessed with.

"Hi, Aggie," I say, barely above a whisper. "Are you ready to come home?"

The tail thumps a little faster. I take that as a yes.

Dr. Kong knocks and enters from the door opposite the reception area. While I pet Aggie's ears and Everett stands nearby, listening intently and nodding along, Dr. Kong talks me through Aggie's medical issues and the prescriptions she recommends, all of which are at least somewhat familiar to me, thanks to my coursework, though the depth and precision with which she can speak about everything illustrate how much I still have to learn. We also discuss diet, movement, and behavioral changes to monitor, echoing a lot of what Sam and Sariah covered with me, and she recommends a vet in Ithaca where I can schedule follow-up appointments locally. She glances fondly at Aggie as she says this, and I get the distinct feeling I'm not the only one who's fallen in love with this dog after only a brief acquaintance.

I give Aggie a big bear hug, nearly tearing up for the umpteenth time since the first call from Andy at the shelter, though this time, there's no grief, no panic, no confusion, no fury at horrible people who shouldn't have pets. There's just an overwhelming surge of gratitude.

I get to love you, I think. *I get the chance to love you.*

While Everett backs his car up to the front of the building, I pay for Aggie's medications at reception, sliding the receipt into my pocket before the voice in my head—the one that sounds a lot like my dad's—asks if I can really afford this. After tucking the bag of antibiotics, thyroid meds, pain pills, and skin ointment into the front seat, I return with Everett to move Aggie from the consulting room into the back of his station wagon. I brought both the sling and the harness. The sling wraps around her midsection and has two handles that can be used by either one or two people to support a dog's weight. The harness wraps around both her shoulders and her haunches, allowing one person to lift the front end and the other to get the back end.

We go with the harness, and it's a bit of a puzzle sorting out how to get Aggie into it, ensuring each length of webbing is in the right place and all the buckles are properly snapped. Thankfully, she can wear it for a while, so I'll only need to do this once a day, taking it off for bedtime. Also thankfully, she's very patient, watching with curiosity and an occasional groan of mild discomfort as we work the straps under her girth and around her legs.

"Just wait," I tell her as I snap the final buckle over her shoulders and test the handle with a gentle tug. "One day, when we come home from a walk, we'll look back on this and smile."

She blinks at me as though she thinks I'm full of crap, which is a reasonable response when she looks like we've dressed her up for an extremely low-budget burlesque performance.

Beside me, Everett suppresses a laugh.

"Sorry," he says. "She just looks so embarrassed."

I tsk at him. "Wouldn't you be if a total stranger strung webbing between your legs?"

His cheeks go a little pink, but he shrugs and says, "Yeah. Yep. Fair enough."

He's very cute when he blushes, and while I have no idea what his kinks are, or if he has any, or if I should be thinking about literally anything *but* his kinks, I can't help but feel a certain tenderness toward him whenever he matches my awkwardness with his own.

As his blush fades, I talk him through where to stand and how to hold the handle. We secure our footing and our grips, and I ask Aggie if she's ready. She looks up at me with so much unearned trust. It's such a gift, and I make a silent promise to her that I *will* earn it. Then I count down from three and we lift, easing her high enough for her feet to clear the floor.

Everett and I both strain and fumble as we balance ourselves, and I feel bad about it, but this is our first time lifting Aggie and the action will get easier with practice. I can also add upper-body strength training to the 5-to-10K runs I sneak in a couple times a week. This poor dog did not get through the past ten days—and the past seven years—to feel like a burden.

The staff cheers when we pass through the reception area, chorusing *Go, Aggie, go!* and *You can do it!* and *Enjoy your new home!* That's the word that follows us out of the office as two vet techs help us ease Aggie up onto her puffy bed and I record a short video of her smiling over her shoulder at us, her pink tongue hanging out and her eyes full of hope and curiosity.

Home.

CHAPTER SIX

Everett needs to return to work for a meeting about a new account he'll be managing—a vegan restaurant chain with a dozen locations across New York and the bordering states—but he helps me get Aggie and her things settled in my apartment, where we place her bed next to mine and cover it with a secondhand leak-proof blanket for easier cleaning. I have no great ambitions for the evening. We won't try to get her situated on the bin or outside for a pee. I just want her to become acquainted with me, the space, and the start of a new routine.

As I see Everett out, he turns to face me from the hallway and a laugh sputters out of me before I can stop it. He's absolutely covered in dog hair. I remember this about Marmie. In many ways, she was the easiest dog in the world. She wasn't demanding, aggressive, territorial, barky, particularly naughty, or desperate for constant input and activity. But she sure did shed.

"Sorry." I pluck a few hairs off Everett's pretty striped sweater. "Though you really should ask before you walk out the door with half my dog."

A smile stretches across his face, wide and bright, as he helps me brush away hair.

"I like the way you say *my dog*," he tells me.

I glance over my shoulder at Aggie, where she's watching us from her bed, though I can't tell from her expression if she's in strict-chaperone mode or curious-onlooker mode. Either way, by the time I pivot back around to face Everett, I can tell my smile mirrors his.

"I like it, too," I say. "And thank you again. For everything. The rides. The help. The shoulder to cry on. I don't know how I would've done any of this without you."

He goes shifty in a way that's already becoming familiar. A little upward jerk of his shoulders. A twitch of his lips. A shift of his stance. An uptick in fiddling and fidgeting.

"You would've figured it out," he says.

"Maybe, but thanks to you, I didn't have to."

He blushes for the second time today but accepts my gratitude without downplaying it again, stepping back and pointing over his shoulder. "I should probably . . ."

"Of course. Yeah. Sorry to keep you."

"You're not. It's just . . ."

"Work. I know."

"And you need to . . ."

"Get Aggie settled. Yep. Absolutely."

He leans around me to wave at her, so earnestly and so sweetly, and I'm struck with a need to do more than fumble my way through another awkward thank you and goodbye.

"Everett?" I ask. "Before you go, can I hug you?"

His smile reappears as his brows flicker with surprise. Then he opens his arms and I step into them, looping my arms around his back and pressing my palms against the planes of his shoulder blades, which I can just discern through his sweater and tee.

Unsurprisingly, Everett Redmond is an excellent hugger. His embrace is firm and earnest as he draws me close and lets his cheek rest against mine, with one hand near my waist and the other perfectly situated on my upper back so the edge of his thumb brushes my bare skin above the collar of my sweater. As he holds me tight, I realize I haven't hugged anyone but my parents in about two years, not since I last saw Hannah when I flew over for a quick trip while she was dealing with a breakup. I miss it. I miss *this*. Holding and being held. People talk about sex all the time. How much they love it if they're having it or miss it if they're not. I miss it, too. I'd be lying to myself if I claimed I didn't, even though I haven't had much to miss.

But a really good hug? I swear. It's life-changing.

Also, that thumb is going to haunt me.

I'm not sure who pulls away first or if we realize at about the same time that we might be hugging too long for a friendly goodbye. As we back away from each other, he waves at Aggie again, and then at me, before heading down the stairs, wisely opting not to wait for the elevator.

I return to Aggie, flopping down beside her on the floor and leaning back against my bed.

"Well? What do you think?" I ask.

She glances at the door and back at me.

"No, not about the guy," I say. "About the apartment. The bed. Your new home."

She blinks at me with her bright, expressive eyes. Then she looks at the door again.

"How about your toys?" I find the stuffed monkey and give it a wiggle near her nose. She sniffs it and then ignores it. I try the squeaky ball. She tilts her head at the noise but shows no particular interest in holding the ball in her mouth or watching it roll across the floor. I also bring her water dish close enough for her to get a drink. She sniffs it, dips her tongue in, and lifts her head as if to say she's finished. By the time I set down the dish, she's looking at the door.

"Okay, fine," I concede. "What do you think about the guy?"

Her funny little tail thumps against her bed.

I break into a laugh as I give her a firm scratch on the head. "Classic. You get a girl everything her heart might desire, and all she wants to do is hang out and talk about boys."

She lowers her head so it rests between her paws, where she looks up at me with a quiet cheekiness that slays me, like she knows I caught her at something and she's eagerly awaiting my reaction. Maybe I'm reading too much into it, but also, maybe it doesn't matter, because there are worse things to do on a Tuesday evening than have a conversation with a dog.

In fact, I can't think of anything better.

"As you've clearly discerned for yourself, he's one of the good ones," I tell Aggie, assuming this is still her topic of choice. "One of the *really* good ones. But don't get any ideas. I'm a week behind on homework already, I have to find a new part-time job that allows me more hours at home but still pays enough to afford rent, groceries, and laundry. And *you* come first. Not a cute boy with floppy curls and swoon-worthy dimples. Everett and I are friends." I roll the word around on my tongue, struck by how foreign it feels to say aloud, which speaks volumes about the sad state of my social life. "Friends," I repeat with more confidence. "*Only* friends."

Aggie gives me another look, eyes raised, brows twitching. She's not buying it.

I'm not sure I'm buying it, either, but I have to. Maybe not forever, but at least while I get a handle on what life will look like for the next few months and how I'll juggle everything without asking my parents for a loan. I appreciate that this is even an option, but it's an option that would come with a lifetime of *making smart choices* lectures and invasive questions about the state of my personal finances. My dad would want to know how I spend every penny, and if I didn't spend it the way he thought I should or pay it back on time, I'd never hear the end of it. Meanwhile, my mom would post on Facebook about how elated she is that she and my dad could "chip in" and help me achieve my dreams. Every neighbor who knew me as a kid would see the post, along with several people I went to high school with, plus two exes I deliberately excised from my life. I don't need any of them thinking I couldn't make it on my own.

Pride is hardly my tragic flaw, but where my parents are concerned, the less evidence they have about how I'm already failing at adulthood, the better.

The rest of the evening is all about getting to know Aggie, and letting her get to know me. I ramble about whatever comes to mind while we hang out on the floor and I try to engage her interest in the monkey, a ball, or a pair of old socks I tie together, none of which sparks much of a reaction. I figure out where she likes to be touched—her ears, her neck, under her chin—and where she doesn't like to be touched—her paws and her tail. I also feed her, which involves spreading digestively balanced canned food onto a grooved rubber dish that's designed to slow a dog's eating. The food has a strong odor and I don't want to think too long or too deeply about the by-product-heavy contents, but Aggie seems to love it, licking away as I hold the dish under her nose and spin it around until she's polished off every last morsel.

After my own dinner of slightly stale granola, I open my pathology textbook and read tomorrow's required chapters aloud, as though Aggie might have use for detailed information about cavitary effusions or tissue aspirates. She humors me by listening with her head on my lap and my free hand stroking her ears. I've always found petting a dog so calming. The rhythm. The soft fur. Even while reading about parasites, I find myself getting drowsy, and by the time nine o'clock rolls around, I'm ready to get some sleep.

I take a selfie of the two of us and text it to Hannah with the caption *We're home!* I've been keeping her posted on the whole affair, and while I've downplayed Everett's involvement, I'm pretty sure she suspects something because she asks more questions about him than she does about the dog. Not that this is surprising. She's known me since kindergarten, and even though she moved away in eighth grade, long before I dated anyone, she's been with me for every crush and every heartbreak. She knew about the first boy I kissed when I was in high school, and my first real boyfriend in my junior year, the one whose wedding my mom was recently gushing about. She knew about the prom date who never showed up, and about the first guy I had sex with in college, who turned out to have a girlfriend, and the second guy I had sex with, who laughed when I asked when we'd see each other again, asking me, *You didn't actually see this going somewhere, did you?* to which, because I was nineteen and mortified, I breezily replied, *Of course not*, and then went to great lengths to avoid him for the rest of the year.

People are complicated. I misread signals. I expect things I shouldn't. I don't understand the nuances of small talk and social greeting rituals. I made an effort for a while, but by the time I got to college and the effort continued to yield minimal results, it became easier to withdraw and focus on school. Then I lost Marmie, and the aloneness I'd convinced myself was a choice became a vast gray gulf of loneliness I'm only able to recognize now because it already feels a little less vast, a little less gray, with Aggie's head on my lap and her hair on my sweater, and a dish I didn't use for my own dinner in the sink.

I change into my sleep shorts and tank top, twist my long hair into a topknot so I can wash my face, and am about to brush my teeth when I hear a light rap on the door to the hallway. Tossing on a cardigan, I answer the knock to find Everett standing on my doorstep, holding a large shopping bag. His eyes dart to my bare legs and up again as he cringes in embarrassment.

"Sorry," he says. "Is this too late to knock?"

I shake my head. "I'm usually up much later. But I got tired early."

"Yeah. Same." His cringe softens as he holds out the bag. "At the risk of sounding like a creeper, I saw the inside of your fridge when I was putting away Aggie's meds earlier. Our client brought food to the meeting. A lot of food. It's vegan and pretty amazing and you know how I am about not throwing things away unnecessarily and anyway . . . I thought maybe you'd like something other than a slice of bread for dinner." He inches the bag forward.

I stare at it, wondering if he's this nice to everyone or if I've done something to warrant extra care and attention, and then wondering why I can't accept the gesture without wondering.

"Thank you," I say as I take the bag. "I mean, I had granola, so I wasn't *that* pathetic."

He frowns at me. "The granola that was on the counter?"

I frown at him. "Yeah. Why?"

"That bag was almost empty."

"It was enough."

"Cameron," he scolds through a laugh. "Almost empty is not the same as enough."

I flinch internally as his words hit like a gut punch, summing up far more than my dinner.

Aggie appears to agree, because she lets out a quiet moan from her bed.

I swear, these two...

"Well, thank you," I say again. "I'd invite you in to share, but—"

He holds up his hands and takes a step back.

"I had plenty at the meeting," he says. "And you can save some for tomorrow."

I peer into the bag. "Tomorrow, and Thursday, and Friday from the looks of it."

His shoulders inch up and he scratches at the back of his neck. "Well. You know."

I do not know, because this whole *being thought of* thing is very new for me, even if he's only bringing me leftovers. It's a big deal, and the food smells amazing, and... and my eye catches on something that doesn't look like a take-out box. I reach in and pull out a paperback book, flipping it over to read the cover. Agatha Christie's *Death on the Nile*.

"That's not to eat," Everett says, making me snort a laugh, which in turn makes his cheeks flare with heat. "Sorry. Obvious. The bookstore near my office was still open. I thought you might like something fun to read. Both of you. As a welcome-home present."

Overwhelmed, I hold it up, pivoting around to show Aggie. "What do you think?"

She lets out a single, happy bark, right on cue.

"I believe that's the official seal of approval," I tell Everett.

He beams at me, still blushing, shifting, and shuffling. Then he gives us each a wave, we say good night, and he heads down the hall to his apartment. I step inside mine and shut the door before he thinks *I'm* a creeper, but after taking another look at the food and the book, I catch Aggie's too shrewd eyes, shake my head, and am forced to agree. I'm totally, utterly screwed.

CHAPTER SEVEN

On Wednesday, after my classes let out, when I get to the pizzeria for my afternoon shift, I ask my boss if I can take Friday evening off again, hoping that with more notice this time, she'll cut me some slack. Instead, she goes into full rant mode about the poor work ethic of my generation, the laziness and rampant irresponsibility, saying that if I don't have time to work fifteen hours a week anymore, if not a full twenty, I should reconsider my value to the establishment. So, I do just that and quit on the spot. This means I'll be short about $200 a week, which I'll need to replace somehow, but I'll figure it out. I was never very good at slinging dough anyway.

This is what I tell myself when I step outside, with my boss's raised voice still audible as she rails against me to the unfortunate coworker I've abandoned to her wrath. Usually, hearing someone tear me down guts me, and I obsess about what I did wrong and how I can do better. But the sun is shining, the lightly burnished September leaves are rustling in a gentle breeze, and whoever runs around town sticking large googly eyes on random things that look like faces has adorned the fire hydrant in front of me. Apparently, even I can't spiral into feelings of low self-worth when a bright red fire hydrant is smiling at me as though it finds my situation amusing.

Thanks, fire hydrant. Same.

With my afternoon suddenly free, I head home to spend time with Aggie, arriving to find her lying on her side with her head on the pillow I *might* have pulled off my bed last night when she looked like she couldn't get comfortable. I also might've pulled another pillow off the bed and lay down with her for a while, but I left no evidence and I doubt she'll rat me out.

"What do you think?" I ask as I kneel by her bed. "Should we try to get you outside?"

She blinks at me dubiously, which is understandable, but we have to start somewhere. It might as well be on a beautiful day during a surprise opening in my schedule. We won't make it to any of the parks that are all within a few blocks of the building, but there's a grassy patch out front by the big old maple tree, so once she tries a pee, we can sit on the grass and read.

With equal parts effort and encouragement, Aggie inches herself up into a seated position, which allows me to wrap the sling around her middle and raise her back end. She can move her legs in a stiff approximation of walking once I've raised her, but we only manage a few faltering steps before I realize there's no way I can support so much of her weight on my own, not for long enough to get her into the elevator, let alone outside into the yard.

As I lower her back end and set aside the sling, she looks over her shoulder at me with the saddest, sorriest eyes in the world, as though any of this is even remotely her fault.

"It's not you, baby," I assure her. "You're perfect. We just need to strategize."

While I'm debating what to try next, I hear the unmistakable sounds of Cycle Guy extracting his bike from the elevator, clunking and banging as he lowers it from the vertical position that allows it to fit in the narrow space, and onto both wheels so he can get it through the door. It's quite the operation, every time, especially when someone else is in the elevator with him, and I've wondered more times than I can count why this building doesn't have a bike room.

I've probably spoken fewer words to Cycle Guy in the fourteen months I've lived here than I had with Everett in the three or four months since he moved into the building, prior to last week. Mostly, Cycle Guy apologizes about the bike, I say it's fine, and we carry on as perfectly amicable strangers. However, I need help, and Everett surprised me, so Cycle Guy might, too.

While Aggie stretches out, half on, half off her bed, I open my door and step into the hall. Sure enough, Cycle Guy is wheeling his bike toward apartment 603, the one to the left of mine. He's in head-to-toe cycling gear, from the bright blue spandex shorts and shirt that are covered in vivid brand logos to the helmet that's still on his head, its chin strap dangling. The saddlebags on his bike bulge, and I've always assumed he commutes by bike, whipping out a nice dress shirt and slacks once he gets to the office, but for all I know, he's a gig worker and this is his work attire. Either way, he's extremely fit, and if he has ten minutes to spare . . .

I flash him an awkward wave, the only kind of wave I know. "Hi."

He flinches at the sound of my voice, looking around as though I must be greeting someone else. Finding no one, he removes his helmet and tucks it under his arm, revealing a head of sweat-dampened black curls he shakes out with a quick finger-comb.

"Sorry," he says. "The bike. The elevator. I get it. I know. I'll try to be quieter."

"Oh god, no." I wave my hands in an unnecessarily manic manner. "I didn't come out here to complain about noise. That's just, I mean, your bike, whatever."

"Okay?" He looks around again, and suddenly I feel ridiculous for barely speaking with any of my neighbors for over a year, even if my gestures are too broad and I can't manage to organize words into a proper sentence. "If you have a problem with the smell of mjadra—"

"If I— Sorry. What?"

"The stew I made last night. If you have a problem with it—"

"I don't. I swear. I love the smell of your cooking," I assure him. It's the unequivocal truth, and now I feel not only ridiculous, but also mortified that my neighbors might all assume I don't talk to them because I don't like them, or worse, because I'm a raging asshole. "I came out here because I need a hand with something, and I'm hoping you have a few minutes to spare. Also, I thought maybe I should introduce myself, you know, since we're neighbors."

He still looks confused. I suppose I would be, too, if our situations were reversed. It's not like we haven't had plenty of chances to do this before now.

"Better late than never?" I attempt a smile that's at least as awkward as my wave. Then I step forward and extend a hand to shake. "Hi. I'm Cameron Goode. I live in 602, but you probably know that already. I'm a grad student in the veterinary program. Second year. Born in Oregon. Favorite color red. Mediocre runner. Appalling vegetarian. I brought home a rescue dog yesterday. She's not very mobile and I'd love to get her outside for a few minutes, but I need a second pair of hands. I'd be happy to return the favor if you"—I falter, unsure where to go from here, given how little I know about him—"if you need your tires pumped or something."

Cycle Guy stares at me, unmoving, and I relive the last two minutes, desperately wishing I could rewind and record over them with a cooler, smoother introduction. Just as I'm about to apologize for disrupting this poor man's perfectly happy, intrusive-neighbor-free day, he steps forward and takes my offered hand, giving it a firm—if sweaty—shake.

"Nice to meet you, Cameron," he says. "I'm Khalil Khoury, 603, which you also probably know. Third-year engineering with a focus on robotics. Born in Iowa. Let's see, what else . . ." He scratches at his sweat-damp hair. "Favorite color, turquoise, maybe? Decent cyclist. Spectacular omnivore. Oh, and also, I only have a few minutes to help you out before I need to get cleaned up and run to class, but I might have something you can use."

"Really?" I ask through a flutter of joy and relief. "That would be amazing. Thank you."

He shakes his head through a lightly amused laugh.

"Sorry," he says. "It's just . . . it's been, like, a year, right?"

I inch up a shrug. "I'm not very good with people."

His laughter softens into a smile. "We're not a particularly social bunch."

As if on cue, Phone Girl emerges from the stairwell. She's a slight redhead currently dressed in a short, pleated skirt and navy blazer that give off a sexy-schoolgirl vibe, with her bright ginger hair in space buns and two long dangling strands framing her face. I've never seen her in the same outfit twice and often wonder where she keeps her expansive wardrobe, given the size of the closets in this building. Her eyes are locked on her screen as she pivots cleanly toward her apartment door, keys in hand, somehow intuiting where the keyhole is, though she looks up as she unlocks her door, as if her inner Roomba sensor realizes she's not alone.

"What?" she asks us. "Is there a gas leak or something?"

Khalil shakes his head. "We're just chatting."

She blinks at us like this doesn't quite compute.

"Okay," she says. "Cool." Then she returns her attention to her phone as she swings open her door and enters her apartment, leaving a waft of weirdly pleasant fruity perfume in her wake.

Khalil flashes me another quick smile. "Case in point."

I glance past him at Phone Girl's closed door. "At least she said we were cool."

"I don't think that was a direct compliment."

"A goal for next time, then."

This makes him chuckle a little, and after dropping off his bike and helmet, he comes with me to meet Aggie. In the short time since I left her, she's managed to inch forward about a foot so her back legs are stretched out behind her with only her feet still on the bed. She sends a guilty look my way, as though I've caught her trying to escape, Shawshank-style. I drop to my knees beside her and tell her she's allowed to move anywhere she likes, earning me a tail wag.

"Aww," Khalil coos behind me. "What a sweetie. What's her name?"

"Aggie. Short for Agatha." I give her a scratch on the head. "Aggie, meet Khalil. He makes robots and he's very nice and he's going to help us get you outside."

He crouches down and lets her sniff his hand. She immediately starts licking him, and not in a polite way with a delicate flick of her tongue, but a sloppy and rather forward lapping and slurping. I expect him to withdraw his hand, but he does the opposite, nudging it forward.

"I grew up with Labradors," he says, catching me watching the interaction. "I used to get a full tongue bath after a long ride, and then needed a real bath after." He rotates his hand so Aggie can access more of his sweat. It's sweet of him, and she's having a fabulous time, so while she licks every inch of his fingers, I tell him a bit about her history and health, and my hopes for the weeks ahead. He listens with interest, and with sharp indignation toward her previous owners that cements my already high estimation of him as a genuine and caring soul.

Before Aggie can start on his arm, he gives her a quick pat on the head, runs back to his apartment, and returns after a couple of minutes, rolling a collapsible wagon behind him.

"It's perfect!" I exclaim. "I should've thought of a wagon."

"It's not *totally* perfect," he says. "It's old and dented, and the extension doesn't have a proper handle since it's designed to attach directly to a bike." He points out the bolt holes and security strap at the end of the metal arm. "But you can tape a towel around this part so it's easier on your hands. The wagon's sides also drop down, which should help with loading and unloading, and I haven't used it in ages, so it's yours for as long as you need it."

I gush with gratitude while Khalil dismisses my gushing with a humble "No worries" and a flick of his hand. He lets me get a feel for handling the wagon and shows me how to drop the sides. I put a blanket in the base and slide the sling under Aggie again. Then I take one handle, Khalil takes the other, and we lift her in. She settles in with her tail wagging and her head held high, like a queen on her palanquin. She looks so happy, and I take a moment to marvel at how she could be treated so badly for so long and still look at us with such love, trust, and joy. It's both a gift and a lesson, and not for the first time, I silently promise her I'll earn it.

I tuck a textbook, a bowl, and a bottle of water in the corner of the wagon. Khalil helps me get the wagon out of my apartment, into the elevator, and out again at the ground floor, holding the front door for me as I wheel Aggie into the sunshine.

"Will you be okay from here?" he asks.

"Yeah. I think so. I'll get the hang of it."

"Cool." He gives Aggie a quick scratch on the top of her head as she blinks up at him with delight, a russet-furred, shaggy-browed mountain of joy and innocence, with her tail lightly thwapping against the back panel of the wagon. Between her clear adoration of Everett and now Khalil, I'm starting to think she's a serious flirt. "Knock anytime you need a hand, okay?"

I almost tell him I'll be fine but stop myself before reflexively rejecting his offer.

"Thank you," I say instead. "You too. And I'm glad we finally met."

"Better late than never," he echoes from earlier.

"Exactly." I flash him an only slightly less awkward wave this time. Then he heads inside, and Aggie and I set off on our first grand adventure together.

PEOPLE OFTEN THINK of New Hampshire when they picture New England parks colored by fall foliage and speckled with cozy benches or neatly landscaped around a romantic gazebo, where lovers can steal kisses in the rain, but Ithaca holds her own on this front. Within only three blocks of my apartment building, Aggie and I hit the start of the Cascadilla Gorge Trail, which follows a creek for about a mile and includes views of half a dozen waterfalls, ranging up to eighty feet in height. It's like a little paradise right in the heart of the city, connecting downtown to the Cornell campus. The trail has too many steps for me to wheel Aggie the entire length, but we find a bench tucked back from the trail with an open patch of grass that's perfect for us.

For the next three hours, we work in shifts. I read Aggie a dry but informative chapter from my immunology text on a topic like hyperproteinemia or antinuclear antibodies testing. Then I help her out of the wagon and we do some brief walking exercises on the lawn, exercises that are more like standing, but she does take a few faltering steps while I hold her up. When we both tire of the exercise, we return to reading. When we tire of reading, we return to exercise.

Despite Aggie's obvious effort at managing forward motion, she seems genuinely engaged in the process, like she wants to not only walk, but to run, and she'll work as hard as she needs to, to reach her goals. I praise every step she takes and gush with hugs, love, and a few carefully apportioned liver treats when we manage a full minute of standing and stumbling. Her skinny tail wags at high speed and my heart nearly bursts. It's astonishing, given her history, how she hasn't become completely defeated, and when people pause on their trail walks to ask what we're doing or if they can say hi while Aggie reposes in her wagon or on the grass after a few hard-earned steps, I find my pride and joy mirroring hers.

Look how amazing she is, I think. *Look what a fighter she is. Look at this glorious, miraculous being I've known for less than two weeks, who's already teaching me how to live.*

Two teen girls in running gear pause mid-jog to hear Aggie's story and cheer her on.

A guy with a brace on his knee tells me about his rehabilitation and how similar it seems.

A kid with what looks like strawberry jam all over his face insists on giving Aggie a hug and kiss, giggling while she licks his face and his mom digs a pack of wet wipes from her bag.

A woman breaks down in tears about her own weight-loss journey, horrified that anyone would euthanize a dog for being overweight.

It's a lot, talking to all of these people, but Aggie makes it easier with her open, amiable demeanor, and since she's the obvious conversation starter, I don't need to hunt for things to say. I just follow the other person's lead, and Aggie's. Several people ask if she has a social media account they can follow. I smile politely and say no, holding back the rant I thrust on Everett that day in his car, but the more people ask, the more I wonder if it's time to reconsider my complete avoidance. If Aggie's inspiring strangers while hanging out in a park for a few hours, setting up an account for her could be kind of fun. Nothing fake. Nothing overly curated and manufactured. Just this beautiful, tenacious girl and her fight to rebuild her life in a happy, healthy way.

"What do you think?" I ask her when we're on our way home. "Do you want your own Instagram account? Or would you prefer TikTok?"

She smiles at me like she's up for anything. She probably is. I'm the one resisting.

"I'll think about it," I tell her.

And I do.

CHAPTER EIGHT

For the next three weeks, I catch up with my classes, do my weekend job with a new determination to hold on to it despite its frustrations, hunt fruitlessly for remote work that will supplement my reduced income from quitting the pizzeria job, and assist with Aggie's recovery. Aside from her carefully monitored diet and meds, on most days her rehab includes spending time on the upturned bin, draped over it like a big, furry, limp starfish, while I bounce a ball in her direction and she watches with only nominal interest until we give up on catching practice and read or watch TV together. We also take a lot of wagon walks with exercise sessions in nearby parks, enjoying fall while it lasts, with its crisp blue skies and the cozy smells of chimney smoke and pumpkin spiced lattes scenting the air, conjuring images of hearth fires and big, plush armchairs to curl up in. Everett joins some of our walks, though he's overloaded with work and rarely has time. I take him at his word that he's busy, but some unavoidable insecurities bubble up as I wonder if I was the only one who felt a spark of attraction between us.

Did I imagine it?

Was he just being nice?

Is this high school and college all over again?

You didn't actually see this going somewhere, did you?

The questions only annoy me, remnants of a past that's better left in the past, so I shake them off as best I can and enjoy Everett's company whenever I can get it.

Meanwhile, Aggie's improvement is slow but steady, and at her first weigh-in at the vet's, she's down six pounds already. She's also able to support more of her own weight on her legs as we walk, allowing us to go farther with the help of the sling. There's still no sign of hair on her tail, but Dr. Beinecke, the vet we're now seeing, is pleased with Aggie's overall progress and encourages me to stay patient. This was never going to be an overnight transformation, and I knew that going in, but I appreciate her perspective so I don't feel like I'm not doing enough.

Thankfully, the vet's office is close by so I pull Aggie home in her wagon while she's greeted by people who recognize her from prior walks. Some just say hi while others ask how she's doing and are elated when I share her progress update. She beams with pride as relative strangers shower her with praise, and I love seeing her drink it all in, hoping that in some small way, it helps compensate for years of neglect no living being should ever experience.

My mom texts when I'm halfway home, letting me know she had a fabulous time while out for dinner with some neighbors I knew when I was growing up in Roseburg, and I should check out her latest Facebook post to see her photos and all the nice comments people made about those photos. I'm tempted to remind her I don't use Facebook, but instead I text back that I'm glad she had a good time, and hope that's the end of the conversation.

It's a minor interaction but it gets me thinking about the social media account I still haven't created for Aggie. Mostly, I've been busy, but also, I found it all so draining when I used to be on it. The FOMO. The parade of cliquish friend gatherings and happy-couple photos. The travel diaries and award announcements that made my life seem so small and inconsequential in comparison. I had enough social struggles in real life. I didn't need to amplify them online.

However, Aggie and I have concrete progress to share now, with her first six pounds gone and her mobility increasing. I'm so proud of her, and other people will be, too, once I update them. People like Hannah, who can be hard to connect with directly, given our time difference. Or Andy and Nora from Hounds and Hearts, who aren't in town. Sam and Sariah from Ruff 'n' Rescue, who've done so much for Aggie and for me. The regulars who pass our favorite bench along the trail, always inquiring about how she's doing. My dog is amazing. I want everyone to know that, and recording her journey for a few friends and acquaintances to follow doesn't mean I'll get swept back into everything I deliberately stepped away from.

When we get home, I get Aggie settled on her upturned bin, where she paws at the monkey she's recently become curious about. I sit beside her on the floor, scrolling through pics and videos while asking her opinion on which ones to share. We start with the first video I took of her, the one where she's in the back of Everett's station wagon, and I cue up four others: one of her propped on the bin, chewing on her monkey; one riding in her wagon with a big smile on her face; one sleep-twitching on her bed with her head on the pillow I now think of entirely as hers; and a brief selfie I shoot of the two of us. I compile them into a single video, hunt for an appropriate song, and write a short caption introducing people to Aggie, noting how her first seven years were spent, her current weight and health concerns, and how we'll be chronicling her recovery under the TikTok account name Goode Girls. I tag Ruff 'n' Rescue, noting their invaluable support in her journey, and before I can overthink it, I post.

"Away we go!" I tell Aggie as I pocket my phone.

She wags her tail and smiles at me, like she already knows she's a star.

I give her nose a teasing smoosh. "Flirt."

Her tail wags harder, confirming my suspicions. Definitely a flirt.

As evening rolls around, I become keenly aware that it's Friday night, I no longer have a job to go to, I need a break from homework, I'm down to half a box of Raisin Bran and no milk of any variety to go with it, and even my dog might be bored with my company. So I reach out.

> **CAMERON:** Any chance you're free for dinner tonight? I still owe you

The response doesn't come right away, but after a few minutes, my phone pings.

> **EVERETT:** You don't owe me anything. But tonight's not good. Sorry. Another time?

I stare at my phone, willing it to deliver a more thorough explanation. *I'm working. I have plans with friends. I'm on a dangerous and daring plant rescue mission that could change the future of our imperiled planet.* Not that he owes me any explanation at all, but my mind has a tendency to fill in blanks when blanks are provided, and given how little I've seen of him in the past few weeks, those blanks feel especially large and especially empty.

I look over to find Aggie watching me intently from her bed.

"What?" I ask. "I'm not allowed to be curious?"

Her eyes dart around the room, glancing past my scattered textbooks, my overflowing laundry bin, my kitchen counter with the teetering stack of mail I unearthed from its drawer but still haven't sorted, and my outdated laptop with a zillion tabs open on job listings I don't quite fit but keep applying for anyway. When she's taken in everything, her eyes return to me.

"Yeah, I know I said I was too busy for a guy," I concede, duly chastened. "But then he got us that book, and the food, and he showed up for walks looking cute and snuggly in his fall-colored sweaters, he talked about brand position and key performance indicators in a way that got even me interested, and if something's important, you *make* the time, so . . . a girl's allowed to hope, isn't she?"

Aggie blinks at me as her tail thumps quietly against her bed.

"See? You like him, too."

I might be imagining it, but I swear her tail thumps a little faster. I also swear that while the average trained dog supposedly knows about a hundred and sixty-five words, this one understands everything I say. Especially if I'm talking about Everett.

Everett who's busy tonight, leaving me to sort out dinner on my own. Like usual.

CAMERON: Sure. Another time. Enjoy your evening

EVERETT: Thanks. You too

I wait a moment in case another text is forthcoming. When nothing appears, I set my phone face down on my coffee table, where I hope to forget it exists.

In true Cameron Goode fashion, I settle for Raisin Bran directly out of the box, too lazy and too broke to go rustle up something more appealing if I'm eating on my own. As I snack on dry cereal, I continue trying to get Aggie interested in her ball. Sitting a few feet away, I toss it gently toward her nose. It bounces off several times, and sails past her several more times, due to my mediocre aim, even at such short range. I cheer her on through each throw, telling her how fetch was Marmie's favorite game, and how she never played with sticks, rope toys, or stuffies, but she always went wild about a ball. I even pull Marmie's photo off the fridge and hold it in front of Aggie's nose as though the two dogs can channel some sort of cosmic energy between them. Then I realize I'm being ridiculous, set aside the photo, and return to tossing the ball.

"Come on, girl," I encourage as I prep another throw. "Just once. Catch it once and I'll let you pick out a movie for us. I know you have a fan crush on Ryan Reynolds, and I'm pretty sure we haven't exhausted his Netflix offerings yet. I'll suffer through another one if you catch this."

Her expression doesn't change but she knows the carrot I'm dangling. It's not like *I* want to watch a kind, funny, hot Canadian be all kind, funny, and hot. That's Aggie's thing. Not mine.

When three more ball tosses fail to spark her interest, I up the stakes by turning on the TV and opening the search window on Netflix so it lists all available Ryan Reynolds titles.

"See that?" I wag the remote at the screen. "We can double-feature it. All for *one* catch."

Aggie looks at the screen, looks at me, and looks at the screen again.

"C'mon," I encourage, readying my next toss. "Do it for Ryan."

She watches me closely. I bounce the ball so it's right on target to hit her mouth, and this time—after countless hours of practice and encouragement—she opens up and catches it.

I shriek with joy as I scoot across the floor to throw my arms around her neck, planting mushy kisses all over her head and showering her with praise while she wags her entire body from the top of the bin. I can't tell who's prouder. We're both buzzing from the high. It's *so good* to see her being a dog, engaging in play. Obviously, her weight and mobility are our top priorities, but her mind needs a reboot, too, neglected for years without sufficient interaction to occupy it. If she'll catch a ball, it's a good sign—a *really* good sign—she'll also engage in other forms of play as she continues to learn, heal, and feel more secure with her new life.

I toss about a dozen more times to make sure her first catch wasn't a fluke. She doesn't catch every ball, but she reaches for the closest ones, and catches about one out of every three. She definitely understands the game now, and her instincts are taking over.

"Who's the best dog in the universe?" I coo as I give her another hug and she nuzzles into me. "That's right! You are. You're the best dog in the universe."

I'm carrying on like this, blathering away, when I hear Everett's voice in the hall. Still buzzing with excitement I'm eager to share, I leap up, jog to my door, and fling it open.

"Everett! You're home!" I call out as I stumble over my threshold. "I need to—"

My voice catches in my throat. He's not alone. Like, *really* not alone. His apartment door is ajar and he's standing by the elevator, embracing a beautiful woman with alabaster skin and platinum-blond hair that falls straight down her back as though it's never seen a tangle. She's even wearing a romper. I can't pull off a romper, not with my gangly limbs and nonexistent curves. But this woman looks amazing, with a pronounced hourglass figure, a sexy cropped leather jacket, badass cuff bracelets, and coral fingernails that match her lipstick, something I've never even attempted, let alone pulled off. She seems so put together, making me newly aware that I'm in cheap leggings, an old Mother Mother concert tee with a neckline I cut away when I couldn't stop tugging at it as though it was tight even though it wasn't, and a stretched-out cardigan I should've replaced at least a year ago. My not-quite-blond-not-quite-brown hair is in its usual hasty topknot, my fingernails are chewed to stubs, and my socks don't match.

Somehow, I'm able to note all of this in the span of a single second, while also noting that the embrace I've blundered my way into witnessing isn't giving off *thanks for popping by* energy, and the woman is not one of Everett's sisters, whose photos he showed me weeks ago.

In the next second, I register the surprise and painfully clear discomfort on Everett's face as he and his date step away from each other, not like they've been caught at something, but like their embrace has been interrupted by a manic woman running into the hall. Because it has.

"Cameron, hi," Everett manages, pulling at his ear and scratching at his neck.

"Sorry." I wave my hands in that way I do, like I can Etch A Sketch a moment away.

"No, what?" he asks. "You were about to say you needed something?"

"Yeah, just, um"—I rack my brain for a neighborly request—"flour. For baking."

His brows shoot up and his lips twitch with the threat of a laugh. "You're baking?"

"Yep." I inch backward over my threshold. "Brownies. From scratch. Grandma's recipe. Famous. So good. Ran out of. Obviously. Anyway." I take another step back, reaching behind me for my doorknob, unable to take my eyes off Everett and his date, who's glancing between us with a little too much curiosity for my liking. "Never mind. You're busy. Hi. Sorry. Cameron. Everett's neighbor. Haveagreatnightseeyoulater!" I swing my door shut, slowing it just enough to prevent slamming it before sinking to the floor with my face in my hands, muttering curses.

Sure, it was only an embrace. They weren't all over each other like The Lovers, and I don't want to leap to too many hasty conclusions here, but I definitely witnessed an intimate moment, and I should at least allow for the most obvious reason for that intimacy.

So what if Everett bought me dinner? And a really thoughtful book? And he went out of his way to help me with Aggie? He also hauls lonely plants out of alleys and rescues discarded sweaters.

He's a nice guy. That doesn't mean he's interested in or attracted to me.

"This is why dogs are better than people," I tell Aggie. "No guessing games. No major misunderstandings. No romantic relationships that somehow never came up in conversation."

She watches me from her bin with concern in her eyes, and understandably so. She probably has emotional whiplash from seeing me exit the apartment elated, only to return ten seconds later in the throes of dejection. I crawl over and bury my face in her neck, raking my fingers through her soft, thick fur while I reiterate that she is, in absolute fact, the best dog in the universe.

Fifteen minutes later, I've hauled her onto the futon—a new thing we're trying—and we're watching *The Proposal* with my feet kicked up on the coffee table, her head on my lap, and the bitter sting of jealousy slowly ebbing with the help of sharp banter and a storyline with a guaranteed happy ending, when I hear a light knock on my door.

I tense at the sound, snapping into fight-or-flight mode, or really, just flight. Despite a growing acquaintance with Khalil, I'm pretty sure only one person would knock on my door after 8 p.m., and while I want to hear what Everett has to say, I'm not up for talking to him right now, not when I'm so raw. I'd rather wait until I can at least pretend to be happy for him.

"Stay really, really still," I whisper to Aggie. "Maybe he won't realize we're here."

She blinks at me, her head still resting on my lap as I set a finger to my lips. On-screen, Ryan and Sandra bicker a little too loudly for my liking, though I can't exactly mute them now.

"Cameron?" Everett's voice comes through my door. "Aggie?"

Her head jerks up and she lets out a happy bark. Traitor.

I shoot her a glare. "Fine. Have it your way. But no more flirting with him!"

The look she gives me suggests this is a futile request, which I suspected before I made it, so I resign myself to my fate, give her a quick scratch on the head, and get up to answer the door. I assume I'll find Everett with his hands jammed into his corduroy pockets and an apologetic look on his face, prepared to talk. Instead, I find him with his arms full of baking supplies.

"Hi," he says. "From what I've seen of your kitchen, I figured if you really wanted to make brownies, you probably needed more than flour. I'm also a pretty decent baker if you want some company and you're up for diverging from your grandma's famous recipe."

"I don't have a recipe," I admit.

"I kind of figured."

"And I wasn't baking anything."

"I figured that, too."

"And I barely knew either of my grandmothers before they died."

"That... is new information. And maybe something we can talk about?" He adjusts the unwieldy baking supplies in his arms as he manages a smile, though it looks conflicted.

I don't manage a smile. And I'm definitely conflicted.

"Everett—"

"Can I come in? Please? I think it's important." He pleads with his pretty hazel eyes.

I take a breath, wonder if I'm up for this, glance over my shoulder to find Aggie watching us with her head resting on the back of the futon, and decide there's no such thing as an ideal time to hear Everett tell me about his girlfriend or date or whatever she is to him. Might as well get it over with.

"Okay." I step back from the door so he can enter. "But only if you're serious about baking."

He steps past me and heads to the kitchen. "Did you have cereal for dinner again?"

I notice the open box of Raisin Bran on the counter at the same time he does.

"I wasn't feeling inspired," I tell him.

"Then let's see if we can change that."

I frown at him, unsure I can handle his sweetness right now, not while I'm trying to eradicate feelings I haven't even fully identified yet. Aggie has no such qualms, wagging her tail as he empties his arms and then gives her a proper greeting, scratching her ears and asking if she's been up to no good, and if she hasn't been up to no good, what is she waiting for?

My frown softens of its own accord. This man is impossible to dislike.

I turn off the TV and pad my way over to the kitchen, which consists of a chipped two-by-two-foot laminate counter, a crappy sink, a two-burner gas range, a compact fridge, and a few serviceable cabinets. It works fine for my purposes, but the lack of space would probably frustrate anyone who actually cooks.

Poking through the items on the counter, I find a baking pan, eggs, flour, sugar, butter, a fancy-looking canister of cocoa, a spatula, a wooden spoon. He brought everything. I don't even need to provide a saucepan or mixing bowl, which is good because I don't own any.

Everett steps up beside me while I'm still marveling at his thoroughness.

"You want to measure or mix?" he asks.

I'm not entirely sure what's happening here, beyond the obvious, but I play along.

"Mix," I say. "Seems more forgiving for an amateur."

He nods as if considering this while he sets a saucepan on a burner and hands me a wooden spoon, nudging the ingredients out of the way and pulling up a recipe on his phone.

"So . . ." He checks the recipe, turns on the burner, unwraps a stick of butter, drops the entire thing into the saucepan, and motions for me to stir, which I do, while the agonizing tension of his unaccompanied *so* stretches out between us. "So, when I was a junior in undergrad, here at Cornell, I fell for a girl in one of my marketing classes." He checks the recipe again while I keep an eye on the melting butter, ignoring a growing knot in my gut. "We started dating and things got serious pretty fast. We bought a condo together after we graduated. It wasn't large or high-end and it was pretty far out of town due to our budget, but it was cozy, and ours, and it felt like home." He glances over, notices I'm barely moving, and gestures for me to get more aggressive.

I do, sort of, too distracted to really commit to the task, while he measures sugar as if we're chatting about the weather and I'm not side-eyeing him like I'm bracing for a bomb to drop.

"We got along great while we were in school," he continues, still focused on measuring. "But once we moved in together, little things that weren't so great became a lot harder to ignore. Differences in lifestyles and interests. We both made an effort, tried to compromise, but by the end of our first year living together, the tensions were palpable. The claustrophobia grew and we started looking for reasons to spend time out of the home. I took on a million projects at work, a choice I'm still digging myself out of. She built a busy social life that didn't include me."

I break the softening butter into smaller pieces, watching them bubble and shrink around the edges while waiting with keen anticipation for the next chapter of Everett's story.

He wrestles with the cocoa canister until it pops open.

"No one cheated," he says as he measures the cocoa. "No one did anything cruel, deceptive, or unforgivable. We simply stopped working as a couple, finding fulfillment outside the relationship instead of within it." He sets the cocoa by the sugar, taking a moment to brush off the counter where he spilled a little. "She recognized what was happening before I did, and one night, when I got home from work, she sat me down and told me she wasn't happy, and she didn't think I was happy, and it was time for us to reconsider our relationship. It sucked at the time, but in retrospect, I'm really grateful to her." He sneaks a glance at me as he reaches for the salt. "You know me well enough by now to know I don't walk away from things easily. I try to save them. She was smart enough to see we'd only end up back in the same place again. So, after a few weeks of hard conversations, I started looking for a new place while she looked for a new roommate, and by the time I moved out, most of the hurt was replaced by a sense of relief."

He pauses there, and my gut finally unknots while my brain catches up, putting the remaining pieces together, what I know of them anyway. A rented apartment at the other end of the hall. A conversation that went deeper than I realized about holding on to things. And...

"She was the woman in the hall tonight?" I ask.

He nods as he checks the butter, turns off the burner, and adds the sugar, cocoa, and salt.

"We put the condo up for sale a few months ago. It sold last week. She needed me to sign the papers, and we both thought it would be nicer to do in person. It's been a while. I had another place for about a year before I moved in here. And Vanessa and I—my ex, obviously—we never stopped caring about each other. It was good to see her. She's doing really well. New job. New place. A recent trip to Croatia with a bunch of her friends. She also met someone she really likes, though she's not sure where it's going yet." He digs around until he finds the vanilla, which he measures and adds to the saucepan, and which I stir in with the other ingredients.

As I stir, I finally realize why he brought the baking supplies. He's not fidgeting. I'm not fidgeting. We both have safe places to look and anchor our hands if we need to. And maybe it's disingenuous to act like we're busy or distracted while he's telling me about his ex, but I don't think so. I think he knows himself, and after only a month, I think he knows me pretty well, too.

"I'm never sure when it's the right time to bring up old relationships. Too soon and it seems presumptuous. Too late and it feels dishonest." He opens the egg carton and examines the eggs, but he doesn't take any out, rotating instead to face me and meet my eyes. "Then I saw your face tonight and realized I waited too long. Or maybe I'm wrong and none of this matters, but in case it *does* matter, I wanted you to know. I got together with my ex tonight so we could sell our place, and maybe catch up, but also . . ." He flicks at the edge of the egg carton, picks at a chip in the counter, and shifts his stance at least three times in as many seconds. "I've been single for about a year and a half now and I'm not seeing anyone. So. Just. There it is. What I wanted to say. In case it's useful information."

I give up on stirring and set aside the saucepan. There's a time for distraction and a time for attention, and this is definitely a time for attention, even if that attention involves fidgeting.

"I panicked," I tell him.

"I had a feeling."

"That wasn't a simple good night hug."

"It was definitely complicated."

"She's really beautiful."

"She is." He picks at the counter again. "She also loves high-end decor, and thinks houseplants are more hassle than they're worth, and she's ruthless about cleanliness, and really particular about her hair, her nails, and her clothes, and she thinks cuddling in front of a movie is boring when she could be out at a club or trying a new restaurant, and none of these are bad things, but relationships aren't so much about who people are, as who they are together."

A warm, expansive feeling spreads through my chest as I exhale slowly and the last of the tension in my body eases. What a gift, for him to lay everything out like this, so clearly and candidly. It's new to me, and unexpected, and I feel like I should offer him something in return.

"Everything you said," I tell him. "It does matter. And for the reasons you think."

He bites down the start of a smile as a hint of pink colors his cheeks. "Yeah?"

I nod, feeling suddenly shy for some reason. "Yeah."

We look at each other like newly smitten idiots for a few seconds. Him with his flushed cheeks, his tousled curls, his grandfather's glasses, and yet another sweater I want to curl up in, this one fuzzy and olive green with a Charlie Brown zigzag in a deep eggplant running around his chest. Me with my mismatched socks, my barely legible concert tee, and my tangled topknot nearly falling out of its overburdened elastic. And suddenly it doesn't matter anymore that I'm not as beautiful and put together as the woman in the hallway. She wasn't the right partner for Everett, or maybe she was, for a while, but she isn't now, and now is what matters.

Who we are—or at least who we *could be*—together is what matters.

I take a step forward, putting me nearly toe to toe with Everett.

He walks his fingers along the edge of the counter, inching closer until the pad of his index finger makes contact with mine, tapping it like an invitation to come out and play.

"Everett?" I ask. "Can I—"

"Yes."

"You don't know what I was going to—"

"Doesn't matter. The answer's yes."

I almost call him on this, tell him I was going to ask if I could compost his plants or get rid of his Neil Diamond CDs. But the warmth in my chest takes over, and the softness of his skin where it's barely touching mine, and the look in his eyes, the anticipation, the vulnerability, the heat, the want, the will, the care, the trust. All that in a look. He deserves the same in return.

So I don't make a joke. Instead, I close the distance and kiss him. Or maybe he kisses me, leaning forward at the same I do as his fingers slide between mine to knot our hands together on the counter while his other arm wraps my waist and draws me against him. His lips are warm. His hands are firm. His eyelids drift closed and I let mine do the same, relaxing into the feel of him, into knowing I didn't imagine anything after all. I didn't get it wrong this time, which is good, because *nothing* about this feels wrong. Not his arm against my back and his hand in mine. Not his lips gently parting so his tongue can slide against mine, sending a jolt of liquid heat through my entire body. Not the breath that rushes out of him. Not the softness of his hair as I slip my free hand around the back of his neck and tug at his curls. I like his height, only a few inches taller than me, and his build, strong, solid, but like a guy who spends a lot of time in an office, not a gym. I like the press of his chest against mine. Everything about him just . . . fits.

A soft *thump, thump, thump* halts my thoughts. And our kiss.

Everett pulls back at the same time I do, not far, but far enough for us both to glance over at the futon where Aggie's watching us intently with her head resting on the cushions between her paws as her skinny little hairless tail plays a happy drumbeat.

"Someone has a lot of opinions tonight," I tell her in a faux-scoldy voice.

Everett's chest shakes with a silent laugh. "Maybe she's excited about brownies?"

Her brows twitch as she looks back and forth between us, her tail still wagging.

"*That* is not about brownies," I tell Everett.

He turns his smile on me, and it's a hell of a smile, with his lips reddened from kissing, his cheeks flushed, his dimples on full display, and his eyes sparkling behind his glasses in a way I haven't seen before. It's magical, this post-first-kiss moment, as the armor we've both been wearing falls away and the little voice that's been whispering quietly but continuously *What if it's just me?* finally goes quiet.

"I'm glad your dog likes me," he says. "It could be a real problem if she didn't."

I trace the zigzag pattern on his chest with my index finger. "It's the sweaters."

His brows rise. "She likes my sweaters, does she?"

"I mean, they're pretty cute on you. All these mushy yarns and cozy fall vibes."

He unlinks our hands where they still rest on the counter, looping me within both of his arms and giving my nose a quick nuzzle. "What if I also have a winter collection?"

I huff out a laugh, already picturing it. "Do you?"

He shakes his head, echoing my laugh. "No, but now I kind of want one. Just so I can hear how cute *your dog* thinks I am in those, too."

My face goes hot and I can tell I'm blushing, which is ridiculous when he already knows I like him. Any attempt at hiding that—however futile—ended when I kissed him.

But just in case . . .

"Everett?" I say. "I really like you."

"Good," he says. "Because I really like you, too."

Then he kisses me again, while over on the futon, Aggie's tail thumps away.

CHAPTER NINE

HANNAH: When was the last time you checked your TikTok account?

CAMERON: Yesterday when I created it. You find it ok?

HANNAH: Girl . . .

CAMERON: If you can't find it, look up Ruff 'n' Rescue. They might've shared

HANNAH: Just check your account. Text me after. I'll wait

I blink at my phone, rereading her text. Hannah's usually very direct so her ambiguity unnerves me a little, like I'll open my account and find it's been suspended for inappropriate content for some strange reason, or one of my high school boyfriends found it and commented.

Aggie's in her wagon and we're halfway to our usual bench by the big scarlet oak and the little green lawn, where we do our walking exercises every weekend before I go to work. Given the ominous tone of Hannah's text, I decide to wait until we reach the bench so I'm sitting down when I check the account and not weaving around joggers, coffee-walkers, and stroller moms. It's a beautiful morning, with the trees donning their mid-October finery in bright yellows, reds, and oranges against an equally vivid blue sky. It even smells like fall, in the indefinable way that converts the sharp tang of newly decaying foliage into thoughts of hot apple cider or pumpkin pie. Posters for bonfire parties, orchard hours, and hayrides wrap lampposts. People I pass chat about Halloween. Hand-knit scarves flutter gently around necks and cozy wool coats abound.

If all that wasn't autumnal enough, I'm wearing Everett's olive and eggplant sweater. He left it with me last night after we finished making brownies and watched *The Proposal*. Well, Aggie watched *The Proposal*. Everett and I mostly made out on our half of the futon, though we agreed to not rush things. While I have extremely mixed feelings about this decision, I don't have a good track record where sex and relationships are concerned.

I don't want to get scared. I don't want to screw this up. I don't want—

"There she is!" says an excited voice just ahead of me. "I told you it was her."

The voice, I realize, is coming from a jogger headed my way on the trail. She's with two other joggers, all of them in trendy, body-hugging athletic gear, slowing as they approach.

"This is Aggie, right?" says one of the other joggers.

"Um... yes?" I say, trying to recall if I've talked to any of these women before, and if I did talk to them, how the conversation went. Most of the people who ask about Aggie are super-friendly and supportive, but I also encounter the occasional random jerk who leaps to criticizing me for overfeeding or mishandling my dog, or who spews unsolicited advice about supplements I know more about than they do or hydrotherapy she's not ready for and that I can't afford.

"I can't believe someone left her outside all that time," says one of the joggers.

"They got her sick and then were going to let her *die* for it? Monsters!" exclaims another.

"People suck," says the third, and in the next moment, the three of them are circling Aggie's wagon, gushing with praise and enthusiasm about losing her first six pounds.

That's when it clicks. If they know about her weight loss, they've seen our TikTok.

This is what Hannah meant. People are already finding us. People I don't even know.

I let Aggie luxuriate in the attention, and soon enough, the joggers carry on with their morning run, departing with eager pleas that I keep posting so they can see how she's doing. I tell them I'll do my best and wave as they disappear around a bend in the trail. Then I wheel Aggie to our bench, let her get in a quick pee and a few steps, and whisk my phone from my pocket.

I gasp when I see the numbers, gaping at my phone with disbelief.

Over fifty thousand views and four thousand followers, in a little less than twenty-four hours. Then there are the comments. People cheering Aggie on, thanking me for saving her, telling stories about their obese dogs and asking for advice about what to do, recommending various therapies and diets, asking questions about her bald tail, offering to walk her or dog-sit if we're anywhere near a number of different cities across the US. On and on they go, with most people posting simple support like *Go, Aggie, go!* and *I'm rooting for you, beautiful girl!*

It's overwhelming. I can't stop scrolling the comments, astonished at how many people have stumbled onto this amateur video with a few details about Aggie, to see something they connect with about her resilience, and about the hardship she's been through and the work that lies ahead. It's not just dog people, though plenty of them are on here, populating the comments with remarks about golden retrievers. It's people who see this beautiful, tenacious being fighting for the life she deserves after years of mistreatment, holding no grudges while finding genuine joy in the world around her. Anyone who's been through tough times and is finding their way forward can probably relate on some level. If people with widely varied backgrounds and personalities can draw inspiration from comic book superheroes, why not from a dog?

CAMERON: Holy s**t

HANNAH: Right? Your dog's an inspiration

CAMERON: I mean . . . OF COURSE SHE IS!

HANNAH: Going to make it hard for you to keep avoiding social though

CAMERON: I guess. Though I can't possibly reply to all of these comments

HANNAH: Of course you can't. Just do what feels good for you

CAMERON: Like hire a social media manager?

HANNAH: Can you afford that?

CAMERON: I can't afford full-price bread

HANNAH: Doesn't Hot Sweater Guy do social media?

CAMERON: When did he stop being Plant Guy and become Hot Sweater Guy?

HANNAH: When you started wanting him to nail you to a wall

CAMERON: Sounds painful. Not sure I'm interested

HANNAH: Aren't you, Cam? AREN'T YOU???

I have to laugh. She has a point. One night of kissing and a lot of things hold new appeal. I'd love to tell her all about last night, and get her advice on how to handle the jumble of intense feelings I woke up with this morning, but unless I want to cut Aggie's exercise short or lose my only remaining source of income, I don't have the time.

CAMERON: I need to walk the celebrity and get to work. Chat later?

HANNAH: Damn straight. I want to hear how she's handling her fame

I slide off the bench and throw an arm around Aggie, snapping and sending a quick selfie.

CAMERON: So far, pretty chill

HANNAH: Aww, look at you two! A match made in heaven

CAMERON: Maybe I'll use it for the next TikTok

HANNAH: Good idea. Or should I say Goode idea?

CAMERON: Cute. I might steal that

HANNAH: Wait. Is that a new sweater? 👀

CAMERON: 👀

HANNAH: 😲

CAMERON: I'll fill you in later

HANNAH: My phone won't leave my side

I check the time and decide I can afford *one* more minute on my phone, firing off a quick text to Everett with a link to the account and a long row of shocked-face emojis. The dots appear right away and his reply comes a moment later.

EVERETT: Wow. Very cool. I thought you hated social media

CAMERON: I'm . . . turning over a new leaf

EVERETT: Looks like you turned over a whole tree

CAMERON: It's just for fun. I'm not going pro like you

EVERETT: Give it time, Goode. Give it time

I bite down a smile, reveling in the knowledge that I have two people to share things with now. Maybe that shouldn't feel so huge, so like a foundational shift in my universe, but it does.

> **CAMERON:** Speaking of time, I have to head to work soon. Talk later?

> **EVERETT:** I'll stop by after work. Can't wait to hear more. Xo

I'm grinning hard as I pocket my phone. Between Aggie's overnight fan club and my giddiness about Everett, I'm brimming over with happy feelings that can't be contained. I don't completely trust them, but when Aggie stumble-walks across the entire thirty-yard span of lawn with me only supporting her back end, like she knows thousands of people are cheering her on now, I stop worrying about what might go wrong and decide to enjoy the ride.

THE LINGERING JOY of my morning quickly dims when I pick up my mail in the Maple Lane Apartments' lobby after work at Loden and Linden, where I was a model employee for once, infusing my sales pitch for $140 artisan-made Turkish linen hand towels in colors like Night Moth and Misty Vale with genuine enthusiasm. I even talked a customer buying a hammered-copper soap dish into several artfully branded mason jars of hand-rolled soap balls to go with it, indisputable proof that my brain was flooded with a cocktail of happy-making chemicals.

Now, once again, my mail includes charity donation solicitations that keep finding me for some reason and coupons for local establishments I can't afford, even with a discount. I ignore all of it, as always, but I can't ignore the envelope with the bold red letters that say *Final notice*. It's from my telecom company. They've sent emails, too, which I've ignored as consistently as I've ignored the stack of mail on my kitchen counter. I eked out my October rent but let most of my utilities slide at the start of the month, having maxed out my credit with the loss of my pizzeria income and the expenses that came with adopting Aggie.

I'm still staring at the envelope, afraid to open it, when I hear Khalil's voice behind me.

"Get something good?" he asks as he nudges the front of his cycle through the main door.

I grab the door to hold it open. "Does anything good come in the mail anymore?"

"I don't know. Birthday cards, maybe?"

"It's been, like, ten years since I got a physical birthday card."

He nods like he gets it and we step toward the elevator together. I'd take the stairs but I kind of like the idea of chatting with Khalil for a few minutes, even if it means being stuck in the steel box while imaginary hamsters on tiny treadmills try to get the damned thing to move.

"Bills," I tell him with an annoyed wave of the envelope. "I've been looking for a second part-time job, ideally something I can do on weekday evenings from home while Aggie's going through the most critical stage of her recovery, but I haven't had any luck yet."

Khalil gives me another commiserating nod. "Good thing grad school's so cheap."

I snort a laugh. "And great that Congress isn't obstructing student loan forgiveness."

He laughs with me, and when the elevator arrives, I let him get on first so he can swing his cycle into position, well-practiced at how to rotate it so it fits.

As the doors shut and we start our slow ascent, my mind recycles old questions, ones I'm tired of wrestling with, and ones Aggie has graciously distracted me from over the past month, but I can't shove them aside forever, as the ugly notice in my hand insists on reminding me.

"Is it worth it to you?" I ask Khalil.

"Grad school?" he asks, and when I nod, he pops the chin strap on his helmet and scratches his chiseled jawline. The man is all hard edges with zero body fat. One day I'll ask him how far he rides, but only when I'm sure I can do it without sounding like I'm hitting on him.

"I just wonder sometimes," I say. "It's so much debt. And so much work. And so much stress. What if we don't build successful careers in the fields we're studying? Or what if we do, only to find out we don't like the careers we've chosen? What if it's all for nothing?"

"Well . . ." He considers this, still scratching at his chin as the elevator dings on two. "I get to play with supercool toys most days. The lab I'm in is working on robotic prosthetics for amputees. Pretty sure I won't find out I don't like that work. Or that it's all for nothing."

I feel my eyes go wide with astonishment. "Like, the real-life Bionic Man?"

"Something like that." He unbuckles a saddlebag and carefully peels back the lid to reveal several zip-top bags full of gears, wires, and other mechanical parts. "Pretty cool, huh?"

"*Extremely* cool." I gawk at him, blown away by what he does.

He accepts my gushing with a humble shrug and a self-conscious smile that only increase my awe. The more I learn about my neighbors, the weirder I feel about not speaking to them for so long. All this time, I've been living between a literature professor and a robotics genius and I had no idea, though I guess that's modern life. We're more connected than ever, but also . . . not.

"Do you really think you might not like being a vet?" Khalil asks as the elevator inches toward three. "Seems like a natural fit. Taking care of animals like Aggie."

"It is, and always has been, though it's harder than I used to imagine, seeing animals in pain all the time, or dying. I barely held myself together when Aggie was in intensive care. And her vets haven't just been great with her. They've been great with *me*. That's the part that scares me most. The people part. And then there's this to deal with." I hold up the envelope again. "If I was working full-time, I wouldn't have to worry if my Wi-Fi was about to get cut off."

Khalil winces. "Maybe you'll feel better when you find that job you're looking for?"

"Maybe." I prod a blackened gum spot with the toe of my only decent pair of shoes, which I probably shouldn't be doing but the spot's been here as long as I have. It's not going anywhere. "I have classes Monday through Friday and a weekend job, so I'm only available weeknights, and I need time for studying and Aggie and dealing with dumb stuff like laundry."

"It's the laundry that screws you every time," Khalil jokes.

I laugh, but with effort, and he deflates at the same moment I do.

"Does it have to be remote?" he asks.

"I'd prefer it, for Aggie, but I may have to reconsider."

"If you do, a guy in my lab does custodial work to make a few bucks. They're always hiring. It's after hours so it might fit your schedule. It's not glamorous work, though."

"I'm not expecting glamour." I take a moment to imagine it,

mopping floors and cleaning toilets while Aggie spends more time home alone. The work can't be that much less inspiring than my pizzeria job, but even considering it is like taking one more step away from the life I thought I'd be living at this point, the one I dreamed about when people asked me what I wanted to be when I grew up, and when I played doctor with my stuffed animals. It makes the question *Will it all be worth it?* flash in hot pink neon, bolder and brighter than ever.

Khalil must read something of my thoughts in my face, because he taps my elbow with his and tells me there's no rush. I can let him know anytime if I'm interested. We swap numbers while the elevator's still creeping toward our floor, and leave the conversation there.

When I enter my apartment to Aggie's eager, tail-wagging greeting from her bed, my mood is instantly buoyed. How I ever thought I could live without a dog is beyond me. All that unbridled joy. It's contagious, and a surefire protection against wallowing. I get her outside for a little exercise, and feed her, and play ball, which she's really getting into now. I make off-brand mac 'n' cheese I try to fool my brain into thinking is gourmet by sprinkling pepper on top. Then I force myself to go through my mail. All of it. Sorting student loan statements into a pile I don't have to deal with yet, and outstanding bills and credit statements into a pile I do have to deal with, plugging the information into a spreadsheet so I can plan out a rough monthly budget, something that feels more essential now that I'm not just taking care of myself.

It's daunting, the bottom line, both what I owe now and what I'll need to bring in each month to cover expenses beyond what my loans afford. I consider the custodial possibility, or waiting tables if anyone's hiring, but Aggie's *so* happy to have me home in the evenings, and finding times to keep up her exercise routine will get harder as the weather gets worse. She's my priority right now, and I don't want to abandon her all hours. It's unthinkable after how she spent her first seven years. So, after considerable thought, and a sharp pang of regret that I can't afford to hit a liquor store first, I brace myself and call my parents.

"Cameron, hi!" my mom says when she answers, as chipper as ever, with a musical lilt to her voice that serves her well in her receptionist role at a local medical center, where she makes everyone feel welcome. For all my complaints about her incessant bright-siding, her warmth is genuine, and my nerves loosen a little at the sound of her voice. "How are you?"

"Good. Fine. Well, um, more like okay, but sort of dealing with some stuff." I grimace at my verbal clumsiness, and how I always autopilot to saying *I'm good* and have to course correct.

"Whatever it is, you'll work it out," she says. "But classes are going well?"

"Mostly. It's a lot of studying. My immunology professor is a really hard grader. And my pathology prof must think we're all speed readers with how much reading she assigns."

"They wouldn't set high standards if they didn't think you could live up to them. And you've never been afraid of hard work."

"I know." My teeth clench the way they always do when she willfully misses the point. "What I mean is that I'm having a hard time keeping up with everything. And not just classes."

She tsks and I try to convince myself I didn't hear it.

"Give it time, sweetie, and keep your chin up. It'll be the end of the term before you know it."

I take a deep breath and let my annoyance out in a slow exhale while Aggie shifts her head on my lap and I bury my fingers in her soft fur, more for my benefit than for hers. We're on the futon, where she already has a favorite side and I always let her have it, along with her favorite blanket, favorite pillow, and the stuffed monkey she's starting to like.

"Have you given any more thought to Christmas?" my mom asks. "Your dad and I can't imagine the holidays without you. And we're still happy to cover your ticket."

"Actually, is he around?" I ask. "I'd love to talk to both of you for a minute."

She sighs, barely, but enough for me to pick up on a hint of frustration that often slips out when my dad comes up in conversation, though she's always quick to suppress it.

"You know your father," she says brightly. "Straight from work to the gym to the television, but I can go see if he'll step away for a minute, if it's important."

"It is. At least, I think it is. It's a conversation for both of you, anyway."

A beat of silence follows, and I can picture my mom rallying to tamp down the worry I've sparked. A swallow. A brow flicker that's quickly smoothed. A smile that snaps into place.

"Okay, sure," she says without a jot of concern in her voice. "Give me a sec."

She steps away from the call to retrieve my dad while I replay her comment about his routine. When I was a kid, the three of us did a lot of things together: watching movies, playing board games, taking summer vacations on the coast, going out for ice cream, hiking nearby trails, swimming with Marmie in the river that weaves through Roseburg, and eating most of our meals together. My dad was pretty hands-off as far as parenting went, busy with his work managing a network of school buses for several regional public-school systems, a job he got by starting as a driver and working his way up. But he made time for my mom and me. I always felt that.

Has this changed since I left for college? Would either of them tell me if it has?

Eventually my dad joins the call, and before we can return to the topic of the holidays, I ask my parents to switch to video. Then I show them the face resting on my lap.

My dad blinks in confusion while my mom gasps and presses a hand to her mouth.

"Oh, Cameron!" she says. "Look at that beautiful dog!"

"Her name's Aggie," I say. "Short for Agatha."

"Look at those ears!" my mom continues to gush. "And those sweet, gentle eyes."

I hold out the camera to take in more of Aggie as I pet her head.

"She's pretty perfect, isn't she?" I ask.

My dad nods slowly, echoing, "Perfect," so quietly I almost don't hear it. He was the one to bring Marmie home as a puppy, and she was as much his as she was mine or my mom's.

"Are you dog-sitting for a friend?" my mom asks with what I suspect is equal curiosity about the dog and the hypothetical friend I haven't told her about.

"Um. Well. No," I manage. Then I tell my parents about the foster applications I filed last year, the call from the shelter, the rehabilitation plan, and the adoption papers I signed before bringing Aggie home. "I fell in love. And I think I needed her as much as she needed me."

"Of course you did," my mom says. "Who wouldn't fall in love with that face? And you'll get her weight down in no time. What an angel. I hope you send me *lots* of pictures."

I almost laugh as I tell her about the TikTok account, and how I'll be posting updates there. She's not currently on TikTok, but I bet she will be within minutes of ending the call.

She sets a hand on my dad's shoulder. "Look at that face, Hank!"

He nods again and musters a smile, but remains notably quiet. It's tough. I know he's happy to have a dog in the family again, but I can practically hear the questions he's not asking. Questions about how much taking care of a pet with major health issues costs.

"Hank?" my mom repeats. "Don't you have anything to say?"

He looks at me, looks at Aggie, and looks at me again.

"It's a big responsibility," he says.

"I know," I say, already tensing again.

"With everything you have going on . . ."

"All of which I'm aware of."

"Are you still working at that pizza place? And only weekends at the fancy soap store?"

"I'm"—I cringe as I search for an acceptable answer—"dealing with the job situation."

Another beat of silence. Not a long one, but a heavy one.

"Cameron," he says.

"Dad," I say back.

"I just want to ensure you're making smart choices," he says with unfortunate predictability, and I know by *smart*, he means *affordable*. I also know there's no arguing him out of this position, even while he's gazing with warm affection at Aggie.

I'd planned on introducing my parents to Aggie, telling them we were spending the holidays here, and then asking if they'd loan me the money they would've put toward a plane ticket, which should be enough to cover what I can't of my November rent while I keep hunting for work. But if we're already talking about smart choices, asking for a loan will only invite a lecture, a lecture will become a fight, and I'd rather leave the conversation on a positive note.

"Actually, I have to run," I say. "I just wanted you to meet Aggie. And to let you know we'll be spending the holiday break here, so I won't need that plane ticket. But thank you for offering and we'll find another time to visit, maybe in the summer when classes are out."

"Oh, I hope so!" my mom exclaims.

My dad nods and smiles. He's trying. It's something.

We sign off with the usual *I love you*s, which we all mean, though it's a complicated love, making me extra grateful for the soft, sweet head that's still resting on my lap, soaking up my affection like it's all she needs to make her world go around.

"What do you think?" I ask as Aggie lifts her head and blinks up at me. "Can you handle two or three nights a week on your own if I can sort out some cleaning work?"

She looks at me for a few seconds. Then she grabs her monkey and drops it in my lap.

"Oh my god. You're killing me!" I moan, but I pick up the monkey and we play for a few minutes as I hold it just out of her reach and then let her snatch it from my hand and shake it in a way that gets her tail wagging. When she refuses to give it up again and sets to chewing it, reveling in the sound from the squeaker, I locate Khalil's number and shoot him a text.

CHAPTER TEN

I'm still in bed Sunday morning at around nine, lazily leaning over the side to pet Aggie while talking myself into getting up, when I hear a carefully controlled light rap on my door.

Aggie lets out a trio of cheerful barks. I'd like to think they're because she knows who's at the door, but I suspect she'd greet anyone who knocked with a similar welcome.

"Worst watchdog ever," I tease with a scratch between her ears.

She smiles as if I paid her a compliment, mouth ajar, tongue out, eyes bright. It's a look that always ignites a spark of joy in my chest. Yes, she's a responsibility, like my dad said, but she also feels like an inevitability. Like I was meant to be hers just as she was meant to be mine.

"Aggie," Everett's lowered voice comes through the door. "Tell your mom to open up."

She barks again, her tail wagging harder as she hauls herself into a seated position, which still takes her some effort, but is already much easier for her than it used to be.

Not wanting to wake our neighbors, I find my phone on the nightstand.

CAMERON: I'm still in bed

EVERETT: Yes, and?

CAMERON: And I'm not ready for you to see me first thing in the morning

EVERETT: I can't tell if I should be flattered or offended

CAMERON: How about well warned?

EVERETT: The possibilities I'm imagining here . . .

CAMERON: At least let me brush my teeth and comb my hair

EVERETT: Spoiler alert: I've seen your teeth unbrushed and your hair uncombed

CAMERON: That was before I was trying to impress you

EVERETT: In case I didn't make myself clear: zero impressing is required here

> **CAMERON:** By impressing I mean letting me woo you with base levels of daily hygiene

> **EVERETT:** Aww. So romantic! Is that Shakespeare or Keats?

"Go away!" I call across the room. "We'll be over in ten!"

Everett's muffled laugh makes its way through my door.

"Don't eat breakfast," he says. "I have plans. You know. Once I'm wooed."

I send a wary look in the general direction of my door. We didn't talk about getting together today, and while I'm elated he's taking the initiative and making plans, I'm nervous about what he might've cooked up. Is this a date? Is *he* trying to impress *me*? Does he remember that I have to work at noon? And that I need to get Aggie outside for some exercise before that? What do I bring? Or wear? Will this cost me money I don't have?

And the big one: Is it a good thing or a bad thing that he lives just down the hall?

Thankfully, I don't have time to spiral myself into a state of high anxiety about what might or might not be my first official date in three years. I rub the last of the sleep from my eyes with the heels of my hands. Then I haul myself out of bed and check the time. Since I stupidly gave myself only ten minutes, I throw on a simple rayon dress I bought in college when I had the time and money to care about things like clothes, and which has weathered the always-changing fashion landscape pretty well. I pair it with cozy cable-knit sweater tights, a long, thick cardigan I picked up at a thrift store last fall, and a densely embroidered scarf Minh Ha would probably like, given the collection of patterned scarves I've seen her wear. With no time to fuss, I yank a comb through the tangled mess that is my long hair—which I've heard described as honey blond by a few generous souls, though it falls more accurately in the dishwater range—and weave it into a simple braid that hangs down my back almost to my waist.

When I'm as presentable as possible, I harness Aggie and load her into her wagon, tucking a ball and an extra blanket into the corner, and a bag of treats into my pocket, before swallowing a flutter of nerves and wheeling her down the hall to Everett's apartment.

After a brief knock, he answers the door in navy corduroys and a rich mulberry roll-collared sweater with a single leather toggle at the base of his neck. I don't know what it is about this man and his sweaters, but each one makes me want to fall against him in a long, lingering hug. Maybe because they all look so soft. More likely because he's the one wearing them.

"Hi," I say, suddenly breathless.

"Hi," he returns, sinking his teeth into his lower lip as his cheeks dimple.

We do that thing we also did in my apartment the other night, mid-baking-confessional, where we get shifty and rosy-cheeked as we look at each other like our minds need a moment to catch up with our hearts, or like all we want to do is look, and be, and share these seconds.

Everett blinks himself out of our locked gaze first, stepping forward to enfold me in the embrace I was coveting a moment ago, and planting a sweet little kiss on my cheek before he releases me to give an eagerly awaiting Aggie a greeting of her own, bending low to scratch her neck with both hands and scolding her for letting me sleep in on a beautiful October day.

"Want to come in for a sec?" he asks. "I just need to grab a jacket, but I told you a while ago I'd show you my place so you knew I wasn't a hoarder. I feel like it's high time I make good on that offer. Consider it my way of wooing you with base levels of human dignity."

I roll my eyes but I'm smiling too hard for my annoyance to be convincing. I like it when he teases me. It never feels mean. It feels like a way of building comfort with each other.

Pulling Aggie's wagon over the threshold, I step into a shockingly bright living room with sunlight streaming through a pair of big, arched windows. I always forget the units at the front of the building look out over the main street, unlike the other units, with our views blocked by adjacent buildings, leaving only dimly lit alleys through any given window.

The kitchen area is significantly larger than mine, complete with a breakfast bar and two stools, full-sized appliances, and a table that seats four. The living room has a wall of tightly but tidily occupied bookshelves and a neatly arranged cluster of furniture that includes a sofa, two armchairs, and a coffee table. The furniture is from different eras and styles, but in good shape and tied together with coordinating curtains, throw pillows, and rugs in olive and teal textiles that give off a mid-century modern vibe. Houseplants perch in corners, on the bookshelves, and on windowsills, maybe a dozen in total, adding color and life without overwhelming the space.

I'm not sure what I expected, beyond a lot of plants and a certain level of vintage eclecticism that mirrors Everett's wardrobe, but I'm struck as I look around by how artistic the space is. It's not assembled by chance, with whatever he found in an alley or thrift store. Every piece feels deliberately chosen and arranged carefully in relationship to the other elements of the room. The space has a mood to it, a design, a personality that goes well beyond functionality, a hint of the outdoors brought indoors, not just with the plants but with the colors and textures.

Now that I see it, it's so obvious. Everett is an artist. He hasn't used that term to describe himself, not directly, anyway. He's said he's in marketing, or makes social media content, or develops branding strategies and improves search engine optimization. What he's grossly undersold is how creative that work must be.

I feel like I've just peeled back a layer of an onion, not to find another layer, but to discover a blossoming flower inside. Also, he has a bedroom, a real one with a door through which I can see the foot of a bed, though I decide to save exploring that part of his habitat for another time.

"Well?" he asks as he shrugs on a canvas jacket. "What do you think?"

"I think I can't believe we live in the same building," I tell him honestly. "That's a real sofa. And a real bedroom. And those are real windows. And real books and framed photos on your shelves. You probably have real food in your fridge, too."

As I spin toward his kitchen, still taking it all in, he steps up behind me, wraps me in his arms, and sets his chin on my shoulder so his cheek rests against mine, smooth and warm. I lean into him, following the instinct before I can second-guess it, and he tightens his hold in response.

"I do enjoy a well-balanced meal I don't pour from a box," he says. "And I make a decent living, though I have to find a way to pull back on work or it'll drown me." He gives me a quick squeeze before releasing me. "But today isn't about work. You have about two hours, right?"

I check the time on a brushed-steel clock over his kitchen window. Just past nine-twenty.

"About that," I confirm. "And I planned to spend it with Aggie."

"I assumed." He gives her another scratch on the neck while she looks up at him with her eyes bright and her tail wagging. "Good thing I have a plan that includes all three of us."

TEN MINUTES LATER, after Aggie's done "her business," we turn the corner onto the Ithaca Commons, the pedestrian mall that runs through the old downtown with its three- and four-story nineteenth-century facades transformed by an urban renewal project in the 1970s and again in the 2010s. It was once home to a lot of banks and department stores, but now it houses galleries, trendy retail outlets and coffee shops, a library I haven't been into yet, and a 1915 vaudeville theater that's been converted into an indie cinema. It's also the home to five of the eleven obelisks in the Sagan Planet Walk, a three-quarter-mile scale model of the solar system that spans several streets across town, and one of Ithaca's quirkiest quirks. It's a tribute to Cornell professor of astronomy, Carl Sagan, anchored in the Commons by the sun obelisk in its black and gold glory, and with Mercury, Venus, Earth, and Mars nearby.

I fell in love with the Commons when I first arrived in Ithaca, which is a big reason I rented the apartment around the corner, despite its deficiencies. It's like a cute small town in the center of a somewhat sprawling midsize city. It has a feeling of overlapping histories to it, like it's been through hard times and come back over and over again, transformed with every rebirth but always bringing its old selves with it. Sure, there's a Starbucks and an Urban Outfitters now. There's also the cutest pastel-explosion bakery I've ever seen, and a bookstore that always has at least one cat sunning itself in the window, usually two or three, and a knitting shop called Wool-to-Wool Yarns. And today, there's a bustling outdoor market, with tents and tables in front of every venue, and a crowd already gathered, inspecting the wares.

"I saw the ad for the market on my way home from work yesterday," Everett says as we merge into the flow of the crowd, him with his arm around my waist and me pulling Aggie behind us. "I thought it would be fun to check out together."

"You thought right," I say, though I refrain from confessing it's the *together* that will make it fun. The Commons hosts a lot of markets and festivals. Earlier this month, it was the annual Apple Harvest Festival. There's also a festival dedicated to chili and another to chowder, as well as open gallery nights and outdoor concerts. I came to a few of the events last fall, shortly after I moved here, but I never feel more alone than when I'm surrounded by people who aren't alone: couples in cozy embraces, parents giving piggyback rides to kids, friends soliciting each other's opinions on handmade pottery or jewelry, and, most notably, people walking dogs.

A year later, being here with Everett and Aggie, I can appreciate the energy without my prior envy toward the lovers, dog walkers, or clusters of laughing friends. I can just enjoy it.

"Tea or coffee?" Everett asks.

"Tea. Always. Coffee is overrated."

"Interesting. And good to know." He steers us around a group of slow meanderers and toward the side of the street. "How about pastries? Streuseltaler or a classic pain au chocolat?"

"I don't know what that first one is."

"Then I believe our decision is made."

We weave through the crowd in no particular rush, which is good, given the not-insubstantial wagon I'm pulling behind me and the way it parts a crowd. When we reach the far corner of the block, Everett stops and pivots us toward Havisham & Harrison's Tea Company. The old-timey storefront is carved from dark, polished wood with delicate gold trim and big bay windows. With the sign's gilded typewriter font, the display of hanging antique teapots pouring lush bouquets of flowers into one another, and the ornate, faux-gaslight sconces flanking the windows and bright green door, the shop is straight out of a Dickens novel. I've admired it every time I walked past it, though I've never been inside, on the solid assumption that it's well above my price range.

"This is my date and my idea, so I'm paying," Everett says as if he's reading my mind, something he's remarkably good at, given our relatively short acquaintance. Also . . . *date*. Good. Phew. Noted. "We only have two hours to spend together before the week gets away from us, and I just want to do something nice for you. Okay?"

Wow. He really does know me, because I instinctively want to put up a fight, and he saw it coming. I'm still replaying my dad's insinuation about my financial irresponsibility on our call yesterday, as well as our fights about the debt I'd incur by attending Cornell, and a hundred other arguments we had about money, security, and independence while I was growing up. However, Everett's offer feels *really* good, like someone's taking care of me for a change, letting me off the hook for taking care of myself. Is it so wrong to let him treat me to breakfast?

Warm lips meet mine, parting softly as Everett's nose bumps my cheek and his hands cup my face. My breath catches with surprise, but as he coaxes my mouth open with his, the surprise fades and I melt against him, still holding the wagon extension with one hand while the other grips his sweater, which proves to be as soft as it looks.

The softness of his sweater is my last coherent thought. The rest evaporate like the flash paper that magicians use, which sparks into fire before vanishing, leaving no trace it ever existed. My knees go wobbly. My toes curl. My skin warms. My tongue finds Everett's, deepening the kiss, but only for a moment before he pulls away, still cupping my face with both hands as his cheeks dimple and his beautiful hazel eyes sparkle with mirth behind his glasses.

"You were thinking too hard," he says. "Did that help?"

I swallow, and swallow again, before managing a nod. Then I notice Aggie watching us from her wagon with her head resting on the front panel, looking as pleased with herself as if she orchestrated the entire morning. Just past her wagon, a pair of googly eyes is glued above a jagged, curved crack in a drainpipe, turning the crack into a crooked smile. It's so silly I can't help but smile back as I give in to the joy around me and steal another kiss from Everett.

"Thank you," I say. "Offer accepted."

A sign on the tea shop door says *No pets*, so Aggie and I wait out front while Everett heads inside to place our order. Several cute café tables are set up outside for the market, all of them occupied with people sipping from antique cups and saucers as a short, wiry woman with a nimbus cloud of unruly silver curls bustles in and out of the shop to wait on everyone. She's in a ruffled eyelet apron over a floral dress and heather wool cardigan, all of which has a fluttery energy to it, though it's her red and white spectator shoes that keep drawing my eye.

As she passes us while heading into the shop for the third or fourth time, her gaze drifts our way and she stops short, pressing a hand to her heart while the other grips a bright blue teapot.

"Are you the Goode Girls?" she asks me.

Heat floods my cheeks at the unexpected attention, which feels different here than it did in the park, where I've grown used to seeing a lot of the same faces as Aggie gets her exercise.

"Um, yes?" I stammer.

"Oh my lord," she lets out in a gust. "What you're doing for that dog is just wonderful."

I send an affectionate glance toward Aggie. "It's a mutually beneficial relationship."

"Well, that goes without saying!" The woman scurries over and crouches by the wagon, giving me a *can I?* look, to which I nod, because Aggie deserves all the affection the world has to offer. The woman asks if we're waiting for someone and I let her know my friend is inside getting tea for both of us. She says she's honored we're here, and introduces herself as Diana, the Havisham half of Havisham & Harrison. Introductions made, she fawns over a delighted Aggie while telling me about the seven or eight wire fox terriers she adopted through various rescue organizations over the years, and how much she loved each one, and what was unique about each, but how it's been harder to consider having a dog now that she and her partner are older. This is something I've already learned about Aggie, that she unlocks people's stories about their dogs, which is a really beautiful gift, now that I'm thinking about it.

"I'm sure we'll be back," I say when Diana straightens up, looking at Aggie like her heart will break if she has to say goodbye. "We live nearby, though I saw your no-pets policy."

Diana flicks my comment away. "We have to put that sign up to comply with city health ordinances, but *queens* of all sorts are welcome anytime." With that, she whisks open the shop door, calling out, "Arthur? Arthur! It's the dog I was telling you about. And the girl who adopted her. They're here getting tea and don't you dare charge them for their order!"

The door swings shut behind her and a few minutes later, Everett emerges with two steaming paper cups and a dark green shopping bag with an H&H logo hanging off his arm.

"So much for my offer to treat," he says through a breath of laughter.

I point an accusing finger at Aggie. "It's her fault. She hooked another one."

She lowers her head to rest it on the wagon's front panel again, the picture of innocence, looking back and forth between us as her brows twitch the way I love so much.

Everett and I share a smile. Then he hands me my cup along with the bag, which turns out to hold half a dozen green and gold tins of loose-leaf tea.

"Apparently those are their bestsellers," he says. "English breakfast. Earl Grey. Mint. They insisted, and I figured their tea was probably better than whatever you have at home."

I stare at the contents of the bag. "They just *gave* you all of this?"

"They gave *you* all of this," he corrects, and at my obvious swell of discomfort, he adds, "Sometimes people do nice things just to do nice things. Enjoy it, Cameron. It's only tea."

I don't have a chance to argue because the shop door opens again and Diana drags a very tall, very lanky man out by the wrist. He's mostly bald with a tidy silver mustache, while his collarless striped dress shirt and black vest give him the air of someone from another time.

"Go say hi," Diana kindly but forcefully instructs him, and he shyly obeys, bending low to let Aggie smell his unusually long hand. Half a second later, she's wagging her tail and inching her head forward for a pet, with her usual gift for overcoming anyone's shyness.

As the man I assume is Arthur—and the Harrison half of Havisham & Harrison—strokes Aggie's head, looking down at her fondly, Everett suggests making a TikTok of her grand day out, exploring our neighborhood and making new friends. I almost laugh. The Goode Girls account has been live for less than forty-eight hours. Everett's known about it for half that time, and his content-creation mind is already at work. But also, his idea is cute and I tell him so, while authorizing him to be our official videographer for the day.

Diana and the man she confirms is Arthur are happy to participate, so Everett gets a shot of them with Aggie and me that includes the adorable store window with its teapots of flowers. Then Arthur heads inside to attend to the growing line of customers, casting one last glance at Aggie from the doorstep while slyly dabbing at the corner of his eye before he steps inside.

"He's always been a man of few words," Diana says, making me realize I'm not sure I heard him speak at all. "But he loved those terriers as much as I did. We carry on, as we must, but the grief never fully goes away. Make sure you come back and see us, okay?"

"Of course." I grip my bag of tea a little tighter as I mentally replay Everett's words.

Sometimes people do nice things just to do nice things.

It's such a simple idea, and deep down, I know true kindness doesn't inherently come with the expectation of a return, but I don't know how to fully embrace that idea. I don't know how to accept generosity at face value, which makes me wonder, maybe the greatest lesson Aggie can teach me isn't how to be happy.

It's how to trust.

THE REST OF the morning follows a similar pattern.

We get free pastries at the German bakery, which is next door to the French bakery. The two have a historic rivalry even I know about, and this is my first time setting foot in either one. Johann Schneider, the friendly owner/manager of the German bakery not only tells us to ignore the *No pets* sign I now know is obligatory, he gives us a bag of the dog treats he bakes, which he sells alongside a mouthwatering array of strudels, cinnamon rolls, cakes, and doughnuts. He's also delighted to be filmed for our account, a sentiment he sings rather than says, displaying a booming operatic voice that has my jaw dropping open with awe, until Aggie lets out a sharp bark at an especially impassioned note, and everyone breaks into laughter, even Johann.

After breakfast, we peruse the outdoor offerings at a toy store, where Everett looks for a birthday gift for his nephew, who's turning two in November. Aggie gets excited when he slips his hand into a big, shaggy Highland cow puppet and teases her with it. Next thing I know, it's coming home with us, thanks to the generosity of the woman running the store, who's thrilled Aggie's showing an interest in the toy. She tells us her sister has retrievers and sent her a link to our account. She takes a selfie with us, eager to send it to her sister, who lives near Melbourne, Australia, which boggles my mind as I think about how far one video has traveled.

Last but far from least, I grab a bright pink tennis ball from a dollar bin outside a sporting goods store and Everett films me lobbing it gently toward Aggie. While seated in her wagon, she makes a concerted effort to catch my throws, until she succeeds on the fifth or sixth try, by which point, several spectators have gathered and break into applause, murmuring among themselves as word spreads about Aggie's history and why her catching a ball is a big deal. The clerk running the outdoor stall tears up as someone shows her our account, and she gives us several balls to take home, insisting we made her day and there's no charge.

Thus, by eleven-thirty, as we wheel Aggie home after her walking exercises, the wagon is full of bags and toys, making her look like a dragon hoarding its treasure. After Everett helps me get her settled on her bed, we perch on the side of my bed and I open Tik-Tok, shaking my head at the growing numbers. Over two days, one video has garnered more than seven hundred thousand views and the account has almost eleven thousand followers. It's unreal.

"Want help with number two?" Everett asks.

"I don't have time before heading to work. We can do it later."

He takes out his phone with the time in bold on the home screen.

"You have ten minutes, right?" he asks.

"Exactly. I *only* have ten minutes."

"Then let's get to it."

He's missed my point entirely—namely, that the first video took me well over an hour to put together—but his cheeks are dimpled with an eager smile and his thumbs are already flying as he scoots closer, scrolling his album from today. Together, we select a few videos, starting with Arthur and Diana at the tea shop and ending with Aggie catching the bright pink ball as the crowd around her applauds. Everett deftly compiles the shots, efficiently cutting and splicing to tighten everything. I dictate a caption about how Aggie's enjoying her Sunday morning. He types it in, adds hashtags, tags the businesses that gave us free stuff, adds a trending pop song without belaboring the choice the way I did, and before I know it, we have a second TikTok up.

"You make it look so easy," I say as he logs out of my account and pockets his phone.

"Only because it's all for fun." His pinkie brushes mine as he sets his hand next to mine on top of my boring and not particularly comforting comforter. The contact is subtle, tender, instinctive, and I silently curse my weekend job for ripping me away from him, and from Aggie. "It takes me a lot longer if I'm developing a new brand, testing posting strategies, targeting a specific type of viewer, trying to meet a performance goal, or otherwise selling something."

I smile at Aggie, who's pawing at a pink ball. "We're definitely not selling anything."

Everett's pinkie brushes my hand again, more deliberately this time, almost like a nudge.

"You could, though," he says, "if you wanted to."

"Why would I want to?"

"I mean . . ." He gives me a look that suggests I should be able to answer this one on my own, and I suppose I can, but didn't he *just* say this was all for fun? Didn't I tell him the same thing yesterday when I texted him about the account? Doesn't he understand that's what I want it to be, for me *and* for Aggie? I'm happy to mention local businesses, especially when they show her special attention or give us free stuff, but I know Everett's talking about sponsorship. Deliberate monetization. Turning fun into commerce. And I'm not interested.

"I appreciate the suggestion," I tell him. "But even posting that first TikTok was a big step for me, and I'm still pretty overwhelmed by the response. I need some time to adjust, so can we park this conversation for another time? Like, a far, faraway time?"

He draws me into a hug, and after only a moment's hesitation, I fall against him, exhaling my little burst of stress so I can relish these last precious seconds together before our beautiful Sunday morning ends, while he gives me a reassuring squeeze and says, "Of course."

CHAPTER ELEVEN

In case there was any doubt on the subject, scrubbing toilets officially sucks. I'm two weeks into my cleaning job at Bradfield Hall on the Cornell campus, where I now work an after-hours shift from 6 p.m. to 11 p.m. Tuesdays and Thursdays, mopping floors and cleaning bathrooms. The job's quiet, I can multitask by listening to veterinary podcasts, and it pays above minimum wage, so I can get by on two nights a week instead of three. All of this is an improvement on my pizzeria job. But still. Little makes me rethink all of my life choices like plunging a stopped toilet.

I'm dragging my feet as I walk home from campus, wondering if this is the best I can do at the adulthood I was racing toward as a teenager and now want to return for a refund. I'm tired of being broke. I'm tired of being tired. Then I walk through my apartment door and find Aggie on her bed, surrounded by a growing collection of toys, able now to scoot herself into a seated position with relative ease, wagging her tail and looking like the sun broke through the clouds.

"Hi, sweetie." I drop to my knees beside her and throw my arms around her neck.

She bunts the side of my head with her cold, wet nose, sniffing every inch of me with a rigorous curiosity I don't examine too closely, given how I've spent my evening. Her tail wags, her entire body wriggles with joy, and within seconds, the best I can do doesn't seem so bad.

I get her harnessed and into the wagon, which remains our easiest way of getting around. She can take a few stiff, shaky steps on her own now, and she supports more of her own weight when I use the sling or harness, but the wagon's still a huge help if we might be waiting for a while in the elevator or traveling beyond the little lawn out front, especially when I'm tired.

With my coat still on, we head out so Aggie can do her final pee for the night. We're in the elevator, watching the doors close, when someone calls out for us to hold them. I reach out a hand to trigger the sensor and The Lovers soon join me, jogging to an abrupt halt as they wedge themselves into the limited space left by Aggie's wagon. We exchange brief, polite smiles, and while the doors close again, I lift my eyes toward the flickering fluorescent lights, praying to whatever's beyond them that The Lovers don't make out all the way to the ground floor.

It's been a little over three weeks since the morning at the market, and I've barely seen Everett during that time. Between his busy work schedule and my busy life schedule, we're lucky to sneak in a couple hours together on a weeknight or a weekend morning. The first time we tried to watch a movie together, I fell asleep on him. The second time, he fell asleep on me.

"No way," says the tall lover, knotting a gray flannel scarf over a navy peacoat.

"Right? I told you!" says the short lover, cutting a sharp contrast with her partner in an embroidered, faux fur–trimmed, ankle-length coat that makes me think of dramatic heroines in old Russian novels, none of which I've read in their entirety. She also has bright orange mittens poking from a pocket, and red earmuffs circling her neck like idling headphones, leaving her natural curls loose, while her partner wears a plain black beanie over her blond pixie cut.

The two of them are looking at a phone together, glancing up at the same time to see me regarding them. I flash them an apologetic smile, hoping I didn't seem like I was showing undue curiosity in their midnight scrolling, and I'm startled when they both break into big, wide grins.

"This is her, right?" says the short one. "This is the TikTok dog?"

"Um, yes?" I manage. After six videos and a little over three weeks, our initial TikTok now has more than three million views, and the follower count is still growing. I appreciate all the support and encouragement, but still. It's . . . a lot. "Her name's Aggie. Short for Agatha."

"Ag-gie," the tall one singsongs, bending down to ruffle the fur on Aggie's neck, a form of attention that always delights her, and this time is no exception. She raises her head to provide better access as her hairless tail wags and her eyes drift shut in ecstasy. "Who's a good girl? Who's *the best* girl? Who's the scruffy-wuffy, goodest, bestest, Aggie-waggiest girl?"

I watch with amusement as Aggie revels in the attention while the other woman looks at her phone again and the elevator inches its way downward at its usual sluggish pace.

"Thirteen pounds, huh?" asks the woman with the phone, presumably referring to the caption on our latest TikTok. We're doing most of our weigh-ins at Ruff 'n' Rescue to limit vet bills, and Sariah and Sam have been amazing at advising on physical therapy and mobility in general, so I don't get too excited by Aggie's progress and overtax her body before it's ready.

"Thirteen pounds in six weeks," I confirm.

"Wow. That's intense." She shakes her head, incredulous. "I'm Regina, by the way." She gestures at her partner, who's now getting a full tongue bath, and apparently enjoying it as much as Aggie is. "This is Tegan. You just moved in a couple months ago, right?"

I suppress most but not all of an embarrassed grimace, though whether I'm embarrassed for her, for me, or for all three of us, I'm not sure.

"Actually, I moved in last July. Like, a year and four months ago."

Regina and Tegan swap a look that's not unlike the one I tried to hide.

"We suck," Tegan says through a laugh. "How did we think you were new?"

"Well, I mean, you're usually . . . busy," I say, and immediately wish I'd let Regina answer.

Fortunately, they find my awkwardness amusing and not offensive.

"It's the elevator," Regina says, also laughing now. "We got so tired of how slow it was, we needed a way to pass the time. Obviously, we came up with one."

"Obviously," Tegan echoes, straightening up to wrap a long arm around Regina.

"Aggie has an elevator activity, too," I tell them. "Sadly, it's farting."

"Oh my god!" Regina sweeps a hand up to shield her nose. "You're kidding, right?"

We all turn toward Aggie, who's looking especially proud of herself, probably for being the undisputable center of attention right now, and not for her small-space farting prowess, but I never know with this one. I still think she understands way more than the average dog.

Sure enough, she lets one fly, though she has the grace to wait until we're almost at the ground floor and we can laugh about it without asphyxiating. By this point, we've expanded our introductions, so I've learned Regina's a fashion designer who recently launched her own brand of locally manufactured streetwear she describes as "color forward" and "typographically whimsical," showing me samples of bright, two-tone baseball tees printed with quotes and word poems in mismatched fonts and placements, sometimes just on a sleeve or near the hem, sometimes spanning the entire shirt. Tegan works at a nearby bank. She doesn't say much about what she does at the bank. I get the impression she's used to Regina fielding a lot more questions about her work in fashion, and she's happy to let her partner enjoy the spotlight.

"You should make Aggie a tee," she suggests as we exit the elevator into the lobby.

Regina grabs her arm, spinning in my direction. "Oh my god, yes! Can I?"

"Sure. Of course. If you want to," I say. "But what would it say? *World-class farter?*"

"Something far more badass," Regina says. "Let me think about it. Can I come take her measurements sometime this week so I can see if one of our current sizes would fit?"

"Absolutely," I say, already picturing Aggie in a custom tee she'd totally rock.

We all swap numbers and part ways, waving on the sidewalk as I wheel Aggie toward the nearest patch of grass, and the couple heads off toward a party they mentioned in the elevator. I watch them walk away, arms around each other, with Regina's head resting against Tegan's shoulder. Before I help Aggie out of her wagon, I find my phone.

> **CAMERON:** You're probably sleeping, but I wanted you to know I'm thinking about you

As I turn off my screen, I make myself a promise that I'll look at my schedule when I get home from classes tomorrow, and I'll find a time to see Everett when I'm not also doing laundry or cramming in homework or exercising my dog or—

> **EVERETT:** I'm thinking about you, too 😊

> **EVERETT:** Date night Friday?

I've never texted so fast in my life.

> **CAMERON:** Yes please!!!

> **EVERETT:** Good. See you then. Now get some sleep you maniac!

I'm grinning as I pocket my phone. Apparently, the best I can do isn't bad at all.

CHAPTER TWELVE

On Friday, when I'm home after classes, Aggie's been out, and I refuse to cram in schoolwork all afternoon, we work on one of the key mobility exercises Sam and Sariah talked us through, with the end goal of enabling Aggie to stand up on her own. She can sit up from lying down but after years of disuse, her back legs aren't as strong as her front legs. We've been practicing for weeks, initially with me helping to lift her back end once she starts to rise, usually using the harness. Later, we added a small, padded step she can perch her backside on so she doesn't have as far to go to reach a standing position. I tempt her with toys, treats, or a spoonful of peanut butter, standing just out of reach. She tries to lift herself. She has the idea, she *really* wants to nail it, and she's so much stronger now than she was when I first brought her home, but she's still struggling, rocking backward and forward but eventually dropping back down.

"You're doing *so* great!" I encourage as I help her up and then return her to the step so she can try again on her own. "You go at your own pace, baby. You'll get there. I can tell."

She blinks at me like she's not so certain, but after a few seconds, she tries again.

We're on our tenth or eleventh attempt when there's a knock at my door. I'd assume it's Everett but it's a little after two right now and he's at work. He said he'd do his damnedest to leave his office right at five so we could have our date night, but I bet he sticks around for at least another hour.

I open the door to find Khalil in the mid-November version of his cycling gear, which means he's swapped his shorts for leggings and added a fleece and a reflective raincoat. I'm sure he has clothes that aren't made of high-tech fabrics, but I've never seen them. He's also soaked from the rain that's pelting outside right now, with his hair dripping and his sneakers squelching.

"Do you have ten minutes?" he asks. "Or, maybe more like twenty?"

"Sure, of course." I step back to give him room to enter. "I also have towels."

"Ack! Sorry. I got excited." He pats at his head while I toss him a towel from the toppling stack beside my laundry hamper. Once I realized Aggie liked to lie down in puddles—of both the water and mud varieties—I stocked up on heavily discounted seasonal beach towels, leaving us with a colorful selection depicting SpongeBob SquarePants, Disney Princesses, and the slightly more appropriate *PAW Patrol*. By pure chance, Khalil gets Elsa from *Frozen*.

"What's up?" I ask as he towels off his hair and greets a tail-wagging Aggie with a vigorous scratch between her ears that *almost* excites her enough to lift her bum off the step.

"I showed everyone in my lab your account." He rummages in the zippered kangaroo pocket on his rain jacket. "They all became instant mega-fans and wanted to do something fun for Aggie. We got to talking about how she loves to play ball, even though she can't chase it yet. We've been doing a lot of work with movement sensors and triggers, and, well, we want you to try this." He holds up a ball he's taken from his pocket. It's about the size of a tennis ball, bright orange, and made of thick rubber with four or five grooves circling the circumference.

"Is that . . ." I swallow an incredulous breath and try again. "Is that a robotic ball?"

He rotates it in his hand, giving it a loose inspection. "We call it prototype Q."

"Meaning there was a prototype A through P?"

"Oh yeah." He nods emphatically. "This was a process."

"I bet." I watch, still flabbergasted, as he digs in his pocket again and takes out a small zip-top bag from which he removes what he explains is the ball's sensor, which he attaches to Aggie's collar near her ID tag. She licks his face and neck with no restraint whatsoever while he's kneeling in front of her, and he gracefully submits to the saliva-fest without complaint.

"Still working on standing, huh?" He taps the side of the step.

"Working on it. She's getting close. It'll come."

"With the two of you working together, I have no doubt."

I smile in gratitude, which Khalil accepts with a smile of his own, and it strikes me in that simple exchange how much he feels like a friend now, and not only because he got a whole team of geniuses to make my dog a special toy, but because he knows how Aggie's recovery is going and that I'm struggling with my life plan. I know his grandmother taught him how to cook, and that she's in Jadra, Lebanon, where he and his sister visit her every summer. I also know he loves Billie Eilish. He knows I'm trying to love Neil

Diamond. These bits and pieces of our lives we share are more than conversation. They're tiny doors we open as we let each other look inside.

That's no small thing, I think. And then I pack the thought away so I can focus on my dog, and prototype Q, and my growing curiosity about what will happen next.

Once Khalil has both the sensor and ball activated, he opens my door and sets the ball near the threshold so it will be free to roll into the hall since there's so little unobstructed space in my apartment. I hoist Aggie off the step and support her back end as she takes a few shaky steps toward the ball. When her nose gets close enough to sniff it, it rolls about a foot away.

Her head jerks back in surprise that quickly morphs into delight as her tail wags and she stumbles toward the ball again. It holds still until she's close, but as her nose nears, it rolls away again, and when it bumps into a wall, it course corrects and rolls a few more feet down the hall.

Aggie looks at me, at the ball, at Khalil, and back at me, like she's not sure what to do.

"Does it keep rolling out of her reach?" I ask, still impressed, but as confused as she is.

Khalil folds his arms across his chest and tips his chin toward the ball. "Wait for it."

After about twenty seconds, when Aggie doesn't go after the ball, it lets out a funny electronic giggling noise that makes her head cock to the side as she renews her interest. When she stalks toward it, curious but wary as she inches her nose closer, it lights up this time, its grooves strobing for a few seconds before going dark again. As Aggie continues interacting with it, it also jiggles, whistles, darts side to side, and slowly rolls toward her, stopping at her feet.

"It currently has a dozen variations," Khalil explains. "All programmed to respond to her patterns of play, learning and adapting with her in order to maintain engagement and motivation. If she disengages, it alters its behavior. We still have some kinks to work out, and I could get pretty nerdy with this stuff, as far as how it ties in with the psychology and physiognomy of rehabilitation work, but I'll be honest with you. We mostly just want it to be fun."

As the ball giggles again while rolling toward Aggie in short stop-start bursts, I have to agree. It's definitely fun. It's also fascinating her. It's fascinating me, too.

"I can't believe you did this," I say. "Your lab mates, too."

"It was a nice break from the usual. We can be a pretty serious bunch."

I flap my free hand at the ball. "Well, that is *seriously* amazing."

Since it's pouring outside and no one else is around, we continue playing in the hall. I support Aggie through short exercise sessions with plenty of breaks. Khalil tells me more about the design and programming process. After a while, the elevator dings and Minh Ha gets off in a yellow rain poncho, dragging a roller bag behind her and with Pilot in her usual quilted handbag, her tiny tufted head peeking out from the hood of a matching yellow rain poncho.

Minh Ha starts as Aggie and I stumble past her, chasing a now zigzagging ball.

"Sorry!" I call over my shoulder. "We're test-driving Khalil's new invention."

Minh Ha cranes her neck to peer at the ball while Pilot lets out a little yip that makes Aggie whip around. We nearly topple but I steady myself on the wall and keep hold of her harness.

"Have the dogs met?" Khalil asks.

"Actually, no, not yet," I say. "I worried Aggie would get overexcited and scare Pilot."

Minh Ha's shoulders shake with a silent laugh. "Pilot? Scared? She's tougher than she looks. Let me get rid of these papers and we'll do a proper introduction." She rolls her suitcase into her apartment, and I try not to think about how many papers are inside, and how long it'd take to grade them all, especially if they're as terrible as the ones I wrote for my mandatory undergrad English class, eking out a C-minus my parents still don't know about. Funny how I naturally absorbed the information in my biology courses but couldn't for the life of me talk about symbolism in *Animal Farm*. Once I realized it wasn't actually about animals, I was done.

By the time Minh Ha returns with Pilot tucked against her chest, Khalil has deactivated the ball and Aggie's resting in the center of the hallway, taking up the least convenient spot for any potential passersby like the queen she is. I make introductions between my neighbors. Khalil explains what he does in his lab and how it relates to the ball we've been playing with. Minh Ha lists the classes she's teaching, which include the Women's Victorian Literature course for which she'll be grading papers. Then she sets Pilot down a few yards from Aggie, and the teacup-size Yorkie-poo struts right up to the mountain of russet fur and licks her nose. Aggie bunts her tiny face in return as her tail thwaps against the floor in a cheerful rhythm, Pilot spins in giddy circles, and just like that, the two have cemented their friendship.

"Took them a lot less time than it took us," I say to my neighbors.

"We can all learn a lot from a dog," Minh Ha says.

Khalil and I nod in agreement as we all watch Pilot continue dancing around Aggie like a tiny black tornado, and as Aggie paws at her or bumps her with her nose, both dogs having the time of their lives, until the elevator dings again, and Regina and Tegan step into the hall.

"Oh my god. Party in the hallway!" Regina enters the space in a burst of colorful clothing and effervescent energy, deftly skirting the dogs, and with Tegan a step behind her.

As improbable as it seems after sixteen months of near silence in this hall, another impromptu round of introductions ensues, after which Tegan plays with the dogs, chasing Pilot in circles around Aggie while cooing endearments. Regina tells Minh Ha she was an English major in undergrad, and they chat enthusiastically about recent reads and favorite books. Khalil shows me how to work the ball and sensor. For the first time since I moved in, I'm witnessing overlapping conversations on the sixth floor of the Maple Lane Apartments. It's bizarre. It's also wonderful, and I don't think any of it would've happened without Aggie.

As I gaze at her with a swell of affection, Regina pulls me aside and takes out her phone.

"I have to show you the shirt samples," she says.

"You already have something?" I ask. "How do you all get so much done in a day?"

My question is addressed to everyone, and they all shrug and wave it off, Regina especially, though she clarifies that she only has sketches and not fully produced and printed garments. We scroll the images together, which include a word poem incorporating *Bark*, *Woof*, and *Yip*, dog-related quotes I'd never heard from figures like Einstein and Mark Twain, and my personal favorite, which says, beautifully and simply, *Love like an adopted rescue dog*. I tear up when I see it, and soon everyone's gathered around Regina's phone, taking a peek and praising the design, which is when the door to apartment 604 opens and Phone Girl steps out, video-chatting on her phone. Today, her bright ginger hair is in a braided coronet, and she's wearing an ankle-length jersey pencil skirt I can't imagine walking in, along with thick-soled combat boots and a bright white cropped faux-fur coat. She halts mid-sentence when she sees the five of us—plus the two dogs—taking up space we don't usually inhabit.

For a suspended breath, everyone goes quiet as if, despite our newfound ease with one another, no one is brave enough to cross this final line and be the first to say hello. This waifish girl with her endless closet and ever-present air of judgment has stymied the lot of us. I'm about to attempt a wave, at least, when she blinks away her surprise, throws open the door to the stairwell, and says to her phone, "Nothing. Sorry. Just my neighbors being weird."

And then she's gone.

After a beat of silence and a round of looks, we all burst into laughter. Then we carry on with the ball, the dogs, the shirts, and the sheer fun of sharing our first collective inside joke.

Eventually, we disperse with a promise to not be strangers anymore. Strange, maybe, but not strangers. Minh Ha offers to loan Regina books. Tegan offers to dog-sit Pilot. We all assure Khalil he can stop apologizing about his bike taking up space in the elevator. I thank everyone for all they're doing to support Aggie and me, and they heap praise and affection on her before disappearing into their respective apartments. I'm the last to get settled, using her harness to help her return to our apartment, where I lower her bum onto her step. We'll give standing a few more tries. Then she can lie on her bed while I shower and get ready for tonight.

As I tuck her robo-ball and sensor into my nightstand for safekeeping, a familiar voice behind me says, "I love that I don't have to text you through the door this time."

I spin around to see Everett standing in my doorway, where I hadn't yet shut my door.

"You're home early!" Before the words have passed my lips, I'm already crossing the few measly steps that separate us, flinging my arms around his neck with no care for his rain-streaked coat and the dripping messenger bag that gets squished between us.

"You'll get soaked," he warns without returning my embrace.

"I have towels," I tell him. "*A lot* of towels. I'm also considering buying a hair dryer."

He gives in to the moment, looping his arms around me as he plays with the hair at the nape of my neck where the soft but defiant curly bits never quite make it into my lazy topknots.

"Your hair is perfect," he says.

"The hair dryer's not for me. It's for—" I stop short as something bumps my thigh. Something I'm ninety-nine percent certain isn't part of Everett's anatomy.

We loosen our embrace, glancing down to see Aggie trying to wedge herself between us, with her face radiating happiness and her wagging tail setting her whole body in motion.

"I . . . she . . . she did it!" I gasp out. "She got up on her own!" I fully release my embrace so I can drop to my knees and fling my arms around the other sixth-floor resident who fills my heart with joy. "Aggie! You did it! You got up!" The rest of my words are incomprehensible, even to me, as I blubber exclamations into her neck, flooded with pride. I think I'm crying. I'm probably crying. She's worked *so* hard. And been through so much. Never losing hope. When I think of all the times I've curled into a sad, lonely ball, buried under my blankets, defeated by a hundred tiny tragedies I desperately wanted to shake off but felt settle on my shoulders instead, I honestly don't know how she does it, mustering this much strength and determination.

I mean, okay. Everett's here. I get it. I sped over, too. He's a spectacular motivating force, simply by existing in our orbit. But Aggie wouldn't be over here if she hadn't worked her furry butt off for the last several weeks. It's not just inspiring. It's a stadium-sellout triumph.

"Think she can do it again?" Everett asks.

I look Aggie in the eyes as I scratch her neck and nuzzle her nose with mine, laughing when her tongue sweeps the underside, warm, wet, and smelling vaguely meaty.

"Oh yeah," I say. "This dog? She can do *anything*."

In this moment, I truly believe she can.

CHAPTER THIRTEEN

Despite how eager both Aggie and I were to see Everett, after we celebrate her triumph by recording her standing up on her own again and posting the video for her fan club, he leaves so I can get cleaned up and put on a cute dress. Not that I own much I can describe as *cute*, given my scant, comfort-first, outdated wardrobe, but surely, I can do better than three-day-old Levi's, a stretched-out plain white tee that should be relegated to sleepwear by now, and a cardigan with so many holes in the cuffs, I can only put it on by fisting my hands first.

When I stand before my open closet after showering, wearing the only two towels I own that aren't printed with last season's trending cartoon characters, I go blank. This is new territory for me: adult dating. What does someone wear on what suddenly feels like a capital-*D* date with a guy who seems to like her just fine when she makes no fuss over her appearance, a guy who might or might not be her boyfriend by now (a distinction to pin for later investigation), and who doesn't need to be "wowed" but who she kind of, sort of, definitely wants to wow anyway?

Fortunately, it's not too late to send a cry for help, even with a five-hour time difference.

> **CAMERON:** S.O.S. Date night with E tonight. Attire suggestions?

> **HANNAH:** Whatever's fun to take off!

> **CAMERON:** Thank you for cranking the anxiety dial to 11

> **HANNAH:** I'm not the one who should be doing the cranking!

> **CAMERON:** Consider me officially disturbed now. Is that a British euphemism?

> **HANNAH:** It's a Hannah euphemism. Coined today. You're welcome!

> **CAMERON:** Gratitude politely withheld. Seriously. Help!

> **HANNAH:** I am being serious. Put on whatever makes you feel sexy

It's obvious advice, but it completely baffles me, leaving me more stressed than ever.

Rather than text back, I call Hannah and she spends the next half hour talking me through my wardrobe and some anxieties I didn't realize I was harboring about Everett. He's *so* different from You Didn't Actually See This Going Somewhere Guy and We Should Probably Cut This Off Before My Girlfriend Finds Out Guy. He's different from my high school boyfriends, too, and not only because he doesn't brag about his stellar AP grades at every given opportunity or perpetually smell like onion rings. I can't imagine him lying about his relationship status or dumping me as soon as someone hotter and more fun catches his eye, but I didn't come through those experiences without scars, and apparently, one of those scars is defaulting to doubt.

I end up in a simple black miniskirt and a black tank top that has miraculously escaped being laundered into a soft charcoal gray hue like most of my black clothing. Together the pieces sort of look like a sexy black dress, and *sort of* is the best I can do. Paired with sweater tights, the ballet flats that are the closest thing I own to heels, and a slate-blue cardigan that's posh-adjacent enough to get by at Loden and Linden on the weekends, I'm no fashion influencer, but I'll do.

"You look gorgeous, dah-ling," Hannah says with an exaggerated British accent that makes me laugh. She's as American as I am, though that might not be true now that she's lived in the UK almost as long as she lived here.

The quick math on that makes me realize she left Oregon nearly ten years ago. *Ten years*, a thought that slams me with a lot of feelings at once. Gratitude that we've stayed close for so long, despite the distance between us. Curiosity about how my life might've unfolded with less loneliness and self-doubt if she hadn't moved away in eighth grade. Frustration at my struggles to form other friendships that are even half as fulfilling. Hope that this is finally changing.

Aggie smiles at me from her bed, where she's chewing on her monkey toy, confident she's wearing the perfect outfit for any occasion. What a beautiful, wonderful way to exist in the world, even when the world isn't beautiful and wonderful in return.

"Any last words of wisdom?" I ask Hannah.

"No big earrings," she says. "They get caught in your hair when you make out. Oh! And hair. Up. Definitely. Show off that neck like the beacon it is. Don't be afraid to ask for what you want, and be clear about what you don't want. Choose your playlist carefully, or better yet, keep the music off because the associations will trail you forever, which is great if the sex is great, and if the relationship lasts, but you don't, like, hypothetically, want to end up popping into Boots to buy a nail file when 'This Year's Love' comes on and some nice lady who looks a little like your grandma asks if you need help finding anything and you can't answer her without breaking into sobs for the smoking-hot guitarist you were sure would disprove the stereotype about musicians only to leave town with a girl named Samantha the day after you told him you loved him."

"Hypothetically," I say.

"Of course!" She presses a hand to her heart in mock indignation, and I laugh when she laughs, but Hannah has her scars, too, though she's acing law school, she runs a zillion miles each week, she's beautiful and funny, and she'll find someone who will adore her. I've always felt that, even when I've been uncertain about my own future, and Hannah feels the same way about me. This is why we need other people. Because sometimes we're so close to our pain we only see our scars, and someone who's standing a little farther away can see us more clearly.

We wrap up the call and I finish getting ready, which doesn't take long since I'm too hopeless with hair and makeup to get ambitious. When I'm all set, I feed Aggie and then slump onto the futon and check our latest TikTok, the one with her standing up on her own. In about ninety minutes, it already has over three hundred thousand views.

Three. Hundred. Thousand. Views. And our first TikTok has over four million.

I wonder if I'll ever get used to this, the voluntary sharing with strangers of Aggie's updates, milestones, and daily fun, and the outpouring of response. It still stuns me at every turn, knowing people are connecting with her story on such a personal level. The tears they mention shedding. The people who've lost their dogs and feel a profound sense of joy at seeing Aggie embrace her second chance at a good life. The people who have golden retrievers and talk about why they love the breed so much. The people who respond not because she's a golden, or a dog, but because she's a living, breathing being who's been through an impossibly hard time, and they feel on a bone-deep level that she deserves to have a happy, healthy, love-filled life. The people who are going through their own rehabilitation journeys, newly inspired to persist.

It's a single step that reverberates around the world. I suppose that's one of the gifts social media gives us: the amplification of a whisper into a shout. It makes me nervous, knowing not all whispers should be amplified, but the reverberations are also giving me hope. They remind me that even in this evolving, algorithm-driven space where vile trolls lurk, popularity is quantified, and the overabundance of aspirational posts can be hard to take, at the heart of it, the driving force is a need to feel connected. It's so human. So universal.

Everett knocks as Aggie's polishing off the last of her food. I open my door to find him in his usual corduroys, Converse, and a moss-green cable-knit sweater that draws out the green tones of his hazel eyes. He looks like he always looks: handsome, boyish, huggable, a little out of step with current times, and kind, but the addition of a collared shirt under his sweater tells me he made an effort, too, and I'm not the only one treating tonight like it matters.

"Hi," he says when I don't assault him with a full-throttle embrace this time.

"Hi," I say back, and before I can get lost in the moment, Aggie shuffle-steps over.

"Look at you, strutting your stuff," he says, bending down to pet her.

She presses her head into his hand, nose in the air, reveling in his attention.

"Now that she knows she can stand up on her own, there's no going back," I say.

"Pretty soon, you won't need that wagon." He tips his chin toward where it's parked by my fridge, the only place it fits, and barely. This apartment was a tight fit for one. For two of us, it's almost comical. Getting rid of the wagon would be great.

After meeting Aggie's most immediate demands, Everett straightens up and his eyes linger on my face as he draws me closer and gives me a quick kiss.

"You look great," he says, and while I pat myself down, holding back the annoying rebuttals and deflections I refuse to let pass my lips, he adds, "I'm glad we can finally do this. Friday night. Dinner out. A real date. Maybe I'll get up the nerve to tell you I like you again."

"Would it help if I tell you that you have zero chance of rejection?"

His smile twitches into view, slow to form but eventually dimpling his cheeks.

"You can keep me on my toes a little, if you want to," he says. "I don't want to take anything for granted here. I think, um . . ." His neck goes blotchy and he scratches at it, running a hand under his shirt collar as he tries again. "I think this could be really good. This." He gestures between us. "Us. I know it's early, but it feels . . . right. Or, I want to get it right."

My heart pinches at the clear evidence that he's nervous, too, and at his willingness to push through those nerves and lay it all out there like he did on brownie night. No games. No dancing around words in a way that so often feels like playing chicken, with no one wanting to jump first. I've never been good at those games. I love that he's not, either.

As Aggie lowers herself into a sitting position on my foot—and possibly on Everett's, too, since we're standing so close to each other with only a dog between us—I take his hand in mine.

"Congratulations," I tell him. "You just nailed it."

EVERETT TAKES ME to a cozy bistro, one that's romantic with votive candles, warm fairy lights woven through the ivy that climbs several columns, and plenty of space between tables to allow for private conversations. It's also not fussy or fancy, which makes it perfect.

Over dinner and a shared bottle of wine, we talk about anything and everything. Holiday traditions. Favorite childhood Halloween costumes. Dream travel plans. Abandoned hobbies. Worst movies we love anyway. We also circle back to the familiar topics of work and school. Everett mentions that an associate creative director position might be opening at his company soon, and the possibility has everyone in his office competing for accounts and trying to prove themselves to their boss. I tell him about the impossible-to-impress professor I keep trying to impress anyway, and about three of my favorite classmates: the quiet one who wants to be a researcher rather than a clinician, the laid-back one who breezes through the work with enviable ease, and the frantic one who always rushes into class late, breathless and dropping things, but yet is mentally so organized, she's the first to finish any test, and with perfect results.

We have our share of awkward silences. Everett plays with a curl over his left ear or rotates a spare fork too many times for me not to notice. I twist the corners of my napkin in my lap. It's not like the first ride we took in his car. We're comfortable talking, teasing, laughing, bumping knees, and letting our feet slide against each other under the table, but after weeks of limited time together, the potential of what might happen after dinner hovers between us, electrifying the air and making us both twitchy with anticipation. We don't need to say it. We both know.

When the waiter asks us about dessert, we swap a sly look and decline, as though another half an hour here would be torture for us both, but on the way home, we swing past Bakehaus, where Johann, the exuberant owner, gave us free goodies at last month's Sunday market, and on another occasion after that, when he waved me in while I was passing by with Aggie, insisted on serenading us with several bars of an aria I didn't recognize, and sent us home with more treats. This time he greets us with open arms and a string of enthusiastic *welcome*s, stepping around the counter to embrace us as though we're all old friends. He's a big guy with a big voice, dark, pin-straight hair he slicks back, a thick beard, and the kind of waxed mustache I usually associate with hipsters, impeccably groomed and perfectly proportioned for his large frame and dramatic personality.

"Dessert for tonight or breakfast for tomorrow?" he asks us.

My face goes hot, and I only manage a nervous stutter of a laugh.

"Both," Everett supplies, lacing his fingers through mine and giving my hand a squeeze. "Whatever you recommend. Plus a bag of the dog treats. And we insist on paying this time."

"*Pssh.*" Johann flicks the suggestion away. "After all the business you've sent my way? I wouldn't dream of it." He steps closer and shields his mouth with a cupped hand. "Just don't start taking your business next door. Madeleine and her silly croissants. They can't hold a candle to my Franzbrötchen." He makes another dismissive noise, casting a narrow-eyed glare toward the brick wall that separates his bakery from Pâtisserie Amour, the adorable French bakery that's all whimsical curlicues and frothy pastels against Bakehaus's warm, solid earthiness.

If the rumors are true, Johann and Madeleine both took over from their parents, who had a fierce rivalry Johann and Madeleine have maintained with equal vigor for about twenty years now. I'm dying to know the details, and to try out the other bakery, but Johann has been so good to us, I wouldn't dream of betraying him.

Also, his baked goods are phenomenal and Aggie loves his oatmeal and pumpkin dog cookies. Coming here is hardly a sacrifice.

Everett slips a twenty into the tip jar before we head out with cheerful goodbyes and enough treats to feed us for a week. He nudges my elbow with his, and I slip my hand through the space he creates for me. I love these moments, these silent conversations where a gesture or a look communicates everything we need to say.

Come closer.

Like this?

Yes. Perfect.

Agreed.

As we turn the corner onto our block, with our building in view, my nerves go taut and my insecurities mount. The night has been *so* great, Everett and I know each other pretty well by now, and we've both been up front about liking each other, so why is this so hard?

My body language must be broadcasting my thoughts, or maybe I spoke them aloud again. Either way, Everett must sense my anxiety because he stops walking, pivots to face me, presses a kiss to the top of my head, looks me in the eye, and patiently waits for me to speak.

"I don't want to be this nervous," I say once I can manage it.

"What can I do to help?" His voice is warm, kind, like always, and I consider his question while drawing curlicues on his soft, cedar-scented sweater where his coat hangs open.

This would be so much easier if I didn't like him so much, if I didn't know with every pulse of my heart that I want more than one night. I want a lot of nights. And a lot of days. And maybe even years. I know I'm getting ahead of myself, but I can picture it, and that's a first for me. It makes the stakes feel high. Yes, this is about sex. It's also about so much more.

"Three things," I say.

"Tell me," he says. "If they're in my power, consider them done."

"One." I hold up a finger. "Can we go to your place? To avoid interruptions?"

"Of course. Whatever makes you most comfortable."

Right, I think. He's getting to the point faster than I am.

"Okay. Two." I hold up another finger. Swallow. Breathe. "Please take the lead. Not forever. But for tonight. I want this. Us. But I need some help getting out of my head."

He nods, once, very businesslike. "Done. Number three?"

I don't hold up a finger this time. I let my hand rest on his chest instead.

"Tell me it means something to you, too," I say. "I need to hear the words. I've gotten this wrong before and I don't want any guesswork about it. Or any surprises."

He nods again, maintaining his formality but inching closer so his toes touch mine.

"This absolutely means something to me," he says. "I'm not a casual dater. I'm not sure I'm a casual anything. I can't predict where we'll be months or years from now, but I knew when we first met, not for a drink after swiping right, but by going on a grand adventure to save a life, that whatever happened between us would be the kind of meaningful that stayed with me forever." As the words *meaningful* and *forever* embed themselves in my brain, the skin near his eyes crinkles in one of his not-actually-smiling smiles, like a secret he's only sharing with me.

"You're so nice to me," I tell him, and to my surprise, he winces, taking a step back.

"Okay, wait," he says as my hands slip from his chest and elbow. "My turn."

"Right. Of course. Okay?" I brace myself, if chewing on my thumbnail counts as bracing.

"Number one," he says. "For the rest of the night, don't call me nice."

I open my mouth to protest, to assure him *nice* is a compliment, but something flashes in his eyes that sparks my curiosity about what a not-so-nice Everett might be like, so I just nod.

"Number two," he says. "My taking the lead doesn't mean you don't tell me what you want or if I'm doing something you don't want. Okay?"

"Yeah. Okay," I say, sweating a little now. In a good way. "And number three?"

"Number three." He closes the distance between us and leans down so his lips brush my ear, making me shiver. "I know we have to get Aggie out, so I suggest we get moving and do that first, because once we get started, I won't want to stop, and if you're not naked in a bed within half an hour, I'm going to yank down your tights and take you against the nearest wall."

My breath catches in my throat as I go stone-still.

Did he just . . .

And am I suddenly . . .

I don't say another word. I grab his hand, and together, we run home.

CHAPTER FOURTEEN

Twenty minutes later, after I've settled a very contented Aggie in front of *Deadpool*, Everett and I burst through the door to his apartment and he kicks it shut as he sweeps me into a kiss. Not a *nice* kiss, but a hot, unrestrained, open-mouthed plunge of his tongue into my mouth. I didn't see him move in. I didn't see his hands move, either, but there they are, one wrapping my neck and pinning my face to his, the other gripping my hip as he backs me against a wall.

I bury my fingers in his soft, dense curls.

His knee presses forward, nudging my legs apart so our hips collide.

I feel how he wants me, and *god*, how I want him, with his hot mouth on mine, his hand fisting my skirt so it rides up my leg, and his tongue demanding *more, more, more*.

In the dim streetlight that filters in through his windows, he moans as he kisses me, lost in his own pleasure, and I make it my new goal to elicit that sound as often as possible.

"Everett," I pant out, eyeing the open bedroom door over his shoulder. "Should we—"

"Anything, anywhere," he gusts out, equally breathless. "I just fucking want you." Then his mouth is on mine again and he's pressing into me and I did *not* see this coming—not the kiss, the cursing, or the hunger—but my body is miles ahead of my brain right now.

I find my way under his sweater, grateful his coat's already open as I yank his tucked-in shirttails free in a frantic attempt to reach his body. I *mmm* with delight as my palms meet warm, smooth skin, running upward over the slight swell of his belly, the harder edges that define his chest, all the way to his collarbones, where I let my nails sink in, drawing out another moan.

"You like that?" I say into his ear, before giving the lobe a good tug with my teeth.

"Ohmygod," he pushes through clenched teeth. His chest is rising and falling so fast. Maybe even faster than mine. "Just let me live long enough to feel all of you."

I shift my hips against him. "Does that mean I get to feel all of you, too?"

"God, I hope so." He drags his teeth down my neck, biting and sucking as he goes. He'll leave marks, but then, so will I. It's all so feral, which I've never experienced before so I didn't know I'd be into it, but at this point, I think I'd be into anything Everett does. The way he teases my skirt higher, but not high enough. The way his tongue flickers across my skin until he finds a place where he wants to linger for a taste or to take another bite. The way his thigh presses forward between my legs, giving us both something to grind against.

I study the contours of his chest with my hands, finding the places where soft shifts to hard and back again until I let my fingertips brush across his nipples, drawing out a shiver.

I pause, intrigued, and then touch them again.

His body jerks in response, and he lets out a stuttering gasp.

"Not fair," he says. "Not fucking fair." Then he's flicking open the buttons on my coat, wrenching down the neckline of my tank top and the top edge of my bra, and taking my bared breast in his mouth, sucking hard and sweeping his tongue over my nipple.

My thoughts go blurry. My knees turn to jelly. My head tips back and my eyes close as I free my hands so I can dig them into his hair, riding the pleasure of his mouth and his hands as his thigh inches higher so I can grind more firmly against it while he sends jolt after jolt of pure, unrepentant, high-voltage want through me.

As my knees buckle completely, I pant out, "Bedroom. Please. Now."

Everett's eyes sparkle as he draws back, letting his tongue drift across his lower lip.

"I thought I was supposed to take the lead," he teases.

"Are you suggesting you *don't* want to get in bed together?"

"God, no," he says through a laugh, spinning me around and pushing me forward.

We stumble into his bedroom and fall onto the bed together, laughing as it creaks under our weight, but then we're kissing again, and I'm hunting for his skin as he hunts for mine. Our coats come off. Then he drags my cardigan off my shoulders to plant hot, wet kisses on my skin while I inch up his shirt and sweater. As we kiss, touch, and pull each other closer, and as I draw another delicious moan from Everett's throat, I toe off my shoes and they clunk to the floor.

Everett makes quick work of removing his shoes, socks, and corduroys.

I make quick work of dragging down my tights and skirt.

He takes off his glasses and sets them on the nightstand.

Sweaters and shirts fly to the floor, leaving me in my bra and underwear, and him in blue plaid flannel boxers. Despite the manic momentum, as we lie down together, everything slows. With our bodies still only dimly lit from the streetlight that comes in through his parted curtains, he takes me in and I do the same with him, savoring the newly exposed details of the man I'm already crazy about yet am still discovering, like the trio of dark freckles on the left side of his sternum. The long, raised scar on his right shoulder, which he once mentioned was from falling out of a tree as a kid after his sisters dared him to climb it. The slightly rounded belly I felt earlier. Even something as ordinary as the tufts of brown hair under his arms. It's all a revelation.

His legs slide against mine, soft and strong, and with more hair than I expected.

His knuckles tenderly brush over my shoulder and the subtle curve of my breast.

His eyes fill with admiration as he follows the path of his hand.

This is how it's supposed to feel, I think. *This is the real thing.*

I kiss him again, before my emotions catch up to my thoughts and I psych myself out with the magnitude of what I've been missing and what I stand to lose now that I have it. He's quick to respond, holding me tight against him as our mouths collide and our legs tangle.

For a while, that's all we do: hold each other and kiss, allowing our bodies to grow accustomed to each other, learning the little dents, swells, and hidden spots that draw out a sigh or a moan. He likes it when I play with his hair. I like it when he wraps a leg over my hip, as if he's embracing me in two places at once. We both like it when we open our eyes to find the other watching, at which point one of us always smiles, and the other can't help but follow suit.

As our kisses deepen and our writhing grows more restless, skin, heat, and movement stir up a new frenzy. He pops the clasp on my bra. The instant I've slipped out of it, he rolls me onto my back, kneeling between my legs and leaning over me as he guides my arms over my head one at a time and pins my hands to his pillow with a single fist around my wrists. Then he studies me with his eyes and his free hand, his fingers splayed wide and firmly pressing into my skin as they travel over me. In any other circumstances, this might make my anxiety spike, being stretched out like this, so blatantly displayed, with all of my flaws in full view, from my bony hips to my too-small breasts to the acne scars just below my collarbones. But I don't feel cataloged or inspected. I feel like he's learning me, the way my pieces come together to make a whole, and it's the whole he's interested in. Not the pieces.

As he secures his grip, I blink up at him, drinking in his smooth skin, the light dusting of hair on his chest, and the boyish face that lacks the hard edges and chiseled features of a classic romantic hero but radiates a warmth and gentleness I'm much more drawn to, even when he's not being "nice." His hazel eyes look bigger and brighter without his glasses, or maybe it's the feeling within them that seems amplified. The desire. The intention. I've always found him attractive, but now I grow breathless at his hunger and his beauty.

Can I? he asks with a look.

Yes, I say without speaking. *Yes. Please. Yes.*

He slips his free hand into my underwear, gliding his hooked fingers directly into me.

I gasp as I arch into his touch, instinctively jerking my arms down so I can brace myself on his shoulders or grip the sheets or... or I don't even know what, but he holds tight to my wrists, keeping my hands above my head as he watches me squirm beneath him, thrusting into his touch with a sense of abandon I never knew I had in me.

"I've imagined this so many times," Everett says, his voice husky with desire.

"Is it, did you, I, um . . ." I give up, lost to the feel of his touch.

He bends lower to steal a kiss, tugging my bottom lip between his teeth as he pulls away.

"It was perfect in my imagination," he says. "Somehow, this is even better."

Then his fingers go deeper. My hips lift off the bed as my heels dig into the tangled sheets. I throw back my head and ride his hand until I can't stand it anymore.

I want all of him. Now.

"Everett. Please."

My voice is barely audible but he must hear me because he tells me not to move as he releases my wrists and withdraws his fingers from inside me. In a quick succession of movements, he drags my underwear down my legs and frees them from my ankles, removes his boxers, and digs a condom from his corduroys where he finds them heaped on the floor.

I watch without moving, without speaking, taking in the full, unobstructed view of him. We're naked in more ways than one right now, and for the first time in my life, that thought doesn't terrify me. It fills me with wonder and affection, and by the time we're kissing again as he guides himself inside me, filling me in a way that feels so good, and so right, I'm dead certain I finally know that not only is this what good sex feels like.

This is what it feels like to be falling in love.

CHAPTER FIFTEEN

I wake with a jolt shortly after sunrise, convinced it was all a dream, only to find Everett sound asleep on the far side of my bed, with his mouth ajar and his hands tucked under his cheek. *Far* isn't that far, since my mattress is only queen-size, but a certain amplebodied, space hog of a golden retriever is stretched out between us. Everett and I came back here after having fun at his place so she didn't spend the night alone, and she decided that if he was allowed to sleep in my bed, she should be, too. I wasn't exactly in a mood to argue.

My stirring wakes her, and the instant I start petting her head, her tail thwaps against the bed. I hold a finger to my lips to shush her, but she only wags harder as she wriggles toward me.

Predictably, Everett's eyes blink open. My anxiety spikes without warning, a knee-jerk reaction to being in a new situation, and one in which wanting too much could shatter me; but before a barrage of annoying questions and reflexive what-ifs has a chance to assault my brain, a sleepy smile stretches across his face and he reaches out to tuck loose strands of hair behind my ear, letting his knuckles graze my cheek and his thumb brush my lower lip where one or both of us bit it last night. I can tell because it's unusually tender. Actually, everything's tender. My neck, my wrists, my breasts, my thighs, my... well. My everything.

"Good morning," he says in a slow, gravelly drawl I find unbelievably sexy.

"Good morning." I try not to look like a lovestruck idiot but I'm pretty sure I fail.

"So this is what you look like first thing in the morning."

"I did try to warn you."

"Consider me horrified." He scoots closer and kisses me before I can apologize for my chaotic hair or my morning breath, neither of which seems to faze him, and he stays close when he breaks the kiss, keeping one hand tucked under his cheek while the other roams my face, tracing my cheekbone, my eyebrows, my jaw. "Last night was *so* good, and the last thing I want to do is start today by breaking your trust, but I have to confess"—he pauses just long enough to make me worry—"I'm pretty sure I spent a significant portion of the night spooning your dog."

As I relax into a laugh, Aggie rolls onto her back while looking adoringly at Everett.

"Enjoy it while you can," I tell her as I rub her belly. "This will *not* become a habit."

She completely disregards me, drinking in attention from both of us.

We spend a lazy half hour lounging in bed together, doting on Aggie, stealing gentle caresses and not-so-gentle caresses, talking about the upcoming week and where we might fit in time together around our busy schedules, and lingering in the afterglow of a night that felt both right on time and long overdue. But eventually we rally and reluctantly get dressed.

Everett fights a smile as he glances at my TV.

"I'm still laughing about *Deadpool*," he says.

I shrug as I zip up my jeans.

"What can I say?" I ask. "If my dog has a fan crush..."

He sidles up behind me and nuzzles my ear with his nose.

"You sure your dog's the one with the fan crush?" he asks.

I reach for the remote. "I know you think I'm lying, but just watch."

I turn on the TV and flip through a quick selection of movie previews while Everett embraces me from behind and Aggie watches from her bed while waiting to go out.

A shirtless Channing Tatum? Nothing.

A broody Timothée Chalamet? Not even a blink.

I click on *Definitely, Maybe*, a 2008 Ryan Reynolds film we haven't watched yet. As soon as he appears on-screen, Aggie's off her bed and sitting in front of the TV, totally rapt.

"Do I want to know how you figured this out?" Everett asks through another laugh.

"You want to be grateful we had two guilt-free hours to do our own thing," I tell him.

"Fair enough," he says.

We let her watch while we finish assembling ourselves. Then Everett joins us for our morning walk and I marvel at the idyllic bubble I've woken up in, where I'm sex-sore, holding hands, and laughing about early Christmas decorations going up while wheeling my dog through the last of the dampened fall leaves on a misty mid-November morning. I can't stop smiling, every time I look at this beautiful man and this beautiful dog, and wonder how I got here.

Everett kisses me in the elevator as we ride upward, and I drop the makeshift handle of Aggie's wagon extension so I can rake my hands through his hair while he finds his way under my sweater to play with my breasts. We pause at each floor but don't fully stop until we pass five, smoothing our hair and clothes just in time for the doors to open, revealing Tegan and Regina in the sixth-floor hall.

We exchange friendly greetings and I briefly introduce everyone as Everett and I wheel Aggie out of the elevator, and as Regina and Tegan step inside, both patting Aggie as they pass.

As the doors close, Regina says in a hushed voice, "Called it."

"Yeah, yeah," Tegan says. "You'll get your twenty when we're back."

Then they're gone, leaving Everett, Aggie, and me alone.

I blink at the closed elevator doors. "Did they just . . ."

"Yep." Everett sets a hand on the small of my back, steering me toward my door so we can enjoy the pastries we brought home last night. "They sure did."

"But we weren't . . . we're not . . . I mean, how did they know?"

Everett's lips press together as he gives me a look that suggests I should be able to figure this one out on my own, which I do, with a pat of my mussed hair and a glance at our rumpled clothes. Everett's lips are also swollen, his curls are especially disarrayed, and I didn't take the time this morning to cover the bruises he left on my neck. In other circumstances I might be embarrassed. Instead, all I can do is smile. I trust what I'm building with Everett. I'm proud of it. And despite my continued wonder about how I got here, I intend to enjoy the hell out of it.

For the next ten days, I find myself suppressing unexpected smiles that threaten to take over my entire face during random moments at work, in classes, and on dog walks. It sounds so cliché even in my mind, but I swear, colors seem brighter. Smells seem sweeter. I'm weirdly inclined to laugh at things that are only mildly funny. I even talk to strangers. *On purpose.* I've spent the last few years desperately, ineffectively trying to talk myself into wanting to engage with the world, and now, without any of the effort that used to exhaust and demoralize me, I not only want to engage with the world, I feel like the world wants to engage with me.

I sit up straight in classes, taking copious notes on biopsies and cytology with renewed interest in my chosen field. I sell $600 sheet sets like I truly believe no one should settle for less than thousand-thread-count cotton. I spend extra time outside with Aggie. I splurge on tea and baked goods so I can visit Diana and Johann. I do all of my laundry and not just whatever load gets me by for another week. I hum like a Disney Princess during my cleaning job, which is especially strange because I'm still listening to veterinary podcasts and not to music.

Perhaps the most significant evidence that I'm under a twinkly love spell arrives when my mom texts to ensure I follow her TikTok account, where she's proudly posted her first video, which is twenty seconds of soft-hued stock sunrise footage with the phrase *Positive vibes only!* superimposed in a scrolling white font. I've avoided directly engaging with her social media content for as long as I can remember, but I don't even hesitate. I go ahead and follow her.

The day before Thanksgiving, I take Aggie to Ruff 'n' Rescue for a weigh-in and to show Sam and Sariah how she's getting up on her own now and shuffle-walking several steps without support, even though I keep her harness on and stay by her side to grab the handle as needed. We record her weight at a hundred and seven pounds, down five from her last weigh-in, and eighteen pounds total over nine weeks. While she still has a way to go, I'm wildly proud of her.

"Think we can aim for double digits by the end of the year?" Sam asks.

I crouch in front of Aggie and stroke her supersoft ears in the way I know she likes best.

"What do you think?" I ask her. "Do I tell them you're a magical, special, celestial being who can do anything you set your mind to, or do you prefer to err on the side of modesty?"

She licks my face and lets out a single, happy bark.

"We'll take that as a yes about the double digits," Sariah says.

"And also about how special she is," Sam adds.

Before I leave, we talk about the possibility of pursuing the hydrotherapy people keep encouraging in the comments on our TikTok account. It would definitely be good for her, once she builds more stamina. She's walking more and more on her own as the weeks pass, but her joints are overstressed from the weight she's been carrying and her steps are still quite wobbly. I'd love to see her run one day, *really* run, the way Marmie used to, flying after the balls I threw no matter how badly I aimed them. Unfortunately, I already researched hydrotherapy, and it costs about $130 for an initial assessment, and $80 for every thirty minutes after that. It's way outside my budget and also halfway across town, so I'm not even sure I could fit in the time.

"You could crowdsource it," Sam suggests. "I bet her followers would chip in."

"They totally would!" Sariah agrees. "You'd have that money in no time."

I nod, still petting Aggie's ears, though more for my comfort now than for hers.

This is where I get squirmy. I know Sam and Sariah are right. I also know Everett agrees with them. He's trying so hard to honor my request to not talk about monetizing the account, but when we were looking at it together a few days ago, stunned that it has almost fifty thousand followers now, he asked if I'd considered hydrotherapy. I said yes but I couldn't afford it. He got *very* quiet, chewing on the inside of his cheek until I put him out of his misery and told him I knew what he was thinking but I needed more time to think about it, myself. I had a hard enough time accepting a few free tins of tea or letting Everett treat me to a nice dinner. Asking strangers to pay for my dog's health care by turning a public space about her joyful, authentic, unfiltered journey into a fundraising mechanism? Or using that space to hawk products like I do on the weekends at Loden and Linden? None of it sits right. Even though I wish it did.

As I leave R 'n' R with Aggie in her wagon, my phone pings with a text.

> **EVERETT:** Hear me out. Orphans' Thanksgiving at my place tomorrow

> **CAMERON:** How many orphans do you know?!

> **EVERETT:** It's a turn of phrase for anyone without a place to go

I frown at my phone, feeling like this is something I should know, especially since I've spent every Thanksgiving since I started college without a place to go. Hannah always called, but otherwise I just hung out in my dorm room—or last year, my apartment—with a single-serving frozen meal I could pop in a microwave. Sometimes I treated myself to a slice of pumpkin pie, always eyeing the whole pies with a quiet longing. Now that I know people host special dinners for loners like me, my early adulthood looks even bleaker than I thought.

> **CAMERON:** It's so last-minute. Would anyone come?

> **EVERETT:** 3 of my coworkers don't have plans. So there'd be at least 5 of us

> **EVERETT:** Sorry. 6 of us. Don't tell Aggie

> **CAMERON:** I wouldn't dream of tainting her idolization

I consider his idea. I've been looking forward to having a little more time with him and Aggie over the holiday break with no classes to attend or cleaning shift on Thursday. I haven't met any of his coworkers yet, and while I'd like to, I'm not sure I want to sacrifice the precious hours we have alone together for hours spent talking to strangers. However...

> **CAMERON:** Can I invite our neighbors?

> **EVERETT:** Of course. Maybe Khalil can make us a robot turkey

> **CAMERON:** Overnight??

> **EVERETT:** I wouldn't put it past him

I have to laugh at that. He has a point. And as I imagine the people on our floor gathering together to share a holiday meal in a way I've only ever seen on TV—with cheerful toasts, plates of food being passed around, and boisterous, overlapping conversations—I find myself smiling.

> **CAMERON:** Let's do it

THE ROBOT TURKEY isn't happening. Khalil's heading to Iowa to spend the break with his family, but Regina and Tegan are excited to come, and while Minh Ha's initially reticent, saying she doesn't want to impose on "a young people's event," she soon comes around.

Despite the obvious route of reaching Phone Girl, I don't have her number, so I knock on her door. When she doesn't answer, I leave a Post-it on her door with the key info. The Post-it's gone when I pass by later to meet Everett, so I assume she got the invite though

I'm skeptical she'll join us. Still, I hope she's only alone tomorrow if she wants to be alone, not because she thinks the best she can do is a microwaved frozen dinner and a marathon of rom-coms about overworked city girls who return to their small hometowns to fall in love while saving turkey farms and pumpkin patches, which I happen to know from experience can fill an entire day.

At the grocery store, Everett and I improvise a mostly vegetarian menu and fill a cart with food. *A cart.* I haven't used a cart since I lived with my parents. I rarely even have reason to use a basket. We also pick up wine and cute napkins printed with autumn leaves, though I talk Everett out of fancy candles. I get enough of those on weekends.

On the way home, seduced by a chalked ad on a sandwich board outside Havisham & Harrison's, we head inside to buy a tin of their limited-edition pumpkin-spice chai. While waiting in line, I give Everett an abbreviated version of Diana's stories about her beloved wire fox terriers: the digger, the chaser, the snuggler. When I finish, he encourages me to go use the restroom. I tell him I don't need to pee. He tells me I'll understand when I get there, and I do.

While the interior of the shop is all classic dark wood against deep green walls, and tastefully decorated with whimsically arranged British antiques, the single unisex restroom is covered wall to wall and floor to ceiling in wire fox terrier art: paintings of both the impressive and comically bad varieties, framed news clippings from dog shows, hammered-tin terriers, ceramic-plate terriers, a terrier street sign, several dog-head brass door knockers. The soap dispenser and wastebasket have terriers on them. There's a chandelier made of tiny crystal terriers. I take it all in with the awe it deserves, and when I return to find out Everett has invited Arthur and Diana to join our dinner, and they've agreed to come, I'm delighted.

Everett insists on paying for everything and I don't fight him on it since we both know I'd be lucky to cover the cost of the potatoes. We haul everything home, drop it off at his place, and I pick up Aggie, who wobble-trots down the hall with only a little bit of help. The sight fills me with joy, and I know it won't be long until she can do the walk entirely on her own.

As Everett and I spend the next few hours peeling potatoes and chopping vegetables to prepare for tomorrow, and while Aggie brings us her ball and we discuss where everyone will sit in an apartment that'll be a tight fit for ten, I think back on all the times my mom said happiness was a choice anyone could make at any time by having a positive attitude and a little perspective, as if we all have a switch in our brains that only requires flipping. That never rang true to me. I don't think happiness is only about attitude and perspective, and it's definitely not as simple as flipping a switch. Sometimes it's really hard-won. Sometimes it finds us by accident. Sometimes it's out of reach for days or years at a time. But right now? For me? Happiness is a dog, a ball, a paring knife, a bowl of bright orange sweet potatoes, a sentimental Joshua Radin song playing at low volume in the background, and a man in antique glasses and a cast-off sweater, telling me a story about a blanket fort he made with his sisters when they were kids.

Tonight, I don't need to wonder what happiness is or how I'll achieve it.

Tonight, I just know.

CHAPTER SIXTEEN

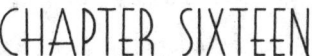

Thanksgiving at Everett's is loud and chaotic in ways that both fill my heart and wear me out. Everett manages the kitchen while fielding holiday greeting calls from his family members. I set the table, answer the door, and find places to put the food, drinks, coats, and bags. Diana holds court on the sofa, an endless well of funny stories about her dogs, the tea shop, and her unruly childhood as one of fourteen siblings on a Vermont dairy farm, rattling on without pause while Arthur smiles at her fondly and barely says a word. Minh Ha sets up a DIY spring roll station and promises to talk us all through the process while Pilot runs circles around our ankles or tries to get Aggie to chase her, running off with Aggie's toys only to return and drop them on her blanket before curling into Aggie's side for a two-minute power nap and then leaping up to play again.

Everett's work colleagues—a Mandy and Mindy I can't keep straight and a beefy blond guy named Brandon who introduces himself as Everett's fiercest competition, earning eye rolls from the others—discuss various marketing accounts they're working on, from a local cheese company to an emerging singer-songwriter to a tech startup exploring AI, before Everett pops over to refill wineglasses and begs them to talk about anything but work.

Regina and Tegan arrive with champagne and charcuterie in hand, wearing *Love like an adopted rescue dog* baseball tees. The shirts are printed in crisp black text against a pink body, with maroon sleeves and neckline ribbing, and a really cute line drawing of Aggie below the text. Regina says they're only samples and she can make changes, but I love them as is. They bring one for Aggie, too, with *Goode* printed across the back like a real baseball uniform. Everyone cheers when I put it on her and she makes a slow, stumbling circuit around the room, collecting praise and pets as she goes. I can't resist sharing something that brings so much joy, so with a little wrangling help from the others, I get a ten-second shot of her with Pilot and post it to our account with a brief caption that says *Happy Thanksgiving, with love from the Goode Girls.*

Shortly before we sit down to dinner, my mom texts me a screenshot of her Facebook post with a photo-perfect meal she prepared and a description about how she and her wonderful husband are spending the day being grateful for each other. Rather than text back, I call right away to wish them a happy Thanksgiving. My mom tells me my dad can't join the call because he's out playing bridge at his club and she's not sure when he'll be back. She goes quiet for two seconds—just long enough for me to peek at her screenshot again—so I ask if she's okay.

"Of course!" she says with her usual cheer. "I'll get all the pie to myself."

I stifle a sigh. She changes the subject by asking how I am. I debate telling her about Everett but decide against it, to avoid her getting unnecessarily invested. We don't stay on the call for long.

Being surrounded by noise, energy, and activity is an adjustment, but not being alone for the holiday feels amazing. The ten of us sit in an assortment of borrowed chairs, crowded around three small tables pushed together end to end, where I let others carry the conversation while I listen, laugh, make heart-eyed smiles at Everett, and eat like I need to tide myself over until Christmas, which is entirely possible given the desperate state of my finances.

Regina tells us how she and Tegan met—showing up for app dates with other people but hitting it off while they were waiting and leaving together instead—while Tegan reenacts the scene with foil-wrapped chocolate turkeys that serve as a low-effort centerpiece.

Minh Ha describes some of the funniest student emails she's received, begging for extensions for hangovers or excused absences for "not being a morning person."

Everett and his coworkers compare stories about the worst things they've found in the communal fridge, from expired cottage cheese to barely recognizable moldy egg salad.

Diana tells us her terriers were all renamed after Irish writers—Seamus, Beckett, Oscar, Joyce—post-adoption, a tradition her parents started and she continued after leaving their farm. This launches a conversation about what everyone likes to read, and we discover I'm the only one who hasn't read *Jane Eyre*, leading to a chorus of demands that I fix this immediately.

We talk. We toast. We laugh. We drink. We eat. It's so ordinary. It's so magical.

As forks get set aside and mostly empty plates get nudged toward the center of the table, Aggie stumbles over to sit between Everett and me, and we both pet her head while sneaking in little caresses of each other's fingertips. I'm sated, happy, and a little fuzzy-headed from three glasses of wine I'm not used to, so I'm unprepared when conversation at the table turns to Aggie's recovery, and Mandy—or maybe it's Mindy—asks about hydrotherapy.

Everett notices me stiffen and scoots his chair closer to set a hand on my back, giving me a look that says I don't have to talk about this and he'll change the subject if I need him to. I'm grateful for the support, but it's a reasonable question, asked with good intentions, and one I'll clearly have to keep fielding, so I might as well get used to answering it.

"I looked into it," I say. "But it's very expensive."

"Easy," Brandon says. "That account's going gangbusters. A little polish and you can double it by Christmas. You hit a hundred K and the offers will start rolling in, if they haven't already. And Redmond can talk you through branding and sponsorship in his sleep."

I force a smile but my hands roll into fists in my lap. Brandon was already my least favorite person at this dinner, full of quick opinions stated like indisputable facts. Now, I kind of want to punch his smug face. From the looks Mandy and Mindy are exchanging, they do, too.

"I'm not interested in polishing my dog," I tell him.

"I meant the account," he says. "Not the dog."

"I know what you meant. That's just . . . not what I want the account to be about."

He scoffs, only a little, but it's enough. "You're the one who needs the money."

"I'll earn it another way." I attempt to look firm, but firmness is hardly my specialty.

Sure enough, he opens his mouth to reply, but Everett cuts in first.

"Cameron's doing an amazing job with Aggie," he tells everyone. "Aggie's well loved and well cared for, and Cameron is carefully considering anything that might help her recovery."

"Whoa," Brandon says through a chuckle that makes my teeth grate. "No offense, but—"

"Oh my god!" Regina pushes back her chair and leaps to her feet, sneaking me a *screw this guy* look. "I totally forgot I brought something for Pilot, too."

"If it's a tiny T-shirt, I'd also love one in my size," Minh Ha says.

"It's better," Tegan says while Regina digs through a big red purse she left on the bookshelves. "Though I'm sure Reggie would be happy to print you both tees."

"I want one, too!" Mindy or Mandy says, and pretty soon everyone's talking about the shirts—everyone but Brandon—and I don't honestly know if they're all colluding to shut him down, or if they genuinely love the shirts, or both, but I'm grateful to not fight this battle alone.

Regina's gift turns out to be a tiny turkey costume made from fabric scraps crafted into an upright circle of tail feathers, and with a bright orange beak and dangling red wattle on a little headband. It's simultaneously the cutest and most ridiculous thing I've ever seen, and when Pilot gets Aggie chasing her a few steps while her tail feathers bounce, I laugh so hard my gut hurts.

Dogs are truly, indisputably the solution to everything.

The topic of branding and sponsorship doesn't come up again, but a couple hours later, after everyone else has dispersed, and only Tegan and Regina remain to help us clean up and set the room to rights, Regina catches me checking the Goode Girls account on my phone, smiling at the TikTok of Aggie in her special shirt, with a tiny Pilot dancing around her. These ten seconds make my heart swell, as does the growing stream of enthusiasm from her fans.

This is what I want the account to be about. My dog. Living a good life. Happy. Loved.

"No offense," Regina says in a mock-bro voice, and we all laugh, even Everett, who's elbows deep in washing dishes while Tegan dries. "But I have a suggestion for you to consider."

I set aside my phone and collect the last few glasses people left around the room.

"I'm listening," I say, genuinely curious what she thinks.

"That guy was a dick," she says. "He needs to stand at the far end of a driving range during a group beginner's lesson." She pauses long enough for us all to swap looks of amused agreement. "I get why you might not be up for corporate sponsorship deals or soliciting personal donations, but after everyone here asked about the shirts, I took a peek at today's comments and saw how many of your followers are also asking about them." She gives her shirt hem a quick tug, smoothing it out so the text is fully legible. "My company's already set up to print these. If you're interested, we can add them to my site as soon as next week. All you'd need to do is post on TikTok telling people where to go if they want a shirt. We'd do the rest, and I'd be happy to split any net profits fifty-fifty with you so you can put the money toward Aggie's recovery. I'd donate all of it but we're a small, new company, and honestly? We could use the business."

Everett turns off the tap.

Tegan lowers her towel.

Regina stands by the bookshelves, patiently waiting, her brows raised in question.

Aggie, exhausted by the day's activity, is sound asleep on her blanket with her head on her shaggy cow puppet and her increasingly distressed monkey tucked under a paw. Despite my reservations about turning her into a sales tool, Regina's offer is a generous one, made in the spirit of friendship and not profit. If people love the shirts, of course she should sell them, and if people buy them to help with Aggie's care, at least they get something cool in return. Everyone wins in this situation—Aggie, her followers, me, Regina, her company. It's perfect.

"Actually," I say, "that would be amazing."

A broad smile breaks across her face while Tegan lets out an excited whoop and Everett walks over to wrap me in his arms, hugging me tight as his eyes sparkle and his cheeks dimple.

"I like this plan," he says. "And I know you and Aggie are in good hands."

"The *best* hands!" Tegan calls from the kitchen.

"TMI!" Everett and I say together.

We're all a little punch-drunk. And a little drunk-drunk.

"Like you two can talk," Regina teases.

I spin within Everett's embrace to face her. "About that. You guys made a bet?"

Regina shrugs. "Saw it coming a mile away. I have a sixth sense about these things."

"She does," Tegan says. "I never should've placed my money on Khalil."

"What? No!" I sputter out a surprised laugh. "You thought . . . I mean . . . really?"

She tosses the towel over her shoulder and counts off on her fingers. "He's smart, he's nice, he cooks, and he's built like an underwear model. If you're into that kind of thing."

I spin around to face Everett, who's watching me with a distinct note of curiosity in his eyes. I could leave him hanging, but one of my favorite things about him is that he doesn't play any games with me, so I see no reason to play games with him.

"I'm into *this* kind of thing," I say, and then I loop my arms around his neck and kiss him. I kiss him for trust. For care. For standing up for me. For letting me make my own decisions about my dog, social media, and money, even when he *really* wants to intervene, and even when we both suspect his ideas are better than mine. For cooking vegetables instead of turkey. For opening his home to discarded plants and discarded people. For the first Thanksgiving I've wanted to remember. And for everything I'll want to remember in days to come.

CHAPTER SEVENTEEN

The first weekend in December, we set up a photoshoot at the studio that's been the source of Everett's secondhand plants. I give him and Regina free rein, not because I can't make a video that mentions the shirts and directs people toward her website, but because this is a world they know better—pitching, packaging, and selling—and they run with it like the pros they are.

The TikTok they create of Aggie and me in matching shirts—playing ball, hugging, happy, and showing off her progress walking a few yards on her own—is carefully edited and synced to music. It tells a story about Aggie's and my relationship. It starts and ends with an animated pink and maroon Goode Girls graphic Everett designs, riffing off Regina's tee. Even the caption is snappier than what I post, tagged and keyworded to increase potential viewership. It's not what I imagined for the account, and I'd never admit this to "no offense" Brandon, but I can see the appeal of a little polish. The video quickly garners hundreds of thousands of views and a load of shares and new followers, along with countless comments from people excited about the shirts, and about having a means of contributing to Aggie's caretaking expenses.

It's a positive start to the month, wrapping a few of the happiest weeks of my life, but I can't float on new-friendship feels and falling-in-love endorphins forever, as becomes patently clear when Aggie's meds require refilling and I can't afford them. Regina's shirts will bring in some income, but we won't have solid sales numbers for a few weeks, and she has to cover her initial costs before there's any profit to share. Thankfully, I'm able to double my cleaning hours for the month, clocking in Monday through Thursday from 6 p.m. to 11 p.m. Not so thankfully, this leaves me with very little time for studying, and when end-of-term exams kick in, for the first time since I started my biology degree as a freshman in college, I'm underprepared.

At the end of the term, on a gray Thursday, I get called in by not one but two of my professors, who are concerned about my drop in performance. I eked out a C on my immunology exam, and a C-minus on my pathology final, while still pulling off an A-minus in anatomy and physiology, so I won't fail anything this term, but for a previously straight-A student, the dip is noticeable. And the grades hurt. I hate not doing well in my classes. It's one of the only areas of my life in which I've never questioned my capabilities, and I'm mortified to have lost my professors' esteem.

"It's not just the exam," Dr. Meacher, my immunology professor, says as I sit across from her in an office that smells like old leather and fresh lavender. A gentle snowfall is drifting down outside the window behind her, and it reminds me I need to get Aggie some traction booties. One more thing to add to the list. "You've been falling asleep in classes. Distracted. Disengaged."

Dammit. I thought I'd hidden that better, strategically parked in the back rows.

"I'm working two jobs right now," I tell her. "But hoping to cut back in January."

She steeples her long, slender fingers and taps them against her lips. She's my toughest teacher, very no-nonsense, and it's not surprising that I'm falling short of her expectations.

I *hate* that I'm falling short of her expectations.

"You're sure it's just work?" she asks.

"Work, life, paying rent. My loans cover my tuition, but not my living expenses."

She regards me with unblinking eyes that suggest a question without asking one. I don't know what she wants me to say, other than something different from what I already told her.

Then she takes out her phone and opens TikTok.

"My teenage daughter showed me your account," she says. "I respect the work you're doing with the dog you adopted, but if you're spending all your time on social media—"

"I'm not," I interject, suddenly furious. She has a right to call me in about my grades. I appreciate that she cares enough about me to check in and not let me slide downhill any further, but seriously? She thinks *this* is what's exhausting me? Making and posting a few short videos about my dog? Not scrubbing congealed dispenser soap off restroom countertops late at night and convincing people with disposable incomes to buy grossly up-charged home furnishings all weekend so I can afford a shoebox apartment and a weekly allotment of generic cereal? Was grad school *that* much cheaper when Dr. Meacher got her degree? Or rent? Or even cereal?

Although, admittedly, adopting Aggie has stretched me especially thin, making my dad's most recent comment about making smart choices echo in my ears for the umpteenth time.

Yeah. Great. Noted. Though a choice doesn't always have to feel *smart* to feel *right*.

"Cameron," Dr. Meacher says, and to her credit, she doesn't say it in a patronizing way. "You're such a smart girl. Hardworking. Good instincts. But this field is competitive, and you'll need to bring your grades up next term if you expect to earn an internship or residency, both of which I think would be good for you, so you get more practical experience."

"I know." My lower lip starts to quiver but I bite it into submission as I repeat, "I know."

She regards me again without speaking, maybe because she knows her next words might unleash tears, and she doesn't strike me as someone who'd want to deal with that. I've always respected her cool, exacting demeanor. It's given me hope about finding my own footing as a vet without being good with people. But today? I can't help but wish she was a little bit warmer.

"I trust that you do know," she says. "Take some time over the holiday break to consider your priorities. Let's see if we can get you back on track in the new year."

I nod and thank her and head out with a sincere but lackluster *happyy holidays*, walking straight into meeting number two, in which Dr. Stean, my pathology professor, exhibits greater compassion for everything I'm juggling and offers to give me a retest in January if I think I can do better then. I gratefully and eagerly accept the opportunity, even though it'll mean studying my ass off over the holiday break, when I was hoping I'd have less to juggle, and not more.

The snow looked beautiful from inside a warm office, but it's cold and wet to walk through, especially since I didn't check the forecast before I left home this morning so I'm in leaky sneakers, I left my scarf behind, and I lost my only hat somewhere between classes last week. Everything around me also feels sapped of color, as though the city's conspiring to reflect my mood. Or maybe my mood's conspiring to reflect the city. Either way, I barely notice the holiday decorations and people bustling about with poinsettias and glittering shopping bags. I'm too busy wrestling with a profound sense of failure, and with an equally intense sense of frustration that once one part of my life comes together, another seems to fall apart.

I try to channel some of my mom's unrelenting cheer but my dad's shadow looms larger right now. I'd never felt his disapproval more strongly than when I committed to coming here to pursue my veterinary degree, despite the cost, and despite Cornell's reputation for intense rigor. I assured my parents I could handle it. Now here I am, not handling it, just like my dad predicted, adding the sharp sting of wounded pride to an already overflowing well of feelings.

The feelings only multiply when I arrive home to discover that Aggie, with her continued gains in mobility, found a way to pull a bag of granola off the kitchen counter. The bag is empty but the slimy, stinky, acid-yellow, granola-filled vomit all over the apartment points a clear finger at the cause. Also, Aggie's not on her bed, where I usually find her when I arrive. She's hiding behind the futon, looking like I'm about to accuse her of murder.

I curse internally, not at her but at the situation, and at myself, at how I've failed in two important areas of my life today: school and taking care of Aggie. If I was home more. If I'd paid more attention to how she's getting around. If I was more careful about what I left on the counter. *If, if, if.* I don't want to deal with this right now, but

I don't have much choice, so I take a deep breath—as deep a breath as I can manage, given the noxious fumes I'm forced to inhale—and count out my exhale—*one, two, three, four*—as I remind myself that life with a dog comes with a few unforeseen digestive issues. Heaven knows Marmie had her fair share. She was like a vacuum, picking up anything that intrigued her and often swallowing it before we could take it away. This was bound to happen at some point, and at least I have hardwood floors.

I weave my way over and crouch before Aggie, stroking her ears as she avoids my eyes.

"You're okay," I tell her. "It's all okay. It's good you got most of it out, though you may have a bellyache for a while. And I guess cereal's going in a cabinet from now on."

Her belly gurgles. Poor girl. She's been on such a strict diet. Her body must be in shock.

"Hey, good news," I say, still trying to catch her eye. "This is a very doglike thing to do. So, you know, good job being a dog, doing dog things, even if they're naughty-dog things."

She lets a short, sharp breath out through her nose. I get the feeling she doesn't believe me. Or maybe she's trying to digest raisins for the first time in her life and she's really confused.

Whatever the case, I get her outside for a short walk, which we can do without the wagon now, just in time to avoid dragging it through winter weather for every quick pee. I wish I had more energy to enjoy her eager curiosity about the snow, the way she sniffs every footprint like it's the key to a great mystery of the universe, but we'll get more snow in days to come, and of the less slushy kind. So I let her sniff for a while, and do her business. Then we return home, where I dry her off and lay clean towels out on the futon before helping her up. She can mostly do it on her own now, but I don't like her to stress her already overtaxed hips and knees.

While she watches me with her head between her paws, the picture of dejection, I use the stand-up shower to rinse the worst of the vomit from her bed, her pillow and blankets, and several small rugs, clean what remains on the floor, and throw anything that's soiled into a pair of bulging garbage bags I load into her wagon. For good measure, I pile my regular laundry bag on top. Might as well get it all done if I'm headed to the laundromat. I really wish this place had on-site laundry, though if it did, I probably couldn't afford to live here.

With less than three hours before I need to head to work, I'll have just enough time to run everything through, and by some miracle of divine intervention, enough washing machines are open for me start all six loads at once, despite the dingy sign that requests patrons limit our use to only four. Whatever. No one's here. I already feel guilty about leaving Aggie alone again when she's not feeling well. I'm getting this done as fast as I can.

While I wait, I slump into the world's least comfortable plastic chair and grab my phone.

> **CAMERON:** If a dog barfs in the woods but no one's there to see it . . .

> **HANNAH:** Uh oh. I'm guessing "the woods" is a metaphor?

> **CAMERON:** "The woods" is my apartment. Every inch of it

HANNAH: Yikes. Is she OK? Are you OK?

CAMERON: She's good. Just needs to ride it out. I'm . . . exhausted. Not my best day

HANNAH: Hot Sweater Guy isn't cheering you up?

CAMERON: Are we still calling him Hot Sweater Guy?

HANNAH: Guy Who Shackled Your Hands to His Bed While Drooling Over You Like the Dessert You Skipped Because You Were Both Too Desperate to Bang doesn't have the same ring

CAMERON: I never should've told you about all that

HANNAH: You ABSOLUTELY should've told me. At least one of us is having fun!

I smile to myself while also sighing. I love how overjoyed Hannah was when I told her about everything that happened that night. But also, I'm not sure how much fun I'm having these days, not with my schedule more packed than ever. Everett's schedule, too, with extra marketing work for the holidays. We make a point of seeing each other on Friday and Saturday nights, but that's about all we can manage. He's been amazing, though, at keeping up by text or dropping by to say hi, and I swear, I'm only avoiding malnutrition because he keeps bringing me food, often couched as "leftovers from a meeting," but sometimes he skips the lie and admits he picked it up on the way home. He's determined to get me off my cereal and toast diet. I've lost the will to fight him on it. Now that I've also lost my appetite for granola for the foreseeable future, I'm even less inclined to argue.

> **HANNAH:** BTW, I checked out his TikTok account

> **CAMERON:** What did you think?

> **HANNAH:** It was cool seeing his work. He's really good

> **CAMERON:** Yeah. He is really good

> **HANNAH:** Wow. Someone's horny

> **CAMERON:** I meant at his job!

> **HANNAH:** Sure you did 😏🛏️

This makes me smile again. She can always get a laugh out of me, even on my grayest days. I also find it amusing that she scoped out Everett's TikTok. It's a small account, with about two dozen videos showcasing some of his branding concepts and animations.

He really is good at what he does, with an eye for creating a unique, catchy look for every product or company. He understands slogans and how to appeal to specific demographics. If the promotion he mentioned last month becomes a real possibility, he deserves to get it.

Hannah and I continue texting until my wash cycles finish. Then I load everything into the industrial-size dryers, but when I put my laundry card into the slot to start the first dryer, I get an error message. The same thing happens on every machine. I swear I had $20 on my card, more than enough to finish today's laundry, but it won't work at all, forcing me to buy a new card, a task that proves impossible when my credit card is declined.

This is *not* happening. After being reprimanded at school, trudging home in the cold, wet slush that soaked my feet, and cleaning up barf for an hour, I cannot be stuck with six loads of damp laundry that includes all of Aggie's bedding, the small area rugs that provide her traction as she wobbles around our apartment, my weekend work clothes, and nearly every towel I own, discounting the ones she's currently sleeping on. But the more I investigate the situation, the clearer it becomes. Unless a holiday elf twinkles his way into the laundromat in the next thirty seconds to tap his sparkly candy-cane wand to the dryer buttons, this *is* happening. And there's not a damned thing I can do about it. Not right now when I'm already tight on time.

The wagon weighs a ton with everything damp, and dragging it six blocks toward home in crappy weather saps every remaining ounce of energy in my body. I don't know what to do with it once I'm home, so I roll the bags out of the wagon and into the shower stall, removing only the rugs, which I go ahead and put down so

Aggie doesn't fall while I'm gone. Then I hang a towel over the bathroom towel rack, hoping it'll be dry enough to use later tonight.

In my remaining free time, I give Aggie some much deserved love, burying my face in her floof, assuring her I'm not mad at her, and apologizing for leaving her alone so much this month. When she finally rallies enough to stop looking like the saddest dog in Sadtown, I feed her a small dinner, make sure she's drinking plenty of water, and eat some cold lo mein from one of Everett's charitable donations. I know he's working late tonight so I text Khalil, telling him I'm leaving my apartment unlocked and asking him to check in on Aggie for me. He texts back right away, no problem. God, I'm glad I have friends now. I can't even imagine...

Before heading out the door, I put on Netflix for Aggie, this time an early 2000s rom-com called *Just Friends*, which the trailer suggests will have its moments, but putting Ryan Reynolds in a fat suit is a weird choice for a multitude of reasons. Aggie doesn't seem bothered by it in the slightest and she settles in to watch while I give her kisses and then leave her with her crush.

By the time I reach campus for the second time today, I'm ready to zone out with a podcast while I mop, scrub, and hope my mood improves before I head home again. This hope is quickly dashed when I learn the Department of Earth and Atmospheric Sciences had a holiday party this afternoon, and one of the floors I'll be cleaning is trashed. Food and drinks have been left out, broken glass litters one of the classrooms, and there's garbage everywhere, not because the trash cans are full, but because people knew someone else would clean up after them.

The carelessness grates but I find my gloves and get to work. No way out but through.

Five and a half hours later, when I get home, sweaty and gross from work, I hang up my coat and fall onto the futon where Aggie's blinking away sleep and wagging her tail.

"Hi, sweetie." I throw an arm over her, using her as a full-body pillow while the emotions I've been wrestling with all day finally burst free and I quietly sob into her neck.

I know it was one rotten day. Only one. A few bad grades. A short-lived digestive issue. A failed attempt at laundry I still have to deal with. A job that on its best days is mindless and on its worst leaves me cursing humanity through an extra-hot, extra-long shower when I get home. None of that can be classed as tragic. But no amount of internal pep talking, pretty sunrises, or positive affirmations in the world would make me feel good right now.

Aggie gloriously, intuitively lets me fall apart, sniffling away while I stroke her ears or her belly. She doesn't tell me to have a little perspective or keep my chin up. She doesn't rattle off ways I could've prevented feeling like this by being smarter or more responsible. She doesn't try to fix me. She gives me free rein to be sad, hurt, lost, stuck, angry, demoralized, drained, and generally beaten down by life, the same way Marmie used to let me be lonely and insecure.

It's such a gift, this level of acceptance. People can't do this, even people with beautiful, caring hearts like Everett, Khalil, and Regina. We have different outlooks, different priorities. Only a dog looks you in the eyes and truly loves you precisely as you are.

Eventually I collect myself, get Aggie outside, get cleaned up and ready for bed, and slide the futon mattress onto the floor so Aggie and I can sleep on it together tonight, since her bed is still at the bottom of a trash bag with all the other damp things I'll deal with tomorrow. As we curl up together to snuggle, two heads on one pillow, I do a quick Google search.

How much can someone make from TikTok sponsorship?

A little bit of digging suggests that for an account the size of mine, I could make $100 to $1,000 per post, pending views, shares, and engagement, more if the account continues to grow. I consider this as I fall asleep with my arm around Aggie, soothed by the gentle rhythm of her breathing, the softness of her fur, and its familiar doggy smell.

In the morning, I send Everett a text.

> **CAMERON:** I'm ready to talk about sponsors

CHAPTER EIGHTEEN

Friday, when Everett comes over after work, he finds me sitting cross-legged with Aggie on the futon mattress, which is still on the floor where I put it last night. She's been napping after a long play session while I've been poring over my pathology notes, wearing my sleep shorts and tank top under my oldest, rattiest cardigan. Most of my other clothes are still damp, discounting the ones I wore yesterday, which are in even less appealing shape. With no classes for the next two weeks, no more cleaning shifts while academic buildings are locked up for the holidays, and no ready means of returning to the laundromat, all I wanted to do today was wallow in front of bad movies with my face buried in Aggie's thick fur while she let me hold her without complaint, but I'm determined to use this time wisely.

"You two look like you're having a picnic," Everett says as he joins us.

I glance around at the textbooks, notes, open laptop, and assortment of dog toys.

"Except there isn't any food," I say.

He drops onto his knees and crawls over to give me a kiss, sneaking in another before crawling past me to attend to the more demanding needs of the overexcited golden retriever behind me. The instant she heard Everett's voice, she jolted from her nap, overcome with joy. Tail wagging. Eyes bright. Ears perked. I sometimes wonder if I should be jealous of how much she adores him, but I know she has enough affection to share, and I love seeing her so happy. I also love that he accepts us as a package deal. She's my first priority. That's nonnegotiable. The only real problem is an unavoidable twinge of worry about how she'll handle it if Everett and I ever split up. It's a small twinge, but I know myself. I don't hold on to things the way he does, and I definitely don't hold on to people who hurt me. I get as far away as possible.

"I'm thinking it's a pizza night," Everett says as I start packing up my books.

"I still have noodles in the fridge," I tell him.

He cranes around to scold me with a look. "Cameron."

"Everett." I attempt to look resolute, and the instinct to resist being treated without the capacity to return the favor is too deeply embedded to skip past entirely, but I'm not fooling either of us. I can't afford principles right now. If he wants to buy us dinner again, I'm all in.

He gives Aggie a vigorous scratch of her fluffy neck while she licks his face like it's a rapidly melting Popsicle and she's determined to catch every drop. Her tail also thwaps away like it always does when he comes over, though the sound is muffled since I've started encasing her tail in a thick sock after I apply antibiotic ointment, a protective measure Sam and Sariah recommended during our most recent visit. I love that it's so cheap and easy, but its effectiveness is impaired by how often Aggie's wagging her tail and shaking the sock right off. Still, with the antibiotics, the thyroid meds, and her improved movement, the scabs and sores have significantly faded and we're all hopeful her hair will start to come in as her health continues to improve.

When Aggie's had her fill of Everett—or close enough, given that this is a logistical impossibility—I tug on his sweater, an especially soft rust-colored one he's been wearing more often since I told him I can't keep my hands off him once I see him in it. Dragging him toward me, we fall sideways onto the mattress, twining our legs as I bury my hands in his hair and he pulls me close, letting out a contented *mmm* as his palm finds its way to my lower back under my clothes. I can't totally ignore the dog breath that's coming from just over his shoulder, but I manage to fit in a good, long snog, as Hannah would call it.

"What did I do to deserve you?" I ask as I pull back far enough to meet Everett's eyes.

"Easy," he says. "You let me attempt to deserve you."

I go all mushy at that, even if he's only saying it to tease me. His smile suggests he's teasing, fully dimpling his cheeks as his eyes dance. Or maybe he's smiling because he's happy. Either way, I'm soon smiling, too, though smiling swiftly turns into laughing as Aggie inches close enough to paw at my head and nudge her nose between our faces, replacing sweet and sexy kisses with an unexpected snort that sprays Everett and me with a mist of cold snot.

"Aggie! Blech," I stutter out through a laugh. As usual, my unconvincing rebuke only encourages her, and she scoots even closer, bunting my nose with hers and snuffling away as though something really exciting might be up my nostrils. I roll away, but she knows we're playing now and she's fully invested in the game so she belly-crawls after me. I cover my face with my hands. She nudges them apart with her nose.

"Good girl," Everett goads, giving her a playful scratch on the head. "You get her."

"Wait! No. Not fair! If it's two against one, shouldn't she be on my side?"

"No way," he says. "My face isn't half so interesting to explore."

"That's patently untrue. And I say that from personal experience."

"Agree to disagree. But I'll leave you to it while I go clean my glasses." He scoots backward off the mattress while Aggie and I continue playing. A few seconds later, he calls from the bathroom, "Do I want to know why your shower stall is full of trash bags?"

My laughter ebbs and I calm Aggie with a few gentle strokes of her head.

"Long story," I say. "But if I can borrow twenty bucks..."

THREE HOURS, ONE delicious take-out pizza, one walk to the corner and back with Aggie, and one on-Everett's-insistence wash cycle later, the dryers at the laundromat are humming away while he sits beside me in a molded plastic chair that looks even less comfortable than mine as he talks me through the basics of social media sponsorship. Rates. Posting expectations. Timelines. How we might increase followers and engagement to improve said rates. I'm not excited about any of it, but I am excited about what it could mean, and when he suggests we start by opening the DMs I've been ignoring to see who's reached out already, I'm stunned by all the messages.

The majority are generic pitches and start with something to the effect of *We love your account and want to work with you!* But even the briefest investigation reveals that they've been cut and pasted by shell accounts, linking me to companies that would expect me to pay them and not the other way around. Other messages are deeply personal, reflecting the tone of a lot of the comments over the past several weeks while going into more detail about individual weight loss journeys or dog adoption stories, or inquiring more directly about Aggie's hairless tail, or asking if she's taking pain medication for her joints (yes), what her goal weight is (we don't know yet), and if she likes certain games or toys (almost always a resounding yes).

Amid these is a handful of messages from dog-oriented companies, reaching out with sincere, personalized inquiries. With Everett's help, I pick three. The first sells therapeutic beds that would be much better for Aggie than the soft, pillowy one I bought. The second sells outdoor gear like brightly colored raincoats and the winter traction booties that are already on my list to buy. The third does monthly boxes of dog toys that simply look like fun. Aggie would be so happy opening something like that, and her enthusiasm would reflect how far she's come since her first days with me, when I could barely incite her interest in the ball or squeaky monkey.

Everett's thumbs fly as he types a response for me, starting with the dog bed company, explaining that I've researched the company and am interested in discussing sponsored posts for their beds. A familiar knot of unease coils in my belly as words like *reach* and *ROI* flash past my eyes. Everything's quantified into follower numbers and visibility statistics that can be plugged into sales projections. He even proposes a fee range, deftly sliding into a transactional language I avoid whenever possible. It's so much more official than chatting with Regina about her shirts while we cleaned up on Thanksgiving, and I can't help the discomfort that creeps in.

My face must reflect something of my concerns—it always does, even when I'm not accidentally speaking my thoughts aloud—because Everett rests his phone on his thigh.

"You're still not sure," he says.

"I wish I was," I tell him. "It's one thing to sell thirty-dollar candles to people who come into Loden and Linden specifically to buy thirty-dollar candles, and who can easily afford them. But this is the space where I celebrate my dog, not where I sell stuff, and to people who aren't on her account to buy stuff. It feels less joyful. Less . . . *Aggie*. And those things I never wanted to matter, like follower numbers and view counts, suddenly become important. I don't want to care about that stuff. I'd much rather buy the bed, the booties, and the box of toys outright."

Everett doesn't say anything, watching me with all the patience in the world and knowing neither of us needs to articulate the obvious, i.e., that option B isn't actually an option.

"No one will expect you to make a big sales pitch," he says. "Just mention the product."

I nod while chewing my chapped lower lip. We've been over this already and I know he's right, but even that phrase grates. It's no longer *the bed* or *the toys*. It's *the product*.

"Think about Aggie on that bed, or in the boots," he says. "Think about having your evenings back to hang out with her or study or have some fun with your boyfriend."

My eyes jump to his. We haven't used that word yet. Not out loud.

"Sorry," he says, reading my expression. "Was that okay to say?"

"Yeah," I say, though it comes out a little breathless. "Of course. I like it. I just . . . I haven't had a boyfriend since high school, and the definition was pretty shaky back then."

"Everything was pretty shaky for me in high school," Everett jokes as he takes my hand in his, knitting our fingers together while his thumb caresses my knuckles and we both watch the gentle movement. "This doesn't feel shaky, though. If that's okay to say, too."

"It's more than okay," I assure him with a squeeze of his hand. "And I agree. It feels good. Right. Solid. Not *boring* solid. *Great* solid. Or *sexy* solid. Or something like that." I'm babbling, which appears to amuse Everett but which is making me deeply annoyed with myself, so I stop there and lean in to kiss him, letting our knitted hands fall so they rest on my thigh.

We kiss for a minute, stopping when a zoned-out woman in a caftan and Crocs rolls a squeaky cart past us at a rate so slow, entire empires are raised and toppled by the time she loads her sheets into a dryer at the far end of the aisle. A long-limbed guy with his black hoodie pulled up is slouched in a chair by the windows, speed-reading what looks like a horror novel while he chews on a black fingernail. Another guy, who may or may not be doing laundry, is napping on a row of chairs, using his puffy parka as a pillow. Otherwise, we're the only ones here, the Friday-night glamour squad, passing time to the steady rhythm of spin cycles and thumping dryers.

Everett picks up his phone and opens the screen to his unsent message.

"We don't have to pursue sponsorship," he says. "Say the word and I'll delete the message. But I promise. There's a huge gap between posting three or four sponsored TikToks and mustache-twirling corporate greed. We're talking about a few nice things to make Aggie's life more comfortable, and a little money to make your life easier. That seems like a win to me. And you don't have to do any of it alone. I'll help with whatever you need."

He knows me so well, Everett Redmond, *my boyfriend*. Despite my anxieties, I agree with what he's saying, and I know he's only encouraging sponsorship because of what it could mean for Aggie and for me. It's that thought, above all others, that has me nodding and telling him I'm ready. He finishes the message and hits *send*, copying and pasting it with the necessary tweaks until all three companies have a reply. Then he logs out of my account, pockets his phone, and draws me into a side hug, kissing my head when I tip it onto his shoulder.

"One day, you'll be a successful veterinarian with a long client list of happy dogs, cats, parakeets, and hedgehogs," he says. "Then you can buy everything for Aggie, yourself, and treat me to pizza, and maybe even live in a place with an on-site washing machine."

I let out a humorless laugh. "Hashtag living the dream."

"Listen to you, using social media lingo."

"Yeah, from, like, ten years ago."

"Still counts." He tightens his embrace.

I sigh against his shoulder, but I'm smiling while I do it. I'm also drawing little hearts over his chest, though as soon as I realize I'm doing it, I switch to lazy circles. I'm ready to call him my boyfriend. I'm even ready to picture myself buying him pizza three or more years from now, but I'm not sure I'm ready to say the word *love*. It'll be a first for me, and after what happened to Hannah, getting ditched the day after she said it, I'm a little gun-shy.

Thankfully, I can still rest my face against Everett's firm shoulder and soft sweater. I can spend a Friday evening in his company, even if we're redefining the notion of a date night. I can admire how deftly he navigates a space in which I feel completely out of my depth. I can listen to him imagine a future in which I'm successful, solvent, and no longer drowning in doubts.

"Did you always know you wanted to go into marketing?" I ask him.

"I wouldn't say *always*." He kisses the top of my head again before resting his cheek there. "They don't sell a lot of associate creative director costumes for the under-ten crowd."

I try to picture him at eight or nine, with a big notepad draped over an easel, nudging his glasses up his nose as he informs his fellow third graders about search engine optimization.

"I bet you were cute at that age," I say.

"I was a total dork. Overly studious. Giant glasses. Baby face. Way too much hair."

"Like I said. Cute."

His chest shakes with a quiet but resonant laugh. It's a beautiful sound, heard up close, and when the thought comes—*that's my boyfriend's laugh*—I can't help but smile.

"Honestly?" he says. "I thought I might be a furniture designer. Or maybe graphics like book and album covers. Then I took a marketing class in my freshman year and I was fascinated with the ways marketing can link people with what they want or need. And sure, numbers matter, but it's not necessarily about selling *more*. It's about selling *better*, directing attention, knowing how to match a product to its likeliest users, how to take something people might otherwise pass by and turn it into something they can't miss. There's a magic to that, as long as I'm working for companies I believe in. At this point in my career, that's usually the case."

I nod against his shoulder, and before we can say more, the first of my dryers dings and I extract myself from the blissful nook of Everett's warm and cozy side embrace to fold laundry. He joins me and together we make quick work of all six loads while I ask him a variation on the question I asked Khalil a few weeks ago, the one that continues to haunt me.

"How did you know it would be worth it?"

"Going into marketing?" he asks.

I nod, and fold, and wonder, and worry. My life in a nutshell.

"How did you know it was the right choice?" I clarify. "How did you know *that* was the dream to put your energy behind? How did you know you wouldn't end up regretting it?"

"I didn't know. Not with a hundred percent certainty. No one does." Everett's response comes quickly but his brow furrows as he slows his folding, like he's giving the matter further consideration. "Some luck was involved. I got a job at a company I liked right out of school. It was only entry-level, but I worked my way up pretty quickly due to some personnel shuffling. Landed some interesting accounts." He folds the last vivid dog towel, setting it on the stack before pivoting to face me. "I think, at some point, I weighed my options and made the choice, and now I do my best to *make it* the right choice." He stops there, and I do, too, letting the last of the laundry idle while I slip a hand under his sweater and press my palm to his chest until I feel his heartbeat, its even rhythm a steadying force I've made a habit of seeking out in recent days. He might not have the chiseled jawline and hard, muscular planes of an athlete or an action hero, but *here*, he's so solid, and *here* is where he makes me feel solid.

"In case you haven't noticed," I say, "I'm somewhat prone to second-guessing."

He sets his hand over mine so both rest against his chest. I expect him to tease me about my gross understatement but he remains serious. No dimples. No creases beside his eyes.

"Carefully considering your choices isn't a bad thing," he says. "But Cameron? I've seen you with Aggie, and with Pilot. I've seen you pore over your textbooks with genuine interest. If this isn't the right time or place for you to pursue becoming a vet, I'd understand why. The cost. The workload. The lack of time for Aggie. But I also think, even while I can't *know*, that if you keep going, you'll be a great vet one day. And I can't imagine you regretting a life that's centered around helping animals in need."

My chest swells with a powerful surge of gratitude and affection I suspect I should be calling something else by now. No one but Hannah has ever had this kind of faith in me, and maybe I should be able to find it in myself, to not need it articulated outside the confines of my circular thoughts, but it feels *so* good to hear. And from Everett, whose opinions I value deeply, and who knows me so well already.

"You sure I'm not the one who has to work to deserve you?" I ask him.

He extracts my hand from under his sweater and places a soft kiss on my fingertips.

"How about we head back to your place, put this stuff away, and spend the rest of the night deserving each other."

I beam at him, this beautiful man with his beautiful heart.

My boyfriend.

"Now, that's a choice I don't have to second-guess at all."

CHAPTER NINETEEN

The rest of December flies by. Everyone on the sixth floor of the Maple Lane Apartments is leaving town for the holidays, jetting off to various family gatherings. Everett invites me to come with him to New Orleans, where his parents are currently teaching, but he knows I want to stay with Aggie, and that I need to fit in as much studying as possible. Also, I'm not sure I'm ready to meet his family. I'm still trying to wrap my mind around having a boyfriend.

Before people disperse, at Regina's suggestion, we hold a Secret Santa gift exchange. I put a Post-it on Phone Girl's door with an invite and my info, but she ignores it as resolutely as she ignored the Thanksgiving invite. Everyone else is eager to participate. We're all on a tight budget—though not all *quite* as tight as mine—so we agree to a spending limit of $10.

I draw Tegan, who I don't know that well so I recruit Regina for intel. In a plot twist I maybe should've seen coming, given her sense of humor, Tegan has her own TikTok account: one she calls I Only Have Eyes for You. Not only is she responsible for the adhesive googly eyes all over town, she makes up brief dating profiles for them. *Harry Hydrant. Done some hard time on the street. I like my* romance hot, hot, hot. Personal motto: hose before bros. Rusty Pipington. Feeling drained by love. Favorite actress of all time: Farah Faucet. Currently looking for a partner in grime. Naturally, I buy her a bag of googly eyes. And I follow her account.

Minh Ha gives me a used copy of *Jane Eyre*, and I promise everyone I'll read it soon. Regina makes Minh Ha and Pilot matching bucket hats in a beautiful blue and teal abstract-print fabric she designed herself. Everett gives Regina a trio of antique thimbles we find at a holiday market. Khalil gives Everett a tiny red windup watering can that clips to the edge of a pot, tilting and pouring when the gears turn. Tegan gives Khalil a T-shirt Regina and Everett helped with, custom-printed to say *Some days I just want to run away and join the circuits*, with a ridiculously cute cartoon of a robot in a clown nose and hat.

And everyone gets something for the dogs. Balls, toys, bandannas, Santa hats, chew bones, a Deadpool action figure we all have a good laugh at. It's all so joyful, and I love that I can look around and see how we've gotten to know each other, maybe not as close friends who hang out together on Friday nights, but as a hell of a lot more than strangers in an elevator, politely avoiding eye contact or apologizing when we invade each other's personal space.

Christmas Day is quiet. I study, play with Aggie, video-chat with Everett, with Hannah, and with my parents, and make nonfrozen meals in the kitchen Everett fully stocked for me before he left, despite a firm agreement that we wouldn't buy each other presents. He swore it wasn't a present. It was an insurance policy that he wouldn't return after a week away to find me passed out from hunger and stubbornness while Aggie was left to fend for herself. He's become very clever about finding work-arounds for my resistance to letting him buy me things while I can't do the same for him. If his gesture isn't meant to spoil me, but to make me laugh, how can I say no?

In return, I'm watering his plants while he's away, which is small compensation, but at least it's something, and I like that it's a gesture of care. I also like that he's trusting me with keys to his apartment. So far, I've resisted the temptation to snoop.

It's the first Christmas I don't spend with my parents, and I expected to get sad about that, but I don't. My dad has never understood the fuss of the holidays, complaining annually about the crowds and the cost while leaving the decorating, meal planning, and gift shopping to my mom, including whatever she wanted for herself. She'd sign a card from him and make a joke of it every year, examining a beautifully wrapped present and saying, *I wonder what this could be!* Meanwhile, she got us to smile for family photos she could post, dragging my dad away from the sports he was parked in front of and me from whatever pulpy novel I was devouring in my room as a much-needed break from schoolwork. Over time, I began to associate the holidays not with happiness, but with a pressure to perform happiness, no matter what I was actually feeling.

Now it seems odd to me that I clung to that routine, even after I left for college and my parents had to fly me home. Granted, until this year, I had no one else to spend the holiday with, not without flying overseas, which I couldn't afford, but still, as I look at the screenshot my mom sends of her Facebook post, with her and my dad posing in front of a beautifully decorated tree he definitely didn't help with, and the ill-considered caption *So happy we're together for the holidays*, I can't help thinking of what Everett said the day we brought Aggie home.

Almost empty is not the same as enough.

No, I think. *It's not*. And I suspect I've always known that, but the emptiness wasn't as obvious until I had something to compare it to. Until I knew what it felt like to truly be full.

On Monday, December 30, I wheel Aggie to Ruff 'n' Rescue for her end-of-year weigh-in. We're all crossing our fingers for ninety-nine pounds or less. Given her rapid weight loss in her first two months, averaging an astonishing two pounds a week, and her increased movement as her mobility continues to improve, eight pounds in five and a half weeks seems reasonable to expect. However, she's been building muscle, and as is often the case with significant weight loss, the initial drop has leveled out, and she weighs in at a hundred and one.

A tiny flicker of disappointment passes across all of our faces as Sam records her weight, Sariah holds out a liver treat, and I guide Aggie off the scale, but by the time I'm crouching in front of her to scratch her neck and kiss her furry face, the disappointment's already gone.

"You're doing *so* great," I tell her as I find all the places she loves to be touched. "Do you realize you've lost almost one-fifth of your initial weight? That's incredible."

"It really is," Sariah echoes. "And look how she holds herself now. Her coat's so much healthier, too. That's a totally different dog than we met in September."

As always, Aggie soaks up the praise and attention, and she's very patient as we examine her joints and movement together, comparing a video of her walking down the hall to one Sariah took a month ago. Her steps are less shaky. Her pace demonstrates more confidence. She walks farther without a toy or reward motivating her. She raises and lowers herself without my help, though I stay close, just in case. All that in three and a half months, and if it wasn't enough to fill my heart with pride and joy, a shadow of golden stubble now runs the length of her tail. Every time I notice it, my chest practically bursts open. Maybe it's not as significant a change as her weight and movement, but her naked tail has been such a clear sign of her mistreatment, and seeing it start to look like a dog's tail *should* look is like seeing her fully become herself.

Before we leave, I reach into the wagon and take out the gift I brought, grinning ear to ear as Sam and Sariah tear through the paper together and pull on the shirts Regina made for me, printed with *Every time a dog is adopted, a rescue worker gets their wings* on the front, and with a whimsical line drawing of a pair of wings that sits between the shoulder blades on the back.

They both melt before me, as if fighting back tears, which means I do the same. We all hold it together, but barely, especially while Aggie smiles at us, with her brows twitching as her eyes shift from face to face and her slightly less hairless tail wags. I don't know how I would've taken her in without R 'n' R's help, or if she'd even be alive without their immediate support after Andy's call back in September, and I can't imagine a life that doesn't include her. My beautiful, funny, resilient, trusting, curly-eared fluff ball of love and acceptance. My dog.

When we finally collect ourselves and I stop gushing with gratitude, Sam and Sariah surprise me with a present of their own, a gift certificate for a half-hour consultation at Aqua Paws, the hydrotherapy clinic we've been discussing over the past several weeks.

"We think she'll be ready soon," Sam says.

"With a few more pounds off to reduce strain on her heart," Sariah says.

"Or when she can walk about twenty minutes on her own," Sam suggests. "Even better if she can manage a full mile with a steady heart rate and even breathing."

"We're getting there," I say, though it'll likely be a few weeks yet. I haven't gone into this with everyone who asks, but cost aside, the three of us understand that if Aggie doesn't have enough stamina to walk for more than a few blocks, putting her on an aquatic treadmill won't do much good. The reduced impact will be easier on her joints, but the water's resistance will make her work harder. Bodies are complex puzzles, and rehabilitation has to account for all the pieces. Rushing to strengthen one piece could injure another. Besides, Aggie's pretty good at knowing her limits. If I just want her to get wet while she lies down, I have a shower for that.

"It's only a consultation," Sariah adds. "You can make your own choices after that."

"It's wonderful," I say, and I mean it, newly hopeful my finances will be more stable in the new year, between Regina's shirts and the sponsorships that are already underway. I heard back from all three companies Everett and I contacted, and all have sent products to post about once they arrive. Despite my earlier reservations, I'm genuinely excited to see what shows up.

I blubber out several *thank-you*s. Sam and Sariah give Aggie hugs that leave a layer of dog hair on their new shirts. We all have a good laugh about it, fully accustomed to the inevitable fallout of embracing a golden retriever. Then I hoist her into the wagon, which Regina and Tegan decorated with tinsel and battery-powered Christmas lights before they left town, eager to ensure

Aggie's first Christmas in a loving home was as festive as possible. I laughed at their suggestion that I get a tree, gesturing around my cramped apartment until they conceded the point without my having to explain it, but they strung lights, left me a plug-in evergreen air freshener, and hung mistletoe over Aggie's bed, which I love, even though she's hardly wanting for kisses.

A dense but gentle snowfall begins as I wheel her home, the distance still too far for her to walk. The snow isn't gray slush like earlier in the month. It's bright white, with big flakes that nestle in her eyelashes and along her back. It's the kind of snowfall I always picture when I hear "White Christmas," and it blankets the parks and sidewalks like it's tucking them into bed for a long and cozy nap. Even better? When we get home, a padded envelope is waiting in my mailbox. Aggie's winter booties have arrived, just in time to play in the snow.

"Okay, sweetie," I say once we're settled and I join her on the futon with the package in hand. "You ready to check out your winter footwear? You're going to look so cute!"

She leans over my lap, sniffing the package as I tear it open, revealing a flash of red.

"What's this?" I ask, a question I answer for myself as I pull out the plastic-wrapped black and gray booties, along with a red hooded raincoat, its soft lining printed in cartoon dogs holding tiny umbrellas. It's ridiculously cute, way higher quality than the cheap plastic poncho we've been getting by with all fall. It's also designed to wrap her entire torso, so I might go through fewer towels every time we come in from the rain or snow.

The package includes a printed form letter from the manufacturer, thanking me for working with them. A handwritten note on the bottom says *We couldn't resist including the coat. We hope Aggie loves it and it keeps her warm and dry this winter. Can't wait to see it on!* I love the note. It makes me feel like I'm working with real people and not a faceless corporation. Maybe it shouldn't matter but it does, and already I'm more invested in the sponsorship.

I get Aggie dressed in the coat and booties right away. She's unsure about the booties, plucking her feet off the floor one at a time and planting them again immediately as though she's trying figure out why they feel funny, but she doesn't seem to mind the coat at all.

I take a pic and send it to Hannah and Everett. Hannah's probably asleep by now with her early morning running schedule continuing through the winter, but Everett replies right away.

EVERETT: Cute redhead alert!

CAMERON: Right?! They threw in the coat for free

EVERETT: It suits her. But what does she think?

CAMERON: Thumbs up on the coat. Booties TBA. But we're about to find out . . .

I film a five-second video out my window and send it. The shot's terrible thanks to my dismal view, just the crumbling brick warehouse and rickety iron fire escape on the opposite side of the alley, but the falling snow is visible, lining the railings and the edge of the roof.

EVERETT: I'm missing the first good snow of the season with you? ☹️

CAMERON: We'll get plenty more ⛄⛄⛄

EVERETT: I should've booked an earlier flight back

CAMERON: You'll still be here by dinnertime tomorrow, right?

EVERETT: As long as there are no weather delays

CAMERON: There will NOT be weather delays. I forbid it

EVERETT: As you have spoken, so shall it be

I smile at my phone, imagining him here in time to enjoy New Year's Eve together. Ever since I was six or seven years old, watching the ball drop on TV with my mom, I've wanted to kiss someone at midnight. Despite forcing myself out to a few parties over the years, where I pep talked myself into painfully awkward attempts at flirting, I never came close.

EVERETT: Charlotte and Dakota want you to know they're sorry you couldn't come with me this Christmas. Apparently, I can't stop talking about you. Also, they love Aggie's new coat

CAMERON: You already showed them? Are they with you right now?

EVERETT: We're out getting ice cream. It's 65 degrees here. Definitely not snowing

CAMERON: I'll catch a few flakes on my tongue in your honor

EVERETT: Please don't mention what you'll do with your tongue. Not when I'm not alone

My cheeks heat and I have a feeling I'll be rereading that text later. Several times.

CAMERON: Enjoy your ice cream. Can't wait to see you tomorrow

EVERETT: Enjoy your snow. I'll be home soon

This time I smile so hard, I swear, the Google Maps satellites might pick it up. But I don't let myself linger in a giddy, infatuated haze, because I have a dog who's bundled up for winter weather and a pile of textbooks I'm eager to ignore for an hour.

"What do you think?" I ask Aggie. "Are you ready to play in the snow?"

She blinks at me from her bed, where she was inspecting the booties on her front paws while I was texting Everett. She makes no move to get up, but when I put on my coat, scarf, and boots, and ask her again if she wants to go play, she eases herself into a standing position and trots over to her toy box, burying her head in it until she emerges with a pink ball in her mouth.

That's a totally different dog than we met in September, Sariah said this morning.

No kidding, I think with a swell of pride and affection, and by the time I remove Aggie's leash off its hook, she's already by my side, ready for our next grand adventure together.

CHAPTER TWENTY

A sharp, shrill noise wakes me from sleep, and I blink my way into a squint to see Aggie lying on her bed with her squeaky monkey in her mouth, pausing mid-chew as I meet her eyes. Dim, colorless daylight comes through my alley-facing window where I forgot to close the blinds last night. I didn't set an alarm, either. For a moment, I forget why, but the arm draped around my waist and the warm breath against my upper back provide a quick reminder, and a happy one.

Everett's flight was delayed yesterday, due to more snow, but he got home safely, and just in time for my long-awaited midnight kiss. A kiss that led to a lot more.

The squeaking resumes in a series of short ear-piercing bursts.

"Aggie, really?" I mumble against my pillow. "It's too early."

She stares at me, unmoving, for a beat. Then she eases her mouth closed so the monkey squeaks again, this time in slow motion, as though making the squeaker squeak doesn't count if she's sneaky about it. The resulting sound is less like shrieking in terror and more like dying in prolonged agony. I pull the covers over my head with a groan. Behind me, with his head tucked against my neck and his naked body loosely spooning mine, Everett shakes with quiet laughter.

"Happy New Year," he murmurs into my ear.

"Happy New Year," I say through a sigh that's part resignation about the noise, part pure contentment to start the year with Everett's warmth and Aggie's playful, cheeky silliness.

She squeaks her monkey again, even more slowly than the last time.

"Make it stop," I beg through a weak laugh.

Everett snuggles closer, pressing his newly obvious erection against my naked backside.

"Aggie," he says calmly but firmly. "Sweet, considerate, understanding Aggie. I'll be your personal belly rubber for the rest of the day if you'll give us five minutes of total quiet."

We both wait, barely moving, though I'm sharply aware of every place our bodies touch.

When Aggie stays quiet, as requested, Everett sneaks a nibble on my neck.

"Think we're good?" he asks against my neck.

I press into him, making my invitation clear. "*So* good."

With an appreciative *mmm*, his hand drifts lower on my belly. I guide it where I want it until he takes over, cupping me between my legs, then parting me with two fingers while a third draws circles over the tight bundle of nerves that's soon slick to the touch. Gentle at first, but with growing pressure and friction, he teases out my arousal while I grind my ass against his hot, hard length, more turned on by his arousal than my own.

I've never felt wanted like this before and it still surprises me, the intensity of Everett's desire, the hunger in the moans and gasps he releases against my ear, the tightness of his fist as he tugs at my hair, drawing my head back so his teeth can skim my neck, the way he dances on the edge of control as his sex-slicked fingers enter me then toy with me then enter me again, the heat and sweat between us, the words that blur together in his stream of panted dirty talk—*wet, tight, hard, cock, clit, cum, fuck*—and the rapid heartbeat hammering against my back that tells me no matter how much he enjoys teasing me, he's as desperate for it as I am.

"I missed you," he says against my ear, and this time the words are clear.

"I missed you, too," I manage through a shallow exhale.

"And I missed this." His fingers dance across my swollen flesh, this time with almost no pressure at all, and I twitch against his barely there touch, a reflex he elicits again as he *mmm*s against my neck, his smile audible as I grip the sheets in front of me, white-knuckled and wordless, trying not to combust from the feather-light flicker of his fingertips.

I love how well he knows my body already, how it responds to him, how I crave his closeness, how he withholds it from me until I beg. He likes it when I beg. I like it when he makes me beg, probably because I trust that this is a game we're playing and we both know the rules. When we're not having sex, he's always giving, freely and intuitively, fulfilling my needs even when I'm resistant to his assistance. Here, and only here, he makes me ask for what I want. And when the escalating sensation becomes too much to bear, I do precisely that.

"Please," I say, a gusted breath of a word that's all I can manage.

"Say it again," he demands, already shifting to ready himself behind me.

"Please," I gust out again. And again, "Please, now, I can't, I need... please."

When he enters me from behind—skin to skin now that I'm on the pill, a choice we made together once we started having sex—my breath catches in my throat. I feel him everywhere. Inside me. Behind me. Around me. In my body, in my thoughts, in my heart.

"Is it too much?" he asks, breathless, and with *so much want* lacing his voice.

"It's perfect," I say. "I love the way you feel inside me."

"It's fucking amazing," he says. "But I want to watch."

With a quick jerk backward, he pulls out, rolls me from my side onto my stomach, and yanks my hips up so I'm on my knees with my face nestled in the pillows and my hands fisting the sheets. I barely have time to part my legs before he's easing himself inside me again, gripping me by the hips as he guides me over his length, slowly at first, like he's testing how far he can push into me from this angle. It definitely feels different, deeper, fuller, but as our bodies adjust and I relax into his rhythm, guiding becomes rocking, then thrusting, gasping, gripping, bruising fingers in soft flesh, and hard, fast friction, two bodies pounding together, chasing sensation like it's the only thing that matters, racing after every new pulse. Every spark.

I squeeze my eyes shut.

I cling to the sheets.

I ride the waves of pleasure that overtake me slowly, and then so suddenly I cry out. The noise I make is garbled and incomprehensible, but there's a *yes*, and there's an *Everett*, and the rest is as irrelevant as whatever he says behind me when his release comes a few seconds later and he shudders against me, still clinging tightly to my hips, holding me against him as we pulse together, riding this incredible feeling we made with only our bodies and our trust.

The word reverberates in my mind, every iteration more powerful than the last. It's what makes the sex so good, and everything else between us. I don't know how Everett managed it, or maybe we managed it together, but somewhere along the way, I stopped bracing for something to go wrong. I tore down the walls I've learned to put up, dismantled the barricades, and left my squishy, beating heart open to whatever's in store.

I trust Everett. I trust us. I trust this.

I let my body go limp and we collapse together, lying flat against the sheets with him on top of me, both of us panting from exertion. While I catch my breath, he plucks a few sweaty strands of long hair off my face, and I blink my eyes open to find him smiling down at me.

"You really are absolutely hideous first thing in the morning," he teases.

"I hope you kept your eyes closed," I play along.

"And miss the sight of your ass quivering as my dick disappeared inside you? God, no."

I fight a smile at that. He really does like to watch, which took some getting used to since I've never been comfortable in my body, but I've never felt this good before, either.

Everett inhales deeply, resting his cheek against mine as he finds my hands on either side of my head and laces his fingers through mine, gently, sweetly, like he's resetting our connection from the incendiary heat of lust to the gentle warmth of mutual care. For several seconds, we breathe together, his front to my back, spent and happy. And then, perfectly timed, in the quiet of our postcoital bliss, the tiniest, faintest, high-pitched hint of a squeak peals from Aggie's bed.

Neither of us can hold in a laugh this time.

"She gave us our five minutes," I tell Everett. "Belly rubs will be expected."

"Worth it." He plants several kisses on the side of my face. "C'mon. Let's give her what she wants. And get that video shot before the snow gets trampled and gross."

I squeeze his hands like I might hold him against me forever, but we can come to back to this, a thought that makes me glow inside as I rally to start the day.

THE SNOW IS gorgeous, newly blanketed with a few inches that fell overnight. We bundle up and head to the park, where the big scarlet oak under which Aggie took her first shaky steps with me is now barren of leaves, but no less beautiful in its winter attire. Aggie's in her new coat and booties, which she's getting used to, though I don't think she'll ever be a big fan. I'm in my usual bland all-weather coat, with its flannel lining zipped in for winter, and the plain wool scarf I've had since I was a kid, plus a black beanie Tegan thrust on me when I told her I lost my hat last month and she informed me she had spares. Everett's in a vintage peacoat with an adorable striped scarf and puff-ball hat that are recent handmade Christmas gifts from his sister Charlotte. We take one look at each other once we're settled by the snow-covered lawn and do a swap. If we're going to depict an idyllic winter outing, Aggie can't be the only one to look cute.

Playing in the snow with Aggie is ridiculously fun. She loves to roll in the soft, powdery areas with her feet in the air and her tail carving arcs like a windshield wiper. She also loves to bury her entire face, following mystery scents until she emerges with her nose, ears, and lashes flecked in white. She catches snowballs that break apart in her mouth. She barks at a teetering snowman someone made overnight. Then she pulls out the carrot nose and trots away to a snow mound where she attempts to eat the carrot, realizes she doesn't like it, and lets me take it from her so I can perform an embarrassing and ineffective snowman rhinoplasty. She's joyful, she's silly, and she has the time of her life, which means I have the time of mine.

However, it doesn't take long for me to recognize the differences between filming with an eye toward marketing and filming entirely for fun. If I didn't agree to highlight the booties, I could post our first shot, in which Aggie takes two steps into the snow and promptly lies down to tug off a bootie and flick it aside. It's funny and it's her being herself. No filters. No faking. And while she's walking on her own now, she's still carrying a lot of excess weight on bones that've been overstressed for years, so she has a tendency to lie down after a minute or two if I'm not walking with her on a leash or she's not chasing a ball. We try the ball and it helps, but we end up with several shots of her out of frame or turning away or distracted by footprints to sniff or with her feet too deep in the snow for the booties to show up clearly on camera. Also, I'm not an actress by even the farthest stretch of the word, so when Aggie grows tired, I grow tired. It shows, and even the world's cutest colorful puff-ball hat can't save us.

"Anything?" I ask as Everett scrolls his phone while Aggie rests in her wagon.

"Maybe?" He attempts a smile, but his brows are pinched together behind his glasses and his attention stays on his phone. He's in work mode, which I can recognize pretty quickly now.

"It doesn't need to be professional standard," I remind him.

"I know. But we still want to sell a story here."

I hide a wince while he's not looking. *Sell* a story. Not *tell* a story. I know they might mean the same thing to him in this context, they probably should, and I'm so grateful for his marketing eye, but the longer we struggle to get usable video, the more I miss the time I spent with Aggie yesterday, just the two of us, slowly walking to the corner and back while she sniffed footprints and I watched giant snowflakes collect on her eyelashes, and none of this mattered.

"Sorry," Everett says without looking up. "I just want to make this good for you. I want it to reflect you, Aggie, *and* the product. If we can do that, and continue to build your engagement and follower count, you can make more money from the same amount of work."

"I know," I tell him, and I do, even though my heart's not in it.

"Give me another minute," he says. "Let me make sure we have something."

"Everett—"

"One minute. I swear." He pleads with his pretty hazel eyes.

I frown at him, wondering if I should push back, but deciding there isn't much point.

"Okay. Thank you." I kiss his cheek and leave him to it as I trudge over to join Aggie at her wagon, crouching down to adjust her hood so I can give her neck a good long scratch. When considerably more than a minute passes and my patience dwindles, I lean in and whisper, "What do you think? Should we remind him this is supposed to be fun?"

She bunts my nose with hers, panting out little clouds of warm, meaty dog breath. It's an ambiguous reply but I take it as a definitive yes, and make a snowball I toss at Everett's back. It hits his neck instead, bursting on impact and spraying his bare neck above his scarf.

He spins toward us, wide-eyed. "What the—"

I point at Aggie. "I tried to stop her. But you know how much she likes to flirt with you."

He pockets his phone as a sly smile dimples his cheeks. "So that was flirting, huh?"

I pretend to consider. "I mean . . . it wasn't *not* flirting."

His eyes narrow. "Oh, you're going down, Goode."

With a swiftness I didn't see coming, he lunges toward me, his arms spread wide until they clamp around me and we topple into the snow. I shriek with surprise as we roll over one another. Aggie barks from her wagon, pushing into a seated position before easing herself off the open side so she can trot over to join us. I usually help her with level changes, but she manages this one on her own, just like she's been growing more comfortable getting on and off the futon on her own. It makes me so happy to see her becoming more mobile and independent, and when she pushes her nose between our faces like she's determined to be part of the game, we invite her in, laughing and teasing, until all three of us are rolling in the snow like little kids.

Everett gets me back for my snowball by sneaking one in as I scramble away from him. It hits the side of my face with a shock of cold that makes me shriek again. I duck around the tree and fire back, missing Everett completely. He hides behind Aggie—who seems to have taken his side, to no one's surprise—readying another snowball and sending it my way. It smacks the tree at shoulder height, dusting my face with snow for the second time. We end up chasing each other around the tree, the bench, the wagon, and

Aggie, madly making snowballs and pitching them as we run while Aggie wags her tail and barks encouragement at us, sometimes joining the fray but mostly spurring on our mischief from a gentle mound of snow.

It's chaos. It's fun. It's joy. It's perfect. And when Everett catches me by the hem of my coat and pins me against the tree for a long, hot, knee-buckling kiss while Aggie pulls off her front booties like she's done being both a cheerleader and a spokesperson, it's even better. This is her being herself, and us being ourselves, and all of it is for no one's eyes but our own.

"I vote we hit pause on the sponsorship video for the rest of the day and head home for towels, belly rubs, hot cocoa, and gingerbread cookies," I say when the kiss ends.

Everett's brow furrows with confusion. "You have cocoa and cookies?"

I give his chest a light shove as I push off from the tree and sidle past him.

"*Someone* stocked my entire kitchen a week ago," I say.

He looks over at Aggie, lying peacefully in the snow with her front booties off.

"What a sweet idea, Aggie!" he says. "I knew you'd take good care of my girl."

I roll my eyes because it's the intended response, but I can't help smiling.

My girl.

Two simple words.

A million complicated feelings.

A heart that somehow has room for all of them, and for even more to come.

CHAPTER TWENTY-ONE

For a long, cold, dark month, January speeds by, full of highs, lows, and everything in between.

Sponsorship is mostly positive. On our second attempt, Everett gets the footage he wants for the first sponsored TikTok, with Aggie and me playing ball in the snow and a great shot of her doing a slow turn in the booties and coat. The video he edits together is extremely cute, the live footage intercut with sketch-like animated graphics. It's so polished, it's practically a short film. Her orthopedic bed arrives the following week and I make the TikTok on my own. It's simpler than involving Everett, and getting Aggie to lie on a comfortable bed and look happy takes no effort at all. The toy box arrives a couple days later. I invite Minh Ha and Pilot over and the two dogs open the box together, pulling out balls, chew bones, rope tugs, and squeaky stuffies with equal fervor, until my floor is strewn with toys while Aggie flops onto her bed with a furry yellow squeaky ball and Pilot curls up against her with a stuffed duck that's as big as she is. Everett films and edits again even though it complicates things. He really wanted to do it, he did an amazing job with the first sponsorship video, and I appreciate that I get to sit back and enjoy watching Aggie and Pilot unbox the toys while he takes care of filming.

The income lets me cut my cleaning hours back down to two days a week, and with Everett's gentle but persistent encouragement, I commit to a few more sponsorships. I'm less daunted by them now but I find myself caring more about follower numbers, knowing they'll impact my income. I spend time answering more comments and engaging on other dog-oriented accounts, some of which is fun and instinctive, but not all of it. A hum of pressure builds to do more and say more, and to fit Aggie's "brand," making me miss the simplicity of posting and commenting on what I want when I want, without worrying what it might mean for sponsorship deals.

However, with more time to study, I ace my pathology final when Dr. Stean lets me retake it. I'm still questioning my degree, and whether it's really worth it, especially when my term-two loan statement arrives, but I shove it in the drawer with the others and attend to more immediate financial matters instead.

Regina's shirts earn an incredible $3,000 in profits in their first month, which she splits with me fifty-fifty, as promised. She tells me not to expect similar numbers every month, since sales naturally surged after the initial promotion and will likely decrease in coming weeks, but for the first time since I started grad school, between the shirts and the sponsorships, I pay down my credit card so it doesn't get canceled again when I most need it and I buy groceries without panic-tallying the cost before I reach the register. I also get Aggie caught up on some important vet visits involving orthopedic monitoring and metabolic tests that go beyond the weigh-ins and general checkups Ruff 'n' Rescue has been providing us for free. The money seemed like so much in abstract numbers, but when translated into real-world expenses, it disappears fast.

Aside from the uptick in vet visits, which I knew was coming, and some shuffling of meds that has unfortunate digestive side effects, Aggie has a good month. Over four weeks, she loses six more pounds, bringing her to ninety-five, for which she gets a lot of love from her fans, both live and online. Regina and Tegan decorate the wagon again, this time with sports-themed banners that say *Champion* and *Winner*, along with brightly colored pinwheels that spin when I pull her through town, still cautious about how much time she spends on her feet. Johann bakes her a dog-friendly cake shaped like a bone. Arthur and Diana create a special-edition tea called Aggie's Blend that's mostly ginger and cinnamon like her coloring, with a hint of pepper for her lively spirit and licorice root for her sweetness. Khalil and his lab mates add a new feature to the robo-ball so it says "You're amazing!" when she picks up more speed than she used to, chasing the ball down the hall. Phone Girl even pauses after exiting her apartment one afternoon while Aggie and I are waiting for the elevator and asks, "Is your dog, like, smaller than she used to be?"

"Yeah," I say. "We're working on it."

"Okay. Cool." She nods. Then she vanishes into the stairwell in a blur of flame-red hair, pale skin, fur-topped snow boots, and a sexy pleather coat that looks like it's straight off the set of a vampire movie. Given how little I know about what Phone Girl does with her time, maybe she did play a vampire in a movie. Maybe she *is* a vampire.

On a cold, crisp day at the end of the month, after gradually extending our daily walks along the Cascadilla Gorge Trail past the frozen waterfalls and iced-over trees, Aggie makes it to our half-mile target without the wagon, sling, or harness. As she turns to look over her shoulder at me as though she wants to know if she should keep going, I drop to my knees in the snow and fling my arms around her neck, planting a million kisses all over her beautiful face. Four months ago, she couldn't stand on her own. It took four of us to get her into the back of Everett's station wagon from the emergency vet. Her first walking exercises with me were little more than short stumbles between long sessions of lying down. Now? She's ambling along with me, stiffly and slowly but with purpose, sometimes even taking the lead, full of curiosity about her world.

"Do you know how much I love you?" I ask, still nose to nose and eye to eye.

She blinks at me with her brows twitching and her dog breath misting my face. It's smelly but it's her, so I kind of love it, like I love everything else about her.

I boop her nose with a gloved fingertip. "I said, do you know how much I love you?"

This time she sweeps her tongue from my chin to my eyebrows, and I wipe away the saliva, scrunching up my face and laughing as I give her more kisses in return.

"I had a feeling you knew," I tell her. "But I'll keep telling you, anyway."

ON THE SECOND Saturday in February, Everett drives us to Aqua Paws, where I scheduled our hydrotherapy consultation. Things with Everett have also been mostly positive since New Year's, though our time together is as limited as ever, making me resent using the time we do have to deal with sponsorships. Not that I'm not grateful for his help. I am. Hugely. Deeply. I love how easily he identifies partnerships and navigates the correspondence. I love his ability to turn a short video into something I want to watch over and over again. I love that he's full of fun ideas about telling stories and connecting with people. I love that he wants to use these skills to help Aggie, and to help me, but he's always ten steps ahead of me, thinking about who else to partner with, how to use the branding he and Regina developed, or if Aggie's progress has a benchmark we should be shouting about to up engagement. Sometimes I want our online celebration of Aggie's progress to be *only* a celebration, not part of a marketing plan.

Neil Diamond and Barbra Streisand are singing "You Don't Bring Me Flowers" when we pull into the parking lot and I get caught up by the deep longing in the song. Not that I'd ever admit it to anyone but Hannah and *maybe* Everett, but Aggie's not the only one who's changed over the last four and a half months. Apparently, I'm starting to like seventies light rock now.

Although truthfully? I think I mostly like Everett.

Before we get out of the car, I set my hand on his thigh.

"Hey," I say, and it comes out like more of an alert than I mean it to.

"Hey." He wraps my hand with his as his eyes go wary and his posture stiffens, like he's trying to be chill but he's worried I'm about to say something scary, and maybe I am, but only scary for me, and only because I don't want to seem ungrateful and because I have no prior experience with relationships and I really, *really* don't want to screw this one up.

"I have a favor to ask," I say.

"Okay. Anything." He nods, fidgets, waits, listens.

"I know we need to film some of this. So many of Aggie's followers have asked about hydrotherapy and contributed to paying for it by buying Regina's shirts. I want to share this with them. I also know we're still trying to grow the account so the next round of sponsorships brings in more money. But Everett? Can we also enjoy some of this live, without worrying about getting the right shot or tying it in with branding or telling the perfect story?"

His shoulders drop as he lets out a slow exhale, tugging my hand to draw me into a hug.

"Of course," he says. "I'm sorry. I've been pushing too hard."

"Yes and no." I hold him close for a minute. Then I pull out of our hug so I can see his eyes and play with his hair. His loose curls are so soft and springy, and I can't imagine ever not wanting to touch them. "A couple years ago, when I visited Hannah in Swindon, we went for a run together. I max out at six or seven miles. She maxes out at over twenty miles, all of them at a much faster pace than mine. She didn't *push me* to run faster or farther, but I wanted to keep up, so I tried. She'd notice I was flagging and try to slow down, but no matter how often I sped up or she slowed down, we couldn't match each other's pace. I finally stopped altogether, and we had a good laugh about it as we walked home, but you can imagine how I felt at the one-hour mark."

Everett takes my hand and plants a long, firm kiss on my palm.

"So, do a better job of recognizing when we're going different paces?" he asks.

"Something like that. Or at least . . . stop for water when I say I need a break?"

He tips his chin toward Aqua Paws. "Which is what you're doing now?"

I nod, smiling at my unintended double entendre. "Which is what I'm doing now."

He kisses my hand again and gives it a reassuring squeeze before letting go.

"Understood," he says. "I'll get a few shots, and then my phone goes in my pocket."

My smile widens and I feel a bit silly for being scared to talk to him. Although . . .

"What did you think I wanted to talk about?" I ask.

He lets out a breath of jittery laughter as he scratches the back of his reddening neck.

"The last time someone said 'hey' like that, it was followed with 'we need to talk.'"

"You mean . . ."

"Yeah."

"Ouch."

"Exactly."

"Well, you have two things working in your favor." I pivot toward the back of the station wagon, where Aggie's patiently waiting, mouth ajar and tongue out. "One, my dog adores you."

"The feeling's mutual." He shines a full-dimpled grin at Aggie before returning his gaze to mine, stretching out the moment as he swallows, and swallows again. "And number two?"

"Number two is obvious. I'd never do anything to upset my dog."

Everett chuckles under his breath while shaking his head at me. We both know what number two really is. I'm just not sure when I'll get up the nerve to say it.

With that, we lift Aggie out of the car and head inside, where we're warmly greeted and treated to a tour. The facility is bigger than I expected, with an elegant reception room equally suitable for a fancy spa, a large pool ringed with ramps and steps, a non-aquatic rehab room with rubber balls and agility equipment, and several smaller rooms where dogs can get laser therapy, massages, and acupuncture. Aggie's fascinated by all of it—as am I—though she's a little wary when we get to the room with the aquatic treadmill, which is just a treadmill in a plexiglass box, currently empty. She spent so much of her life confined, but she won't be alone this time, or outside, and if she's unhappy, we can stop anytime.

The receptionist leaves us with Georgia, the PT who will be working with us. She's a tall, lean thirty-something Black woman with flat twists, wearing a knit shirt with the sleeves pushed up to reveal heavily inked forearms, and the kind of green rubber waders I've only ever seen in fishing photos. We talk through Aggie's history and goals while Georgia examines her joints and musculature, and Aggie submits to the examination with her usual boundless patience, casting me an occasional put-upon look while I rub her ears and tell her she's doing great.

"What do you think? Should we give it a try?" Georgia asks, and I love that she directs the question at Aggie and not at me, even while I know I'm the one who will answer.

Aggie lets out a single, cheerful bark, proving me wrong. Clearly, she's in charge, though I support her enthusiasm with a *yes, please* and promise Aggie we'll be close by the whole time.

We get her onto the treadmill, with Everett luring her forward with treats and her favorite bright pink ball while I pet her head and coo reassurances. Once she's in position, Georgia steps in and closes the door at the back of the tank. The treats do the trick and Aggie barely seems to notice she's enclosed. She's a little surprised when the water rises, but by the time it reaches her belly, she's biting at bubbles and my concerns that she'd be anxious have melted away.

She spends five minutes in the tank, with Georgia guiding her back legs in an even stride and pausing the treadmill whenever Aggie needs a break. I dole out treats or nudge the ball in her direction for motivation. Everett films what I suspect is more than "a few shots," but he does eventually cheer her on with his phone tucked away, which is good because I don't want to get caught crying on camera and I find myself fighting back tears as Aggie smiles up at us, taking another step while looking for another treat. I'm not sure what it is about seeing her walk through water that gets me choked up. We've logged countless miles together by now, though I suppose I always get emotional when I see clear evidence that she's getting stronger and more flexible, and now we have even more help to continue her progress. For a dog who was so alone for so long, her support team keeps growing. That makes me emotional, too.

While we wrap up and get Aggie dried off, Georgia praises her for being so strong and brave at her first appointment. She makes suggestions on next steps, like setting up once-a-week or every-other-week sessions, and gives me an idea of what we might see for progress over the coming months if we continue. She also mentions a few of Aqua Paws' other services, though she's clear that pursuing any treatment should be at the recommendation of Aggie's vets.

Her comment echoes what I saw on the website, that the PTs here aren't licensed veterinarians, and that clients shouldn't expect medical examinations and diagnoses. It also sparks my curiosity, so before we head out, I ask how Georgia got into canine physiotherapy.

"You're a vet student, right?" she asks, and at my nod, she adds, "That's one way to go about it. I went the physiotherapy route. Thought I'd end up working in sports medicine. The classes were great but one really rotten internship showed me it wasn't the career I wanted, so I pivoted. Got my certification in animal rehabilitation and never looked back." She smiles as she gives Aggie an affectionate scratch behind the ears. "You're one step ahead of me. You already knew dogs are better than people." She glances at Everett. "Better than most people, anyway."

He holds up his hands in surrender.

"Don't worry," he says. "I can't argue that point."

Georgia turns her smile my direction. "I believe that's what people call *a keeper*."

Yeah, I think. *I'm not letting go anytime soon.*

I ask Georgia a few more questions about her work, intrigued at the idea that my career might not be as linear as I've been thinking. I'm not sure why I hadn't fully considered that before now, but outside of classes, my experience with vets has always been in a clinic. Scrubs. Lab coats. Exam tables. Blood samples. Vaccines. IVs. X-rays. Maybe that's a world I'll find fulfilling, but if it isn't, maybe I can pivot, too, and maybe looking into other options will make me less anxious about the degree I'm pursuing.

I'm still mulling this over as we exit the building when Everett's phone pings with a text and he pauses to check it. I wait with Aggie, watching as his brows pinch together and he fires off a reply. Another text pings, and his cheeks puff as he blows out a breath.

"Wow. Okay," he says. "Looks like that retirement I told you about has finally been announced and the associate creative director position is opening up."

A little spark of excitement ignites in my chest.

"That's great, right?" I ask. "You want this?"

He stares at his phone while chewing his lip.

"I do," he says after a long pause. "I mean . . . of course I do. It's more autonomy. An actual office. A chance to help shape the company as a whole and not just individual accounts."

I wait, though when he doesn't say anything else, I nudge him with a gentle "But?"

He inches up a shaky, uncertain shrug as he pockets his phone.

"I was finally wrapping up a few things so I wasn't working all the time," he says. "If I go after this, it means more work, not less, at least until the position's filled. I've been carefully building my portfolio since I heard this might become a possibility, but competition will be stiff, even within the company. I'm terrible at interviews and I'm not sure I have enough range." He goes quiet while running through his usual roster of fidgets: shifting his stance, nudging his glasses up his nose, scratching his neck, adjusting his scarf. Even if I couldn't read his body language by now, I know what self-doubt feels like. Down to my bones.

I step forward and take his hand. "If you want it, you should go for it. Right, Aggie?"

She steps forward, too, nudging our linked hands with her cold, wet nose.

Everett smiles a little, just a twitch at the corners of his lips, but it's something.

"Is this her way of saying yes?" he asks.

"It's her way of saying she believes in you," I tell him. "And maybe that she knows a few things about setting hard goals, and how trying to reach them is worth the effort, even when you fall down a lot while attempting to stand up. Or need more than twenty breaks to walk a mile."

Everett's brows rise with surprise. "Does she give you this pep talk, too, because . . ."

"Yeah, yeah. I know." I draw him into a hug before he can tease me further. His teasing's well-earned but this moment's not about me. "We're here for whatever you need. And if you won't have much time to spare for a while, we'll just make the most of the time we do have."

He relaxes into my embrace, and as his arms come around me, the words that've been dancing around in my mind more and more often in recent days almost slip out. But his mind is miles away right now, lost in portfolio planning and interview strategies, so the words can wait. The feeling's there, and I'll do my damnedest to make sure he knows that every step of the way.

CHAPTER TWENTY-TWO

"You're amazing!" the robo-ball says as Aggie chases it down the sixth-floor hallway on a cold, wet Saturday afternoon in early March, after a cold, wet walk we cut short so we could play inside instead.

"Wow," Khalil says as he watches with me. "We could almost call that a jog."

"*Almost?*" I scoff with mock indignation. "That is *definitely* a jog."

He nods his agreement while Aggie catches up to the ball, grabs it, drops it, and follows it again as it zigzags in our direction. Okay, *jog* is a stretch, but not a big one. Aggie's pace is more than a walk or a trot. A month of hydrotherapy has been really good for her. She can walk four full minutes on the water treadmill before resting now. She's lost eight more pounds. Her once scabby, bald tail is covered in hair. The hair's still growing in, so her tail doesn't yet look like a normal retriever tail, but it does look like a dog tail, no longer a constant sign of her neglect.

"My prof is really excited about how well the ball's working," Khalil says. "We're putting together a grant application to expand on what we've learned with it. See if we can't modify it for kids with mobility issues, combining game play with adaptive movement."

"You're amazing!" the ball says as it rolls toward us.

"The ball beat me to it," I say. "You *are* amazing."

Khalil waves off my praise, like always, but I swear he's standing taller, which is saying something because he's pretty tall to begin with. Tall, kind, and genius-level brilliant.

It never ceases to astonish me that I live near such cool people, and I'm so glad we all finally talked to each other last fall. Well, almost all of us, but maybe one day Phone Girl will come around. Even if she is a vampire, she'll have to feed at some point.

"Can we show off your work to Aggie's fan club?" I ask Khalil.

He flushes but he smiles as he reddens. "Um, I guess, okay?"

I smile back, eager for the world to witness his genius. "Yay! Thank you!"

I grab my phone and film Aggie chasing the ball. Then Khalil talks through the key features, geeking out about actuators, feedback loops, and proximity sensors while standing in our hallway in black and gray high-tech winter cycling clothes that hug his body like a superhero costume. I don't fuss with the video editing, obsess about the caption or hashtags, or ensure the music is trending. With three more sponsored TikToks on the account now, all of which Everett insisted on producing to his carefully branded and highly curated professional standards, I'm ready to post something amateur. Just a dog, a ball, and a humanitarian robotics nerd.

Ten minutes later, as we continue playing ball with Aggie while joking about how the Cornell Alumni Society is already asking us for donations, my phone buzzes in my pocket.

HANNAH: Saw your new TikTok. Was that your next-door neighbor?

CAMERON: Yeah. Khalil. Previously known as Cycle Guy. Why?

HANNAH: Seriously, Cam?!?! You have at least LOOKED at those legs, right?

I swallow a laugh and force myself to keep my eyes on my screen while Khalil plays with Aggie. I should've seen this coming. I know Hannah's type. Tall, dark, and handsome. Muscular. Chiseled features. And it doesn't hurt that he's a high-achieving endurance athlete, just like her.

CAMERON: He cycles over two hundred miles a week. For fun. Of course he's fit

HANNAH: Fit, and with an actual brain! Didn't you say he cooks, too?

CAMERON: Are you telling me you're thinking of visiting?

HANNAH: I'm not THAT thirsty. But your TikTok might hit a record number of views

CAMERON: Speaking of numbers . . . should I give him yours?

> **HANNAH:** God, no. I'd only fall for him, tell him I'm in love with him, and get dumped

> **CAMERON:** That was ONE time

> **HANNAH:** Sometimes one is all it takes...

Oh, Hannah, I think, and wish I had a way to make her forget that guy ever existed, though I guess I wouldn't appreciate Everett as much if I hadn't kissed a few frogs first. Still, Hannah deserves so much better, and I won't stop hoping she'll find it.

After a few more texts, we sign off with the usual heart emojis and I pocket my phone.

"Everything okay?" Khalil asks, now seated on the floor with Aggie basically in his lap.

I consider telling him my best friend thinks he's hot, and that they'd probably be perfect together if they ever met, but since they're unlikely to cross paths, I'm not about to meddle.

"Just my friend in the UK," I say. "The one I've told you about who's getting her law degree and doing Ironman races. She's impressed with the ball you made."

"Yeah? Cool." Khalil flushes again, fighting a shy smile he buries against Aggie's neck.

Okay, maybe I can revisit the meddling idea. But only if the opportunity arises.

Tucking that thought aside, we pick back up where we left off, chatting about everything and nothing while sending Aggie back and forth down the hall so she gets her exercise since it's too cold and slushy outside to enjoy the park. I don't know why I always expect March to feel like spring when it always feels like winter's stubborn refusal to end. There's always one more snowfall. One more freezing rain. One more day to bundle up while wishing I could hibernate.

Khalil's expressing a similar sentiment when the elevator dings and Regina and Tegan stumble into the hall, locked in a tight embrace, hands roving, clothes bunched, mid-make-out.

"Look out!" I shout before they stumble over the ball or Aggie barrels into them.

They pull apart, laughing as they turn and see us.

"Sorry, sorry!" Regina waves her hands like she's erasing the space between us.

"We didn't expect anyone to be here," Tegan says.

"And if you *did* expect someone?" Khalil challenges.

Regina and Tegan exchange a look, then burst into more laughter.

"I don't know what it is about that elevator," Regina says.

She and Tegan both look at me, which means it's my turn to blush. Thankfully, Tegan quickly redirects everyone's attention by holding up a large bag from Pâtisserie Amour.

"Warm croissant, anyone?" she asks. "We got greedy and bought more than we need."

Aggie's first to wander over, because of course she is, but Khalil and I clamber up and join her, lured as easily as she is by the smell of fresh-from-the-oven, flaky, buttery pastry.

I reach into the bag Tegan holds open for us. "I've been dying to try one of these."

"And you haven't had one yet because . . ." she asks.

"Johann's been so generous," I say. "And I know how he feels about his rival."

Regina and Tegan exchange another look before Regina turns to me.

"Oh no," she says. "No, no, no, no, no. You did *not* fall for that."

I glance at Khalil, but he shrugs, looking as in the dark as I feel.

"Fall for what?" I ask Regina.

"Johann and Madeleine?" she says. "They're totally banging."

"They're what?!" I sputter through a shocked laugh.

Khalil shrugs again while Tegan nods in an *oh yeah* kind of way.

"I thought they hated each other," I say.

"Maybe they did, once," Regina says. "Or maybe their parents hated each other so Johann and Madeleine pretended for their parents' sakes. Either way, it has to be a publicity stunt by now because the minute the lights go out, someone's getting their cake frosted."

I almost choke on my croissant. "How do you know?"

"I told you," she says. "I have a sixth sense about these things."

"Also, we've seen them," Tegan adds. "But *after* Reggie told me what she suspected."

I gape, speechless. All these weeks. All the hissed aspersions. Was Johann really faking it while sneaking next door after hours? And why do I kind of love the idea that he was?

We all devolve into speculation, though conversation shifts as we eat our croissants, parking ourselves on the floor so we can also play with Aggie. Khalil offers to let us all try the stuffed eggplant he cooked last night, making us drool as we recall the aroma. Tegan shows us her latest TikTok with googly eyes glued above a jagged crack in some brickwork and the caption *Rosy Muson. Whether you're looking to get stoned or get laid, I won't take you for granite.* Regina tells us about a new sportswear line she's launching this spring, speaking with the unshakable confidence I've come to know her for, the confidence that will likely get her to New York Fashion Week by age thirty, and have her dressing major celebrities shortly thereafter.

"Wait a sec." She glances around as Aggie flops down beside me, tired from playing and resting her head in my lap, where I can pet her spectacular ears. "Aren't we missing someone?"

All eyes turn on me, and a month of complicated feelings threatens to bubble up.

"He's working," I say, and plan to leave it there, but everyone's looking at me like they know there's more to say, and I guess I don't have to keep this stuff to myself anymore, or save it all for Hannah. "He's up for a promotion he *really* wants, which is why he's working on a Saturday. I miss him but I get it because my schedule doesn't leave much room for him, either. I just . . . I wish he could turn off more when he *is* free. We haven't had much fun lately. He's determined to keep helping with my TikToks, which is pretty much all we have time for, and I keep telling him they don't need to be fancy and that I'm not sure I want to keep doing them at all, but he keeps pushing and I want him to feel appreciated, even when he's being—" I cut myself off. I can't believe I'm complaining about Everett. Not when he's been *so* good to me.

"A perfectionist?" Regina fills in for me.

"Single-minded?" Tegan suggests.

"Relentless?" Khalil offers.

For a moment, all I can do is blink. Then it sinks in. "You guys noticed?"

Regina laughs. Tegan smirks. Khalil shrugs. All three responses clearly say *yes*.

"Our walls are thin," Tegan says. "We know when he's pulling an all-nighter."

"And we've seen your TikToks," Regina says. "Yours and Everett's."

Khalil doesn't add anything but the look he gives me says he's seen and heard plenty, and I'm sure he has. We all run into each other often enough to know when someone's having a bad day, having a great day, or too exhausted and preoccupied to talk about their day at all.

"Everett has high standards," I say as a fresh wave of guilt crashes through me. "He puts all that work into my account *for me*. And I need the income. Why can't I just be grateful?"

"Gratitude is complicated when what people give you isn't what you actually want," Tegan says, addressing her point to Aggie and not to me. "Like cold, meaty dog food instead of the warm, tasty croissants your mean old mom won't let me feed you. Right, Aggie Waggie?"

Aggie slides me the perfect resentful side-eye, and I can't help but laugh.

"And being grateful doesn't mean you have to keep going," Regina adds. "Or that you can't pop up an occasional TikTok without Francis Ford Redmond directing production."

I know, I think. But also . . . "It's hard to turn down that kind of help, not when he's so insistent about providing it. He also knows his way around social media so much better than I do. And his TikToks are *so* good. They get ten times the number of views and likes mine do. They bumped my follower count up enough to double my sponsorship income. It's an incredible gift."

Regina, Tegan, and Khalil all regard me skeptically while Aggie lets out a timely groan. Their looks speak volumes, and maybe what they're not saying is exactly what I need to hear.

"I'll talk to him once he gets through this work crunch," I say. "Maybe it's time to be firm about quitting sponsorships. Take the pressure off both of us."

"He might not get it right away, but he'll come around," Regina says. "He clearly wants the best for you and you clearly want the best for him. I'm sure you guys can work it out."

"Yeah. I know. Thanks," I say, and while I may never share Regina's certainty about life, love, or the sexual tension between bickering bakers, I love that I'm hanging out with friends on a Saturday afternoon, with the taste of buttery croissant still on my lips and a warm dog by my side.

This is happiness, too, I think. *Tempered by complicated feelings for someone who's not present, and arriving in a form I couldn't have predicted. But definitely happiness.*

Chapter Twenty-Three

The week after the croissant pep talk, Everett gets an invite to the current associate creative director's retirement dinner, where his boss plans to announce who will take over the position. Everett knows he's in the final running but he doesn't know who his competition is other than Brandon, the beefy blond guy who spent Thanksgiving annoying everyone else, including the dogs. The dinner is planned for Monday, March 31, during my spring break, which gives Everett two and a half weeks to stress about his final interview and portfolio review.

I tell him I want to stop the sponsorships, for his sake as much as mine, but when Aggie's vet suggests hip X-rays so we can make a longer-term care plan for managing the stress her bones have been under, Everett finds my laptop open to part-time job listings and talks me into another sponsorship instead. This time it's a mileage tracker that will log Aggie's walks, allowing her followers to see her progress in concrete terms. Despite my reservations, it's a useful tool. It's also hard to argue with Everett when we both know I'll make more money with a few TikToks about walking my dog, which I need to do anyway, than I would working twenty hours a week at any of the dismal jobs we see in the listings. We also know what happened the last time I filled every free hour with work. So I sign on to the sponsorship and make Everett promise to not obsess about branding and video production.

Predictably, he obsesses anyway.

He swears he's not overdoing it.

I remain unconvinced.

When spring break starts, my cleaning job goes on pause, incessant rains limit outdoor activity, and I don't have a major exam to cram for, so I settle in on the futon with a tired-from-playtime Aggie and finally, *finally* crack open *Jane Eyre*. I've always been a reader but only of fast-paced mysteries and thrillers. Dense classics with symbolic settings and long-winded passages about society and religion generally bore me, so I assume I'll tire of Jane's story within a few chapters, but hours pass before I even pause to make a fresh cup of tea. I thought the book was a romance between a governess and her rich employer, and it is, but more than that, it's a story about loneliness, about a woman whose lack of familial affection, strong friendships, and romantic prospects leads to a kind of rootlessness, and her longing to be fully seen not as one part of herself, but as *all* parts of herself, and to be valued for the whole those parts make up.

Saying it's relatable would be the understatement of the decade.

Also, the madwoman in the attic fascinates me.

Eager to talk about it when I finish the following evening, I head next door with Aggie, only to find Minh Ha worrying about Pilot, who's curled up on a tiny, furry donut bed beside an armchair and a side table stacked with papers. Usually Pilot goes bananas when she sees Aggie, running circles around her and trying to get her to play. Tonight, she barely lifts her head.

"Is she injured?" I ask from the doorway.

"She picked something up on the street before I could stop her," Minh Ha says. "Food waste of some kind that ran right through her. Now she won't eat or drink, and her vet's office is closed on Sundays. I could take her to emergency care but the last two times this happened, they charged me three hundred dollars for the consult, sent us home, and told me to keep an eye on her for twenty-four hours, returning with a stool sample if nothing changed."

I wince at the dismissiveness, but I also understand. Unless a dog consumes something that could cause an allergic reaction or block or rupture its organs, most canine digestive issues resolve themselves in twenty-four to forty-eight hours. A vet could run a lot of tests, some more invasive and expensive than others. When in doubt, tests are worth running, especially if parasites are suspected, but with every new case, a judgment call has to be made, and while it never feels helpful in the moment, *watch and see* is often relatively solid advice.

"Can I take a look?" I ask.

Minh Ha steps back so I can enter her apartment. "Please."

Aggie saunters in with me, bunting Pilot with her nose while I kneel to examine her. Pilot's gums are pale and her nose is warm and dry, but she exhibits no signs of distress when I massage her throat, sides, and belly. While I can't offer an official diagnosis after only a quick evaluation, I suspect she's tired and dehydrated, and probably has a bit of a bellyache.

"Have you tried chicken broth?" I ask. "To get her to drink?"

Minh Ha shakes her head, turning toward a minimal kitchen like mine where she finds a can of chicken soup she opens and strains into a bowl. Aggie's nose works overtime as Minh Ha carries the bowl over, but I swear she knows her friend is distressed because when Minh Ha sets the bowl down near Pilot's bed, Aggie makes no move toward it. Instead, she lies beside me and watches as Minh Ha picks Pilot up, gives her a cuddle, and then sets her by the bowl.

Pilot looks at us as though she knows she's being observed and she's not sure she wants to perform, but after a moment, she steps forward, sniffs the broth, and dips her tiny pink tongue in. One taste leads to another and soon enough, she's lapping up the broth while the worry lines soften on Minh Ha's face and she gushes with gratitude and relief. I tell her it's no problem and I mean it. The assistance I've offered is so small. Although, seeing its impact, it doesn't feel small. It feels big. Huge. Important. And being able to do something important feels really good.

"I should've thought of the broth," Minh Ha says.

"It's what we used to do for Marmie, my previous dog. She was basically a vacuum in dog form. We were lucky she never had to have surgery." I lean into Aggie, drawing her against me with an arm looped around her neck. I'm lucky to have her, too, no matter how many medical appointments lie in our future. It's hard to believe I met her six and a half months ago now. It's also hard to believe I haven't known and loved her forever. In my heart, I feel like I have.

When Pilot finishes drinking, she trots over and curls up against Aggie's side, a tiny gray tuft against a mountain of russet fur. Aggie gives her a little nuzzle before flopping over for a nap of her own. While the dogs sleep, Minh Ha and I talk about how my degree is going (good but hard), and how her classes are going (good but exhausting), before segueing into discussing *Jane Eyre*. I tell her why I connected to Jane, how I've never been good with people and have struggled to form friendships and romantic relationships. Minh Ha listens with interest, full of insight about the author, symbols, and varied interpretations of the madwoman in the attic. I'm mortified to recall that I once told her I couldn't imagine taking one of her classes. Not that I'm about to change my degree because of one conversation, but when she loans me her copy of *Convenience Store Woman* by Sayaka Murata, suggesting I might connect to its heroine, too, I sense the start of a very sporadic but deeply rewarding two-person, two-dog book club.

Eventually we say good night and I head out with Aggie, but I pause at my door when I hear what might be someone quietly crying in the stairwell. I listen for a moment while stroking Aggie's ears, unsure if I should check it out or leave well enough alone. I'm not a likely source of comfort or wisdom when someone's upset. I don't even know how to deal with my own emotions, not after being raised to pretend they don't exist. But when the noise continues, more distinctly like a sob, I turn and head toward the stairwell with Aggie following close behind.

Opening the door, I find Phone Girl sitting on the edge of the landing in thigh-high boots, a tight leather miniskirt, and a fluffy oversize sweater coat that nearly swallows her slight frame. Her head is buried in her arms, which are folded on her knees, but she jerks upright at the sound of the door opening on creaky hinges, her red-rimmed eyes narrowing into a sharp glare.

"I'm fine," she snaps at me.

"Right, okay," I say slowly. "I just—"

"I left my keys at my stupid boyfriend's apartment," she interjects through a sniffle. "My friend's on her way with my spare so I'll be out of here in, like, minutes or whatever."

"Okay," I say again, floundering a little.

She peers around me. "Your dog can do stairs now?"

"Oh. No. She can handle a few, but I'm pretty sure she'll always be an elevator girl."

"Then what—" She stops herself. "Oh. Got it. I don't want to talk about it."

"Okay," I say for what already feels like the hundredth time.

I bury a hand in Aggie's neck fur, desperate to fidget. I don't know what it is about this girl that intimidates me––the wardrobe and flawlessly styled hair and makeup, the combination of tiny body mass and intense fierceness, or the way she passes the rest of us by like she has much better people to spend her time with. Whatever the case, I'm a little at sea here.

A door opens behind me and I turn in the stairwell doorway to see Minh Ha exiting her apartment in her coat and scarf with Pilot in a handbag. They're wearing the matching bucket hats Regina made them for Christmas, and I'm momentarily distracted by the cuteness, but then Minh Ha's eyes dart toward the stairwell and she gives me an *everything okay?* look. I reply with a hint of a shrug and a look I hope communicates something like *I think so and I think maybe the less fuss the better?*

However Minh Ha interprets it, she seems to get the gist because she presses the elevator call button opposite the stairwell and tucks herself out of Phone Girl's view while she waits.

Still standing in the doorway with Phone Girl sniffling on the stairs, Minh Ha waiting in the hallway, and Aggie looking up at me for direction, I brace myself and try again.

"You don't have to tell me anything," I say.

Phone Girl scoffs. "No shit."

"But," I press on, "Aggie's a really good listener if you want to talk to her. She's also great at hugs, so, um, I thought maybe, if you wanted some company while you wait..."

Phone Girl blinks at me through seriously impressive lash extensions.

"You think hanging out with a dog is going to solve all my problems?" she asks.

"No, but for me, my problems aren't as overwhelming when I'm not feeling as alone. Also, as a major bonus, dogs *never* say the wrong thing. They don't make assumptions about your situation or offer solutions you don't want or interrupt to talk about themselves or tell you everything will be okay when you absolutely know it won't be. They just listen. And love you."

Phone Girl continues blinking at me like she thinks I have a few screws loose.

I don't know. Maybe I do. But I also know I'm right about this.

"Your dog doesn't love me," she says.

"You'd be surprised. She's pretty indiscriminatory where affection's concerned." I realize how insulting this sounds the second I've said it, which is why I usually avoid situations like this, but to my immense relief, a soggy laugh bubbles out of Phone Girl's throat.

"Okay, whatever," she says. "Why not?"

The tension in my body eases and I guide Aggie toward the edge of the landing, where she sits next to Phone Girl like they've known each other forever, giving her face a sniff where tears have streaked her cheeks but cordially refraining from her usual emphatic kisses.

Phone Girl watches her, uncertain, but when Aggie simply waits, with no pressure or expectations, she reaches out, wraps Aggie in her arms, and bursts into another round of sobs.

I stand in the doorway, more than a little uncertain, myself.

"I can just, I'll be, why don't I wait in the . . ." I point over my shoulder at the hallway.

Phone Girl's shoulders shake with another sob, but then she lifts her eyes to mine.

"Or you could stay," she says with unexpected shyness. "To keep an eye on your dog."

"Oh, um, sure. Thanks. Good idea." I sneak Minh Ha a nervous look.

She smiles warmly, full of reassurance, before stepping into the arriving elevator while I enter the stairwell and sit at the back of the landing, letting the door close behind me.

For several minutes, Phone Girl buries her face in Aggie's fur and cries. Aggie occasionally looks over her shoulder at me like she's not sure what's going on, but I've cried with her enough times for this to not be a wholly new experience. I assume this is all we'll do until Phone Girl's friend arrives, but as her sobs grow quiet, she surprises me by telling me her boyfriend broke up with her for being too high-maintenance, which made her furious when she only asked him to go out with her once in a while instead of playing stupid video games with his stupid buddies every stupid night. She goes on to call him several creatively insulting names and to detail the many reasons she's better off without him. Despite how vehemently she argues this point, she's clearly crushed, so I do my best to listen without judgment, following Aggie's lead.

By the time Phone Girl's phone chimes with a text and she

buzzes her friend into the building, she's down to gentle sniffles and an occasional dab at the corners of her eyes. I rally Aggie, and the three of us clamber up and step into the hall. The elevator will take a century to arrive, and I'm not sure if I should wait or not, as incapable as ever of judging the right moment and the right way to exit a conversation. Thankfully, Phone Girl speaks up first.

"Thanks for loaning me your dog," she says.

"If you need her again, let me know. She never turns down a good hug."

Phone Girl's lips flicker, not quite easing into a smile.

"Thanks also for . . . you know." She waves a hand in a manner that might indicate my company in the stairwell, the Post-it invites I've been leaving on her door, or something I can't call to mind. It doesn't really matter what she's thanking me for. I'm just glad she let me in.

"I'm Cameron, by the way," I say.

"I know. I started following your account. It's pretty cool."

A ripple of pride runs through me, not that she called *me* cool, but I'm calling this a win.

"Thanks," I say. "It's all Aggie. And a lot of help from my friends."

She nods as she glances around the hall, her expression indecipherable, though I get the sense she's picturing the people who live behind the doors, how she passes us by, gathered in the hallway to chat, share a laugh, or play with Aggie. I have a hard time picturing her joining in, but who knows? I would've said the same thing about all of us a little over half a year ago.

Phone Girl's friend comes barreling out of the stairwell, griping about the traffic, the ignorant asshole who just made the worst decision of his life, and the elevator that never showed up, all of this pouring out in a breathless fury as she sweeps her friend into a side-hug and steers her toward her apartment while pulling a ring of keys from her sparkly cross-body purse.

I take my cue and guide Aggie toward our apartment on the opposite side of the hall.

"Cameron," Phone Girl calls, and I spin toward her in surprise as her friend steps into the apartment, leaving us alone in the hall. "Felicity. My name's Felicity."

The irony almost makes me laugh. The happiest name for the saddest girl.

"It's nice to meet you, Felicity," I say. "I'll see you around?"

She nods and *almost* smiles.

"Sure," she says. "I'll see you around."

Then she steps into her apartment and closes the door.

I take a breath, letting the moment settle. Then I crouch to give Aggie a big, fierce, proud-of-you hug, covering her furry face in kisses.

"I love you so much," I tell her for the millionth time. "So, *so* much."

And then I tell her for the million-and-first time.

I'm still crouched in the hall, gushing over the glorious, magical, angelic being I get to share this part of my life with, when the elevator dings and Minh Ha returns with Pilot.

"Everything okay?" I ask as I straighten up.

"Everything's great." She pats Pilot softly on the head. "And you? Everything okay?"

My eyes drift to Felicity's door, behind which two muffled voices break into a laugh.

"Yeah," I say. "She had a rough day, but her friend's here now."

"Good. I'm glad. Although, Cameron? You're better with people than you think you are."

My throat gets thick with emotion but I swallow, and swallow again.

"Thanks," I say, barely.

"Of course," she says, warmly and kindly.

It's a simple exchange, the last in a series of simple exchanges, but by the time I'm in bed an hour later, I'm rethinking everything about why I've been so worried I might regret my degree and career choice, where all the doubt came from, and why I've let it grow.

CHAPTER TWENTY-FOUR

Everett has always talked about his workplace as a small company, so I'm astonished when I make a rough head count partway through the salad course and tally over two hundred people present to celebrate the work of longtime associate creative director Peter Pollard and to hear the announcement of who will fill his "impossible to fill" shoes. Statements like this have been flying all evening, and I have a new appreciation for Everett's anxieties around his application. He's doing a valiant job of remaining poised as the suspense builds, but anything within reach has been subject to his fidgeting. His silverware, wineglass, water glass, napkin, napkin holder, necktie, belt buckle, shirt and jacket cuffs, hair, glasses, and whenever I can offer it, my hand.

"How are you holding up?" I ask as he pushes a cherry tomato around on his plate.

"Sorry." He lowers his fork. "I promised you we'd have a good time tonight."

"Everett," I say through a breath of astonished laughter. "I don't care what kind of time we have tonight. We knew this would be stressful for you. And whether we eat dessert as a celebration or commiseration, I just want to be here with you."

He exhales as though he's been waiting to do it all night.

"Can I at least promise I'll be a better boyfriend after this is over?" he asks.

"You're not a bad boyfriend because you're busy."

"I am if I'm *always* busy."

I don't contradict him this time. He's right, though this goes both ways.

"How about we both commit to more time for each other," I suggest. "And to not filling the time we do have with anything related to school or work, including the sponsored TikToks."

He nods and finds my hand to plant a kiss on my knuckles as I will him to hear me this time, even though this is hardly the moment for a serious relationship conversation. One way or another, things will change for him after tonight. I can't help hoping they'll change for us, too.

For the next ninety minutes or so, we eat our dinner while people tell stories about Peter Pollard from a microphone at the front end of the restaurant's banquet room. We hear about how a spontaneous napkin doodle earned him the nickname The Logo King and how he once landed a client by joining the company president's weekly karaoke nights. Everyone's in good spirits, even Everett, though his mind is obviously elsewhere. I spot Brandon a few times on the opposite side of the room, looking as overconfident as ever. Not a fidget in sight.

God, I hope he doesn't get this job, even if Everett doesn't get it, either. I heard him tell someone he "had it in the bag" when I got here, and he keeps draping a giant arm over his date's shoulders while she keeps shrugging him off. I'd never describe anyone's face as punch-worthy but I swear, every time that guy grins, my fingers roll *a little bit* toward my palm.

Time wears on, plates get cleared, and speeches wrap up. I take Everett's hand in both of mine, holding it tight while the CEO heads to the microphone and we await the news, Everett in a slick 1960s suit he looks great in, despite its lack of soft, cozy textures, and me in a simple blue bodycon dress Regina loaned me when I showed her my closet and she gasped with despair.

I lean toward Everett and whisper, "By the way. You look *really* hot tonight."

He musters a smile and kisses my forehead.

"You too," he says. "Whatever happens next, I can't wait to get you home."

Same, I think, but I don't get to say anything to this effect, because the CEO has begun, reiterating yet again the challenges of replacing such a gifted and dedicated colleague.

"After an extensive search process," he says, "we were fortunate enough to find the right candidate from within the company. A young man who's proven himself time and again with his impressive imagination, his clarity of purpose, his dedication to quality, and, to be frank, his inarguable results. The accounts he manages trend toward growth, and his clients report sharp upticks in business thanks to clever branding strategies and online traffic direction."

I tighten my grip on Everett's now sweaty hand.

Please don't say Brandon, I think. *Please, please, please don't say Brandon.*

"For someone so young," the CEO says, "our candidate has also demonstrated remarkable range, from manufacturing, to retail, to musicians and artists, to a heartwarming influencer account my wife loves about an adopted rescue dog on a weight-loss journey."

My thoughts scramble.

Did I hear that right? Surely, I didn't hear that right.

"Fuck," Everett whispers as the CEO continues his speech. "Cameron—"

"Did you..."

"No. Well, yes."

"Yes?"

"Sort of. But not, I mean—"

"Yes or no, Everett." I release his hand, balling mine up in my lap as the past three months start to reframe themselves, and conversations that seemed like gentle encouragement threaten to feel like manipulation. "Did you or did you not use the account I repeatedly told you I didn't want to turn into a sales mechanism to get a promotion?"

He opens his mouth but he closes it again without saying anything, which is answer enough, as is the guilt-ridden expression on his face. He looks like he wants to wilt into his chair. I want mine to swallow me, too. All this time, when I was pulling back and he was pushing forward, when I thought we were just running at different paces, he was chasing after *this*.

People applaud and turn in our direction. Everett's name must've been announced. He needs to go accept the position. But he sits there staring at me as if he's waiting for me to give him permission. It only makes me angrier. He did the work. He might as well reap the reward.

"Go," I tell him.

"But—"

"Just. Go."

"Not like this."

"Please. I don't want to make a scene."

The guy on my other side asks if everything's okay.

I channel my best impression of my mom, paste on a smile, and tell him it's great.

Everett leans in and kisses my cheek.

"We'll talk in a minute," he whispers. "I'll explain."

I don't say okay. I don't say no. I just keep smiling, joining the applause as Everett stands and weaves around the banquet tables to the front of the room. His acceptance speech is brief and awkward, a few stammered sentences of gratitude and excitement about the opportunity ahead. I applaud again with everyone else, waiting to hear his explanation, but he gets sidelined by one colleague after another, shaking hands and accepting congratulations as his eyes find mine through the crowd. Every time we lock gazes, another memory reframes itself.

If we grow the account . . .

If we use the branding . . .

If we sell the right story . . .

If we do one more . . .

I know, I know, *I know* all of that work benefited me, but he still lied to me. He said he was doing it for me, and for Aggie. And at every turn, when I told him I wanted to back off, to simplify, or to stop altogether, he argued otherwise. Now I know why.

I feel blindsided. Like always.

And if I sit here any longer, feeling this way, I'll either sob or scream. Easing back my chair, I flash the people nearest to me a stiff, apologetic, and likely unconvincing smile. Then I speed-walk to the coat check, retrieve my coat, and burst through the restaurant doors, filling my lungs with the crisp, cold night air.

With the first exhale, I tell myself not to catastrophize.

With my second exhale, I tell myself to wait and hear him out.

With my third exhale, I overhear a familiar, grating voice say, "Yeah, can you believe it? His fucking girlfriend and her fucking dog. Shady son of a bitch. The only upshot was the look on her face when she found out he used her to get a leg up. That shit was priceless."

It's Brandon, of course, on his phone, partly tucked behind a big white pillar and flicking ash off a lit cigarette. He sees me a moment after I see him, and somewhere, buried under umpteen layers of egotism, he finds the ounce of grace required to look embarrassed.

"Sorry," he says. "I didn't know you were there."

I glare at him, ready to snap back with any of a dozen barbed retorts that rise to my lips. But I don't want to fight with some random jerk right now. In fact, I want to be anywhere but here, so I turn and walk out of his view.

Then I run the rest of the way home.

CHAPTER TWENTY-FIVE

Everett texts, calls, and knocks on my door, begging for a chance to apologize. While I want to hear what he has to say and I don't intend to avoid him forever—a logistical impossibility when he lives down the hall and I have a dog who needs to go out three or four times a day—I tell him I need some time to cool off first. It's the truth, though not the whole truth, and he's kind enough to not challenge it, agreeing to leave me alone until I let him know I'm ready to talk.

Aggie's tremendous company while the sting of betrayal is sharpest, generous with her sloppy kisses and patient with my many smothering hugs, but sometimes even the world's best dog can't provide all the necessary support. So when Hannah arrives at my door two days after Everett's dinner, looking frazzled but beautiful with an impressive tangle of auburn hair escaping its ponytail elastic, a chic wool coat hanging open over a rumpled hoodie and leggings, a faded duffel bag slipping off a shoulder, a sneaker shoelace undone, and her familiar bold red lipstick as on point as ever, I throw my arms around her and dissolve into tears.

"I can't believe you came," I sob into her shoulder.

"You showed up for me two years ago."

"You were heartbroken."

"And you're not?"

I cry harder at that. Of course I'm heartbroken. I've spent the last two days picturing futures without Everett and hating every single one, but at least he didn't ditch town with another girl. We might be able to salvage something out of this mess. Then again, I have no experience rebuilding trust once it's broken. I didn't stay friends with anyone I dated or had sex with once things ended. In fact, I did my damnedest to avoid all of those men completely.

As I release my hold before I leak snot and tears all over Hannah's shoulder, we head into my apartment, where Aggie's sitting a few feet beyond the threshold, patiently waiting while wagging her tail, like she knew we needed a moment before she got her turn to say hi.

"The famous Agatha Goode." Hannah drops her bag while she crouches and gives Aggie a vigorous pet. "You have no idea how elated I am to finally meet you, TikTok influencer and canine companion who brought my best friend back from dark and lonely times."

I choke out a soggy laugh. "You make me sound like a brooding recluse."

She raises an amused brow. "Yes, and that's *generous*."

I concede her point with another breath of laughter while looking around my crowded apartment. It's filled with Aggie's things, and with signs of the friendships I've made. The robo-ball. *Jane Eyre*. A pair of googly eyes over my bathroom doorknob. A pink and maroon T-shirt draped over the rim of my laundry basket, having not quite made its way inside. Customized tea and dog biscuits on the counter. The wagon with its dismantled decorations tucked in nooks and crannies. Group and couple photos pinned up on my fridge, surrounding what used to be a lone photo of Marmie. A super-cozy sweater I don't want to give back, even though I know I should. But a year ago, this space contained a dressed-up futon, an empty kitchen, and little else.

Dark and lonely times, indeed.

Over tea and baked goods, I fill Hannah in on everything we didn't cover by text or phone before she said she'd be here as soon as she could book a flight. Aggie brings us three balls, her monkey, and a rubber bone before settling between us on the futon with her head on Hannah's lap, her backside on my lap, and a limp paw draped over the shaggy Highland cow puppet we got at the fall market, now so matted from months of playing, its cow-like shape is only distinguishable by the horns and tail I keep sewing back on.

"So, the promotion was Everett's goal all along?" Hannah asks when I finish.

"I think so, but I don't know for sure." I tip my head back and send a despairing sigh toward the ceiling, feeling like I should have a better answer to this question. "Encouraging me to pursue sponsorships could mean anything, but he got relentless about them, and about account growth, branding, and all the rest, when we started making the sponsored TikToks in January. The job opening wasn't confirmed until early February, more than a month later, but he mentioned the possibility on our first date back in mid-November, so he saw it coming."

Hannah nods, considering, while she strokes Aggie's ears.

"You think he'll tell you the truth if you ask him directly?" she asks.

It's my turn to nod. This, at least, I can answer with confidence.

"I do. He's been cagey before, like when his ex came over, but as soon as he knew I was freaking out about her, he told me everything. He didn't even lie about liking the CDs I thought he inherited from his grandmother, and that was when he was trying to make a good impression."

Hannah smiles at this. She's solidly alt-rock, and has been laughing about Neil Diamond and John Denver for months, especially once I told her I was kind of getting into them.

"Sounds like you have to talk to him," she says.

"I know."

"And soon."

"I know that, too."

"But..."

I roll my head toward her as I rally the strength to say this out loud. To make it real.

"But if he confirms the promotion *was* his goal all along, I don't think I can stay with him." More tears well up but I blink them away before they fall. "If he'd told me he wanted to put the Goode Girls account in his portfolio, I doubt I'd have minded. I wanted him to get the job. We could've made choices together, found workable compromises. But he didn't tell me. Instead, he manipulated me. He used my financial difficulties and lack of certainty as openings for his ambition. He shattered the trust I gave him. I can't see a way to come back from that."

Hannah watches me with eyes full of sympathy as she continues stroking Aggie's ears.

"So the longer you wait to talk to him..." she starts.

"The longer I put off the breakup," I finish for her.

She sighs with all due despondence for my potential fate while I reach for my umpteenth tissue from the box I've been decimating since we started talking. I have my moments of rational thought, but then I say a word like *breakup* and my composure crumples.

"Think you can maybe stay friends?" she asks.

I give her a look. She gets it instantly. She knows me too well not to.

"You already looked at apartment listings, didn't you?" she asks.

"On the opposite side of town," I confirm, unleashing another stream of tears. "I don't want to move. I don't want a breakup with Everett to mean a breakup with everyone else I've come to care about in the building and the neighborhood. But I also don't want to risk running into him every time I leave my apartment. And I *really* don't want to get home late one night to find him smuggling an oversized plant in with his new girlfriend. Even the thought guts me."

Hannah plucks a fluffy wad of dog hair off her hoodie and lets it float to the floor, the inevitable result of petting Aggie's head, an activity she promptly resumes.

"At least you'd still have this exquisite cuddle monster," she says.

"I don't know. If Everett and I break up, she might never forgive me." I pet the back end she so unceremoniously bequeathed me, as if she's already holding a grudge.

"Aggie will *always* forgive you," Hannah counters.

Maybe, I think. *And maybe that'll be her greatest lesson yet. How to be happy, how to trust, and now, how to forgive. Though it's the trust that got me into this mess to begin with.*

"The real consolation is that my mom doesn't know anything about Everett," I say.

Hannah cringes. "She's still sending you updates on your exes?"

"Yep." I sink lower on the futon while petting Aggie's back end. "I don't know why she has to know what everyone she ever met is doing at all times."

"Curiosity, probably, and not the totally healthy kind, though I also get the feeling she's lonely." Hannah's tone is matter-of-fact, but I reel as if she slapped me.

"My mom's the ultimate social butterfly," I say. "She has more friends than anyone I know. Every conversation is a newsletter about the people in the neighborhood, her book club, wine club, craft club, walking group, and coworkers. She's stayed friends with other parents she met through my *day care*. She knows everyone in Roseburg. And you've seen her social media. If it isn't a *live, laugh, love* sunset, it's a dinner with friends or a perfect date with my—"

I stop myself, feeling like the idiot to end all idiots. I know my mom isn't always as happy as she claims. That's been obvious since I was little. But when did I last see my parents showing genuine affection toward each other? Not on social media, but in real life? And if those posts tell a false narrative, why assume nothing else is curated? Is Hannah right? Is my mom lonely? Has my greatest challenge in life also been hers? And if so, what do I *do* about that?

"Sorry," Hannah says, snapping me from my thoughts. "Was that all right to say?"

"Yeah. I think I needed to hear it, though I'm not sure I can fully grasp it right now. Especially not with—" I wave a hand in the general direction of Everett's apartment.

"God. Sorry. Of course." Hannah takes my hand as I rest it on Aggie's back. "First things first. See if Everett's willing to talk when he gets home tonight. I'll lace up my running shoes and get some miles in while you sort things out. If your conversation goes well, Aggie and I will take the bed tonight while you have insanely hot makeup sex at Everett's. If your conversation doesn't go well, I'll be here to ply you with tissues and comfort food all day tomorrow before I have to head home."

"Okay," I say through a reluctant, teary nod. "Okay. Okay. Okay."

"That's a lot of okays," Hannah teases.

"Because it doesn't sound convincing yet."

"Then say it as many times as you need." She gives my hand a reassuring squeeze.

I squeeze back, overcome with gratitude that she's here, and that even during my darkest and loneliest times, I wasn't truly alone, a thought that nudges me past my shaky *okay*s.

I find my phone and open my screen to my long-running text thread with Everett, but I can't make my fingers move. Once we do this, once he confirms what he tacitly acknowledged on Monday, all the things we haven't done will become things we'll never do. We'll never go to another market on the Commons. We'll never picnic with Aggie under blossoming spring trees. We'll never walk past the waterfalls on a hot summer day, letting the mist cool our cheeks. We'll never sing along to "Sweet Caroline" on a road trip to visit his family with Aggie's head out the back window, her smile wide and tongue flapping. He'll never loan me another sweater that smells and feels like him. I'll never buy him the take-out dinner I still owe him from the day he drove to Syracuse. We'll never wake up naked and tangled together, desperate to collide. He'll never tease me about my textbooks full of parasite photos. I'll never tease him about his plants.

I'll never tell him I love him. He'll never say it back.

I don't want never. I don't even want sometimes. I want always.

Hannah holds out her hand. "Need help?"

I swallow back the sob that wants to emerge as I hand her my phone. She types for me.

> **CAMERON:** Can we talk when you get home tonight?

She hands the phone back with the message unsent.

"You should probably do the last bit yourself," she says. "When you're ready."

I nod again, afraid speaking will unleash more tears. I'm not sure I'll ever be ready. How is anyone ready to sever a relationship that has fundamentally changed them? But as I stare at my phone with my thumb hovering over Send, Aggie stirs, craning around to look at me over her shoulder. Maybe I was petting a sore spot on her hip. Maybe she randomly grew restless. But I swear, as her big brown eyes meet mine and her brows twitch in the way I love so much, she's telling me she understands what it means to do hard things. She's telling me to be brave.

I hit Send.

Within seconds the reply comes.

> **EVERETT:** I'll leave right after my last meeting and be home by 4

"Okay?" Hannah asks.

"Okay," I say, and will it to be so.

CHAPTER TWENTY-SIX

At 3:45, Hannah ties my spare keys onto her running shoe, zips up her reflective jacket, and steps into the hall, earbuds in and ready to run a zillion miles.

"Call anytime." She taps her phone where it's strapped to her arm, cued up with her high-adrenaline playlist. "Otherwise, I'll run for two hours and aim to be back around six."

I shake my head at her, incredulous. Two hours. If she was anyone else, I'd suspect her of spending half that time parked at a coffee shop, sipping a latte. But she isn't anyone else.

"Thank you again for being here," I say. "And also, I guess, for not being here?"

She laughs, and I almost laugh, though I'm too keyed up to do more than muddle a smile.

"You'll be okay?" she asks.

"Maybe not tonight, but eventually."

"It's good to have goals." She envelops me in a warm hug and I squeeze her tight.

As we step back from each other, Khalil's door opens and he

wheels his bike out, halting as he sees us. Hannah spins toward him and she goes still, too.

"Hi," he says, still frozen.

"Hi," she says, equally rapt.

"Are you—"

"Yeah. And you're—"

"Yep." He does a quick scan of her appearance. "Are you about to—"

"Yeah." She gestures at his bike. "You?"

"Uh-huh. Any chance you want—"

"Please. Yes. If my pace is okay."

"Mine's . . . whatever."

"As in fast?"

"As in happy to pace you."

"But that's—"

"Doesn't matter."

"You sure?"

"Absolutely."

"Okay. Cool."

"Yeah. Cool." He hikes his cycle onto his shoulder and opens the door to the stairwell as though he's in such a rush to get going, he can't be bothered to wait for the elevator.

Once he's out of view, Hannah sneaks me a wide-eyed look of surprise and delight. Then she follows Khalil into the stairwell and I watch the door close, too stunned to move. Despite my prior concerns about meddling, no meddling appears to be necessary. In fact, I don't think full sentences were involved. Can two people really fall for each other that fast?

I shake off the question as swiftly as I ask it.

This is not a moment for analysis.

This is a moment for joy.

I'm about to close my door and stress-pet Aggie while watching the clock when the elevator dings and Everett steps out, looking cozy and familiar in his peacoat, corduroys, red Converse, and striped scarf, with his ancient satchel strapped over his chest, but also not familiar with his posture slumped, his face unshaven, and dark circles under his eyes. He sees me right away and as our eyes meet, I'm slammed with several feelings at once: intense longing to run to him, anger that he made this impossible, and a random concern that he might think I've been standing here waiting for him for god knows how long. I swiftly decide it doesn't matter what he thinks. In a way, I've been waiting for him for the last two days. Even while I've also been avoiding him.

"Should I, um, do you want, would you rather . . ." he stammers, and I'm about to save him the effort of asking by inviting him in when Aggie sidles past me and trots over to greet him, completely disregarding the heart-to-heart we had a few minutes ago, when I told her things with Everett might be changing and she shouldn't assume we were still on familiar terms.

Everett bends to pet her head, though he eyes me uncertainly as he does it, like he's not sure petting her is allowed anymore, which is like a knife to the heart. It's one thing to know I might have to live without his affection. It's another to thrust that reality on Aggie.

"Come in," I say, no longer willing to drag this out, not when he looks tortured and Aggie's breaking my heart, nuzzling into his touch and wagging her tail with oblivious joy.

I step back and Everett enters my apartment with Aggie following at his heels. He stands just inside the threshold, clinging to his bag strap with more uncertainty, no longer the boyfriend who's spent countless hours here, but a stranger in a strange land. Until he notices the kitchen.

"You're baking?" he asks with understandable surprise.

"*We're* baking," I amend. "It seemed to help the last time we had a difficult conversation, so I thought maybe, instead of sitting awkwardly on the futon, we could try this again."

His brows flicker. His lips twitch. His grip tightens on his strap. I don't know what any of it means, other than I'm not the only one struggling here, but that's probably all I need to know beyond the obvious, which he can tell me as we crack some eggs.

He leaves his coat and bag by the door and joins me at the counter while Aggie flops onto her bed and watches us with quiet curiosity. I didn't look up a recipe, figuring we could keep it simple and make the cookies on the back of the chocolate chip package, which is what Hannah I rustled up ingredients and tools for this afternoon, all of them laid out on the counter. Everett grasps the idea right away, setting a bowl in front of each of us and asking, "Wet or dry?"

"Dry," I say. "That chilled butter's all yours."

We set to it, me measuring flour and him unwrapping sticks of butter, standing hip to hip but making an effort to keep space between us, which I hate but also need right now.

"First of all," he says as he locates the wooden spoon, "I want to say I'm sorry. I made a choice that hurt you and I knew it was messed up when I did it. While I'm glad I get a chance to explain, my explanation doesn't excuse what I did. So. Yeah. I'm *really* sorry, Cameron."

I nod, and swallow, and let the flour idle until the threat of tears subsides.

"Second." Everett frowns as the wooden spoon fails to dent the butter, but he tries again, and the white-knuckled, neck-tendons-straining effort he puts into it confirms I chose the right task. "I didn't plan to mention your account in this interview process. I need you to know that. I encouraged you to pursue the sponsorships because I hated seeing you spend so much time at jobs you didn't enjoy, or struggle to afford a few basic things for Aggie. And also, I guess, I encouraged you because they were something I could help with."

I carry on with the dry ingredients while hanging on every word.

He brute-forces the butter into the beginnings of submission.

"You're really hard to do nice things for," he continues. "You don't want me to buy you dinner, even when all you have in your kitchen is a literal crust of bread and whatever you can scrape from a nearly empty jar of peanut butter. I had to sneak a Christmas gift in through a loophole in the strict No Presents agreement you forced me to make. You're so self-sufficient you had to hit an extreme financial crisis to let me help with your laundry. But building your account to increase your sponsorship revenue? *That* was something I could do."

I stir the dry ingredients together but I'm too distracted to trust my measurements or put much effort into it. So far he sounds so reasonable, so like the Everett I've always known: kind, gentle, generous, thoughtful, helpful. His criticism barely even feels like criticism. It seems fair and crystallizes a lot of other thoughts I've been wrestling with lately about loneliness and what it means to need other people, having always assumed my self-sufficiency was a necessity, or even an asset, without realizing it might not leave room for someone who's trying to show they care. Releasing myself from that assumption would be *so* freeing, and I want to consider it further.

But I feel like I'm waiting for the axe to fall. And I need him to get on with it.

"The choice you said you made?" I prompt. "The one you knew was 'messed up'?"

"Right. Okay." He scowls at the lumpy butter and goes at it again with full force. "We were headed into the final round of interviews last week when a few of my colleagues overheard our CEO saying the final choice would likely come down to Brandon and me, and if I didn't get the job, it would be because my portfolio didn't demonstrate enough scope, strong on sleek and sophisticated with a lot of prestige accounts, but lacking anything purely whimsical and fun."

I stop stirring, suddenly sensing where this is going, desperate to find out if I'm right.

Everett carries on with the butter, so absorbed by his task he doesn't notice my stillness.

"Word spread," he says. "Brandon's . . . well, Brandon, but he's good at what he does. He also interviews well, which is where I struggle most. I get anxious and fumble my words. Everyone I work with knows this. They also knew Brandon would nail it." He pauses just long enough for me to swallow a swell of nausea on his behalf. "They all follow you on TikTok and knew I'd helped with branding and video production. Someone suggested I add your account to my portfolio before the final interview. I argued against the idea. It felt like an abuse of the rare opportunity you gave me to do something nice for you. But Brandon kept walking around like he'd already picked out wall art for his new office, my colleagues were freaking out that he was about to become their boss, pressure built, and in the middle of an interview I was stammering and sweating my way through, someone asked if I had anything more vibrant and joyful. So I panicked and pulled up your account." He stops there, sets down the bowl of softened butter, grips the edge of the counter with both hands, bends forward, and exhales as though he's been holding his breath for a century. Or at least for the last forty-eight hours.

I reach toward him on instinct, ready to comfort him by rubbing his back, but I retract my hand before touching him. We're not there yet, though I no longer sense we can't get there.

"So you weren't using the account for your portfolio all along?" I ask.

"God, no." He straightens up with a rueful shake of his head. "I made a choice in the moment, under stress. I used the work I did on your account to prove I could do the kind of work the position might require. That's all. And I never said I managed the account. Just that I helped with branding and content creation. But I knew when I did it that I was doing it for selfish reasons. I was exploiting something personal for professional gain."

He pivots toward me. I pivot toward him. For several seconds, we regard each other, standing too close in a kitchen that's only nominally a kitchen, but also not close enough.

"I thought—" I start.

"I know," he says.

"But you didn't—"

"I did. Just not the way you thought."

"It doesn't sound so bad, now that I know the whole story."

"Maybe. I don't know. The look on your face Monday night..."

I feel myself grimace. I can only imagine.

"Why didn't you tell me?" I ask. "If you'd asked about using the account for your interview, especially if you said it might be the only way to keep that toxic waste of a skin suit from getting a job you deserve and he doesn't, I would've been on board."

He flicks at the edge of the counter where the laminate coating is peeling, realizes he's doing it, and busies himself with tearing open the brown sugar and measuring it out.

"It felt so selfish," he says. "Like giving you a gift and then asking for it back. And I'd already been too focused on my application and not focused enough on us. I didn't want to turn the TikToks we made together into *one more thing* that was about my job. I didn't want you to think *that* was what was most important to me. Not you. Not Aggie. My goddamned career." He packs the brown sugar into the measuring cup with fast, fierce punches of his fist, denting it with knuckle prints. "I don't know. Maybe I also thought that if I couldn't earn the promotion with the work I'd done professionally, I didn't deserve it. It should go to someone else. Guess I changed my mind on that one." He punches the sugar again, this time hard enough to make me flinch.

I reach out to halt his motion. "Everett..."

"Sorry." He flexes his hand as I retract mine. "It's just, Monday, when you heard—"

"I was blindsided. That came out of nowhere. After I trusted you so implicitly."

"I know." He hangs his head, shaking it slowly. "I know. I know. I know."

That's a lot of I knows, I think, but it's a joke only I would get.

"Even if you didn't plan to use the account for your interview," I say, "you should've at least told me after you did it. I would've supported you. I would've understood."

"I know," he says again. "I meant to. I *tried* to. But I was so ashamed."

"More ashamed than you are now?"

He lets out a breath of humorless laughter. "Definitely not."

I attempt a smile but I don't get very far with it. All this stress. His and mine. My shock. His shame. The mental contortions I've put myself through, trying to make sense of his actions. Whatever he's put himself through over the last few days. The near certainty we were over. And for something that now seems so insignificant, just a series of small, imperfect choices, their impact catalyzed by an unexpected announcement. I can't even be that mad at Everett for not telling me. Didn't I avoid talking, too, making matters worse? Aren't we both at fault?

"We have to be able to trust each other," I say. "And talk to each other."

His expression grows stern, etching a crease between his brows. "Of course we do."

"How do you suggest we do a better job of that?"

He drags a hand down his stubbled face while his eyes stay locked on mine, their warm caramel-colored centers ringed by mossy green. Fall-colored eyes for a fall-sweater boy. I don't know why I think that in this particular moment, at the critical fulcrum of *What's next?* But my thoughts are a million places at once right now. My emotions are even more fractured. There's such a weird energy between us, a softening of edges but a distance yet to be bridged.

"I can't guarantee I'll get everything right all the time," Everett says. "I'll make more mistakes. A lot more, probably, but I do at least learn from them, so I think I can safely promise you I won't make the same ones twice, not the big ones, anyway. If I know I'm doing something that might hurt you, I'll tell you right away. Even if I really, *really* don't want to."

I nod, considering, as I sneak a glance at Aggie over on her bed. She's lying on her belly with her head lowered between her front paws, still watching us intently. I wonder how much she understands about what's happening right now. She must sense the tension between us. If she didn't, she'd be over here with a ball in her mouth or angling for a pet.

Happiness. Trust. Forgiveness, I think. And also *deep, lifelong, unreserved love.*

"And I won't put off having hard conversations," I say. "Even if I'm really, *really* afraid of what they might mean. I'll also try to be better about accepting help when it's offered."

The first hint of a smile pulls at the corners of Everett's lips.

"Does that mean I can buy you dinner tonight?" he asks.

A familiar snap of resistance straightens my stance and forces my lips to purse. But I heard what he said, and of all the issues on the table, this seems like the most easily solvable.

"Yes. Thank you," I say with noticeable effort. "But we should finish the cookies first."

"Forget the cookies," Everett says through a sharp exhale. "Just let me hold you."

With those five simple but beautiful words, the tension between us breaks and we collide into a fierce embrace, one that feels like we're squeezing the life out of each other, or squeezing the life back into each other. Fingers curl into clothing. Arms tighten into vise grips. Knees bump. Cheeks brush. Hearts pound together. Chests rise and fall as one.

I love you, I think as all other thoughts vanish. *I love you. I love you. I love you.*

He draws back far enough to meet my eyes as something beyond joy sparkles in his.

"I love you, too," he says.

My chest cracks wide open at the sound of those words, as though he spread my rib cage and spoke directly into my squishy, beating heart, where I most needed to hear them.

And then the *too* registers, making me scrunch up my face in embarrassment.

"I said my *I love you*s out loud, didn't I?" I ask.

Everett beams at me, with his glasses glinting and his soft curls begging to be tousled.

"It's one of my favorite things about you. Direct access to your brain." He tips his forehead against mine as if to illustrate. Or maybe to get closer. "Also, thank god you did say it because I've been waiting to say it for months, afraid you'd think it was too soon."

I scold him with a look, but a half-hearted one I undercut with a smile I can't repress.

"No more being afraid to tell me things," I say.

"I'm working on it." He nuzzles my nose with his, softly, sweetly, gently, Everett-ly.

"I'm working on it, too," I say, knowing I was also afraid, knowing I will be again, and he will be again, but maybe we'll be *less* afraid next time. It's enough. It's more than enough. So I close the last inches of distance between us and kiss him, falling into the warmth of his lips, the slide of his tongue, the strength of his arms, and the countless murmured *I love you*s he showers on me between kisses, each one embedding itself in the forever section of my memory.

Not never. Not sometimes. *Always.*

We're going to be okay, I think, or maybe I say it out loud. It doesn't really matter if I do. It's the truth either way, and one I believe more now than ever, because the world may be full of disposable things, but that doesn't mean we should let something die if all it needs is a little care and attention. Care, attention, forgiveness, an occasional mustering of bravery, a lot of love, an impossibly soft sweater, an impossibly soft boy, and the sound of a perfectly timed thumping tail over on a dog bed, ensuring we know she's on board for whatever the future holds.

CHAPTER TWENTY-SEVEN

The rest of the term flies by and before I know it, we're three weeks into May and I've completed my second year of Cornell's veterinary program.

Something clicked into place after I helped Minh Ha with Pilot, a rightness in being able to offer useful assistance while knowing that with my degree, I'd soon be able to do so much more. Also, what she said to me that night—that I was better with people than I thought I was—made me realize I've attached too much of my identity to a single personality trait. Sure, I have a history of struggling with dating and making friends. I gravitate toward solitary spaces, speak before I think, and get anxious in large public settings. But when given a task, whether randomly baking or helping a neighbor feel less alone, I do okay. Something I think my parents know, deep down, even if they couch their love and concern for me in too many lessons about what I should do differently, building insecurity when they're meant to do the opposite.

Funny thing, doubt. All it takes is a seed. The watering comes all too easily.

Everett and I throw a party in his apartment on the last day of my exams, celebrating my new resolve to finish my degree, his promotion to associate creative director, and Aggie's recent weigh-in at seventy-five pounds, marking an astonishing fifty-pound loss since I first met her at the shelter last September. Several of Everett's coworkers attend, a few of my classmates, Sam and Sariah from Ruff 'n' Rescue, Georgia from Aqua Paws, and everyone on the sixth floor of the Maple Lane Apartments, including Felicity, who pops by to say congrats and that she can't stay long, only to end up talking with Regina about fashion for two solid hours.

We also have some out-of-towners. Andy and Nora from Hounds and Hearts drive down from Syracuse, eager to celebrate Aggie after being near certain last fall that she wouldn't make it to winter. Everett's sisters Dakota and Charlotte visit to toast Everett, Dakota on her own and Charlotte with her husband and delightfully precocious two-year-old son. The adults embrace Aggie and me like we're family, as warm and kind as Everett is, while little Liam interrogates his parents about the curious dog-less state of their household. Hannah flies over so we can enjoy a proper visit this time and to check out the Lake Placid Ironman course before she completes the race this summer, though her motivations are suspect since she and Khalil keep making heart eyes at each other. They've been training together through an app since she headed back to the UK last month. He hasn't stopped talking about her. She's never looked happier.

Johann the baker comes by with a Black Forest cake that might be the best thing I've ever eaten, and Arthur and Diana visit with the five-year-old wire fox terrier they started fostering last week.

We all play along with their use of the word *fostering*, but the dog has clearly found his forever home. Diana wasted no time renaming him Stoker in the Irish author tradition she has upheld with all of her terriers. He gets along great with Aggie and Pilot, and the three dogs create no end of chaos, chasing each other around the sofa, playing tug-of-war, sneaking unattended food off the coffee table, and vying for attention. Aggie can't totally keep up with the other dogs, and we'll always be managing the impact of her early years, but her tail never stops wagging. Her beautiful tail, now covered with fully grown hair where last year, there were only sores.

Once people disperse, Everett's sisters head out to their short-term rental, and the party has dwindled to the seven of us—Hannah, Everett, Regina, Tegan, Khalil, Minh Ha, and me—we collapse in the living room with two tired dogs, and I hand out the gift bags I put together this afternoon, waving away questions about why I brought gifts to my own celebration.

Tegan opens hers first with a childlike enthusiasm, reaching in to hold up a pillar candle.

"'Wistful Wishes,'" she reads before sniffing the candle. "More like Whole Lotta Lavender."

Regina gives her a playful swat. "I believe you mean thank you."

"No. It's okay," I say through a breath of laughter as the others examine the candles and soaps in their own bags. "I don't understand any of the names. I just figured I should use my employee discount before handing in my notice. Thought we could all use a laugh."

"Cinnamon apples," Minh Ha says as she sniffs her candle. Then she rotates it to read the label. "Sorry. No. 'Autumnal Caper.'" She holds it out to Pilot, who's curled up on her lap.

Pilot gives it only the most cursory of sniffs before settling in for a snooze.

Hannah smothers a laugh behind a loose fist. Her candle scent is Love at First Sight. She doesn't share this with the group, but the giddy look she sneaks Khalil speaks volumes.

We carry on, laughing about Loden and Linden products in a way that feels deeply cathartic after almost two years of working there, feigning enthusiasm about pretentious home furnishings with politely condescending customers. This Sunday will be my last day. I'm starting a paid internship on Monday with Dr. Stean, the pathology professor who was so understanding about my exam mark last term. She's even letting me bring Aggie to the lab while I work. The job is full-time for the next three months, and while it doesn't pay a fortune, it's enough to hand in notice at both of my part-time jobs. No more weekend candles. No more late-night plungers.

"Think you might go back in the fall?" Khalil asks as he sets aside his Gentle Avalanche candle, one of the most nonsensical scents and therefore one of my favorites.

"I hope not," I say. "I'm applying for teaching assistantships, and my immunology professor recommended me for a scholarship, but I won't know about any of it until the fall."

"If you need another recommendation, let me know," Minh Ha offers.

"Wow, really?" I ask. "Even though you're not my professor?"

"Happy to," she says. "And I can honestly say you never wrote a paper that bored me."

I almost laugh. If she ever read the papers I wrote as an undergrad...

"I can do another shirt," Regina adds from her spot in the middle of the sofa. "I'm dying to launch official fan club merch and Tegan's been begging for an Aggie's Waggies tee."

"Aggie's Waggies," I echo with a smile as I pet her head where it rests on my lap.

"You know I'll do branding and video production," Everett says, seated behind me in an armchair while I lounge on the floor with Aggie. "But only if you want me to."

I give his leg a squeeze in gratitude. He knows I'll want him to. We've already worked this out. I post casual Aggie updates when I have them. He steps in with sponsorship negotiation and video production as official brand manager on an as-needed basis. Neither of us touches the account on date nights or weekends, which we've been better at carving out for each other.

"If it'd help," Tegan says, "I can book you in for a financial planning session."

I spin toward her in surprise. She has only ever said she works in a bank.

"You're a financial planner?" I ask.

"I know." She sighs through an eye roll. "Most boring job ever."

"Most *amazing* job ever," Regina corrects before I can do the same. "I never could've started a business without you. And you look stupid hot in a pantsuit."

Tegan grins at this, and for a moment, the two of them get lost in a love bubble, locking eyes and linking pinky fingers on the sofa, still and forever The Lovers to me.

"If we get seed funding for our grant proposal," Khalil says, "I might be able to pay for Aggie to test demo models. Worth a shot, right? And something fun for your account?"

I gape at him in astonishment. "Something spectacular for the account."

"You know I can't help with money," Hannah says, "but I've got you twenty-four seven for moral support. And I'll visit more often. Also . . ." She sneaks another look at Khalil as her cheeks bloom red, drawing out a blush on his cheeks as well. "Cornell has a hell of a law school, so, you know, we could look into that. See if there's a way to do more than visit."

If I was gaping before, my jaw is now completely unhinged. The room goes quiet, other than Aggie's slightly labored breathing as she twitches her way through a dream. Anticipation hums between us while my friends' generous offers hang in the air. This time, despite a familiar tug of resistance, I don't question the kindness or let my brain twist it into something that has to be transactional. I allow my smile to build, and the burst of happiness and gratitude to expand in my chest, warm, bright, vast, and unfettered by the lessons I'm finally letting myself unlearn.

"I love you," I say. "All of you. You know that?"

They all respond at once, some earnest, some teasing me for being earnest. Minh Ha scratches Pilot's head. Tegan and Regina snuggle closer. Khalil and Hannah make more heart eyes at each other. Everett leans forward and wraps his arms around me, holding me in a snuggly embrace made even snugglier by yet another cozy sweater his sister made for him.

As I lean into him with a heart so full I wonder how it still fits in my chest, Aggie stirs from her nap and blinks up at me, rolling onto her back for a belly rub.

It started with you, I think as I bury my hands in her floof. *It all started with you.*

Everyone soon heads home, with Hannah and Khalil the last to leave after helping us clean up. Maybe she stays at my place but more likely at his, which I look forward to hearing about tomorrow morning while Everett drives us to Lake Placid with the late spring trees in full bloom, Aggie's head hanging out the window, and Neil Diamond blasting at full volume.

Aggie settles in now on the bed we keep for her at Everett's, where we sleep more often than not these days, snuggling with her cow, her favorite pink ball, and her monkey, though we've selfishly removed the squeakers from her overnight toys. She was confused at first, and gave us her most convincing sad eyes, but as always, she forgave us and loves us anyway, a lesson I suspect she'll teach me a thousand times over in the days and years to come.

As I climb into bed with Everett, I take care of one last, unfinished task by finding my phone and opening TikTok to my mom's account. It's filled with cheerful videos of social outings and posed moments with my dad, almost always with her arm around him, much less often with his arm around her. Shortly after Hannah's last visit, I asked my mom if she was lonely or if she ever wished my dad made more of an effort to spend time with her. She expressed astonishment at my questions, assuring me everything was great, wonderful, perfect. Her life. Her job. Her friendships. Her marriage. I may always wonder if I would've handled my loneliness better if she'd been more open and accepting of her own, but I can't change that now. I can, however, accept that social media has given her something more than a platform for relentless positivity. It's where she finds connection, and I understand that a lot better now that I've seen more of its positive sides. So, after years of stubbornly refusing to engage, I get over myself and give her the only reassurance I know she'll accept.

I tap the screen and like her latest post.

"Everything good?" Everett asks as he snuggles close and pulls me against him.

"More than good." I set aside my phone, turn out the light, and rotate to face him, toying with the curls that curtain his forehead while his fingertips brush circles on my lower back. All these little ways we reach for each other, each one a tiny miracle of human connection.

"I love you," Everett says with a gentle sincerity, and no matter how many times I've heard the words now, they still hit hard. I hope they always do.

"I love you, too," I say back.

Thump, thump, thump, says Aggie's tail.

And all feels right in the world.

EPILOGUE

Two Years Later

On a beautiful day in early June, in the tiny riverside town of Little Falls, New York, Aggie watches from the front porch of our cute yellow bungalow while I roll a dolly stacked with boxes up a temporary ramp and past her, gradually unloading the U-Haul that contains all of my belongings, half of Everett's belongings, and an egregiously large collection of dog toys and accoutrement. We pulled in half an hour ago, eager to settle into the house we bought together. It has a fenced yard for Aggie, lots of garden beds for Everett, an on-site washer and dryer for all of us, and no painfully slow elevator to get stuck in, though I suppose that has its drawbacks, too.

After countless applications and interviews, I'm joining a veterinary practice with two Cornell alums who were elated that I was interested in moving to New York's second-smallest city, and that my partner could do most of his work remotely, making the two-hour drive to Ithaca as needed. He's keeping his apartment there, at least until we settle into a routine and he knows how often he'll need to be in the office. He told me to wait on unpacking while he picks up lunch—an errand he was weirdly insistent about since we had breakfast in Ithaca less than three hours ago—but I figured I might as well get started.

I pause after the tenth or twelfth load to sit by Aggie and give her floof a good scratch. She was excited, as always, when we helped her into the station wagon, or as we've come to call it, the adventure box, since she never knows where she's going so it's always an adventure. Now, she seems a little despondent, and probably not only because she's watching for Everett.

"I know it's a lot of change," I tell her. "But we'll have a good life here. We'll make new friends, and explore new parks, and find a baker who bakes you dog cookies."

She drops her head into my lap with a heavy sigh.

"I know," I tell her again. "It's a lot of change for me, too."

I take a selfie and text it to the MLA6 group thread that includes everyone from the sixth floor of the Maple Lane Apartments, plus Hannah, who we admitted as an honorary member, even though she stayed in the UK, opting to finish her degree there before entering Cornell's one-year LL.M. program for graduates with non-US degrees. She'll be here in the fall and I can't wait to have her closer. Neither can Khalil, who's already setting up their new place in a much nicer building and with a guest bedroom Aggie and I will see a lot of in the months to come.

As it turns out, Everett will be the last holdout at the Maple Lane Apartments. Felicity left to room with her friend shortly before my third year started. Regina and Tegan moved to New York City last summer when Regina's latest line of sportswear took off. Minh Ha got a tenure-track job at Brown that she started last fall. Everyone has gone their separate ways, as I suppose happens, making me even more grateful that we all intersected when we did, and leaving me determined to hold on in whatever ways I can.

> **REGINA:** #smalltownlife

> **MINH HA:** I'm so happy for all three of you

> **FELICITY:** How's the closet space?

> **KHALIL:** Can't wait to visit!

> **HANNAH:** Me first!

> **KHALIL:** Pretty sure we can find a way to share 😉

> **TEGAN:** And you called US The Lovers!

> **CAMERON:** It's still apt. And broadly applicable

Tegan changes the name of the group thread to All Lovers All the Time.

Regina changes the name to My Girlfriend's Niche Sense of Humor.

I change the name to My Ridiculous but Amazing Forever Friends.

No one alters it again.

My smile lingers as I pocket my phone and give Aggie another snuggle, both of us watching the road until Everett's ancient station wagon rounds the corner and pulls up by the curb. He gets out with a brown paper takeaway bag and wearing a sweater for some reason, even though it's way too warm for one. Maybe the sandwich place was overly air-conditioned?

Aggie's tail thumps away but she waits with me, still not big on stairs.

"How are my girls?" Everett asks as he leans in for a kiss, thoughtfully allowing me the first go at it before Aggie gives him a much more vigorous greeting, sniffing and snuffling away.

"We're good," I say. "Though I'm missing my friends a little. I think Aggie is, too. She spent so much time with Pilot and Stoker. We'll have to find someone new for her to play with."

"Yeah, um, about that." Everett sets down the bag and sits beside me with a hand pressed to his chest. "I thought that might be the case, and you'll be at work full-time soon, and I'll be going back and forth to Ithaca for a while, and I didn't want either of you to get lonely, so—"

This is when I notice his sweater is wriggling.

His sweater. Is wriggling.

"Everett? What did you—"

Before I can finish, a scruffy black-and-tan head peeks out over his sweater collar, with a tiny black nose and tiny black-bead eyes, and tiny fold-over ears.

Aggie leans in, all joyful curiosity. I tear up. Everett helps the puppy emerge from his sweater and hands it off so I can press it—or rather, her—to my chest.

"I've been keeping an eye on the local shelter since we bought the house," he says. "The whole litter was listed a week ago. I called and asked if they'd save one for us, preferably female. I figured, if two Goode Girls make me this happy, why not three?"

I shake my head at him, wondering how he does it. Just when I think I have everything I want or need—a cute vintage home with the man I love in a tiny town I'm excited to call home, a funny and supportive group of friends only a text away, the best dog in the universe as my daily companion, and a new job in my dream career—he finds a way to make things even better.

Oh, what a year we have ahead of us.

I can't wait to find out what's in store.

ABOUT THE AUTHOR

JACQUELINE FIRKINS is a writer, costume designer, and lover of beautiful things. She's on the full-time faculty in the Department of Theatre & Film at the University of British Columbia, where she teaches character design, world building, and period costume construction courses. When not obsessing about where to put the buttons or the commas, she can be found running by the ocean, eating excessive amounts of gluten, listening to earnest love songs, and pretending her dog understands every word she says.

Looking for more? Check out
JACQUELINE FIRKINS'S
young adult novels

HOW NOT TO FALL IN LOVE

A hardened cynic and a hopeless romantic teach each other about love in this swoony and heartful romance that's perfect for fans of *Tweet Cute* and *The Upside of Falling*.

HEARTS, STRINGS, AND OTHER BREAKABLE THINGS

In this charming debut about first love and second chances, a young girl gets caught between the boy next door and a playboy. Perfect for fans of *To All the Boys I've Loved Before*.

DISCOVER GREAT AUTHORS, EXCLUSIVE OFFERS, AND MORE AT HC.COM.